PRAISE FOR *LITTLE SIBERIA*

'Expect the unexpected from the get-go as the prologue lights the touch paper to an intense, smirky, carnival ride of a fabulous read … sharp, amusing and provocative, *Little Siberia* is also incredibly thoughtful' LoveReading

'The biting cold of northern Finland is only matched by the cutting dark wit and compelling plot of this must-read crime novel' Denzil Meyrick

'Expect the unexpected from the get-go as the prologue lights the touch paper to an intense, smirky, carnival ride of a fabulous read … sharp, amusing and provocative, *Little Siberia* is also incredibly thoughtful' LoveReading

'What seems like a cockamamie crime novel full of dark humour is also a wonderfully poignant piece of writing' Crime Fiction Lover

'The plot is fast paced and well put together. I enjoyed the meteorite storyline and the violence and action that went along with that … So brilliantly written' Mac's Book Reviews

'This is one funny and dark twisty read and I loved it! … A Finnish treat of dark, black comedy wrapped up in fantasy and folklore' The Book Trail

'Dark and funny and it has some startlingly violent moments and a brilliant, sparkling finish. But it is also rather a thoughtful and questioning book about the nature of faith, the value of secrets and the importance of love' Live & Deadly

'A novel as much about faith, doubt, forgiveness and imperfection as it is about greed, ruthlessness and a million-euro rock' Glottal Stop

PRAISE FOR ANTTI TUOMAINEN

'Tuomainen is the funniest writer in Europe' Marcel Berlins, *The Times*

'A cast of misfits, a dead body, and the world's most unlikely holiday resort – *Palm Beach Finland* is the work of a master storyteller at the very top of his game' Kevin Wignall

'Finnish crimin … nelling Carl Hiaasen in this

'This one is a winner right from the first sentence … An offbeat jewel' *Publishers Weekly*

'Combines a startlingly clever opening, a neat line in dark humour and a unique Scandinavian sensibility. A fresh and witty read' Chris Ewan

'Brilliant. Absolutely brilliant. I enjoyed every sentence' Thomas Enger

'Antti Tuomainen is a wonderful writer, whose characters, plots and atmosphere are masterfully drawn' Yrsa Sigurðardóttir

'Deftly plotted, poignant and perceptive in its wry reflections on mortality and very funny' Declan Hughes, *Irish Times*

'The deadpan icy sensibility of Nordic noir is combined here with warm-blooded, often surreal, humour … Tuomainen's dark story manages to be as delicious as it is toxic' Jake Kerridge, *Sunday Express*

'Told in a darkly funny, deadpan style … The result is a rollercoaster read' Laura Wilson, *Guardian*

'An original and darkly funny thriller with a Coen brothersesque feel and tremendous style' Eva Dolan

'This was a truly beautiful book – deliciously dark, thought-provoking, and gorgeously written. It gave me chills … I see why Antti is so revered in Finland' Louise Beech

'Right up there with the best' *TLS*

'The spare style suits the depressing subject and raises a serious question: how do you find hope when law and order break down?' *Financial Times*

'Both a thriller and a dark, laugh-a-minute journey that will keep you hanging on to the end. The story of a man investigating his own death has been done before but not with such gusto' *Crime Time*

'A tightly paced Scandinavian thriller with a wicked sense of humour and a bumbling ne'er-do-well at its centre' *Foreword Reviews*

'The off-kilter, black comedy tone is perfect for such a far-fetched story, guaranteeing plenty of spontaneous bouts of laughter' *Culture Fly*

'A Finnish slice from the comic, crazy, greedy, crime world of the likes of *Get Shorty* or *Fargo*' Euro Crime

Little Siberia

ANTTI TUOMAINEN
translated by David Hackston

ORENDA BOOKS

Orenda Books
16 Carson Road
West Dulwich
London SE21 8HU
www.orendabooks.co.uk

First published in the United Kingdom by Orenda Books, 2019
Originally published in Finland as *Pikku Siperia* by LIKE Kustannus Oy, 2018

A catalogue record for this book is available from the British Library.

ISBN 978-1-912374-51-9
eISBN 978-1-912374-52-6

Typeset in Garamond by MacGuru Ltd
Printed and bound by CPI Group (UK) Ltd, Croydon CR0 4YY

Orenda Books is grateful for the financial support of FILI, who provided a translation grant for this project.

For sales and distribution, please contact *info@orendabooks.co.uk*

'Weird but wonderful and utterly addictive with its fast-paced storyline that can be compared to a Finnish *Fargo*' My Chestnut Reading Tree

'Electrifying and utterly brilliant. This is an author you want to watch out for; each of his books is a joy to read' The Quiet Knitter

'An excellent read and a little gem that brightened up the start of my autumn reading' Mrs Bloggs Books

'I loved the dry wit, the understated humour … So many moments of this book had me chuckling out loud, so many times when I could feel that smile building on my face' Jen Med's Book Reviews

'Alongside the humour, unintentional violence and mayhem is the blossoming friendship between Jan and Olivia. Far from straightforward but very sweet. Just wonderful' Steph's Book Blog

'Completely unpredictable. It is dark. It is eccentric. It is crime fiction with a zany twist. Hats off Mr Tuomainen, you have introduced me to a whole new world … that of Finnish noir' Swirl and Thread

'Sharp and acerbic when it needs to be, dreamy and dozy when the inept enforcers are the focus and frustration is evident when nefarious plans come unstuck. Loaded with dry humour' Grab This Book

'A tightly written novel – funny, clever, slick. A must' The Literary Shed

'A uniquely irreverent, very cleverly crafted story which kept me guessing throughout as to the eventual outcome and left me smiling long after I finished it' Hair Past a Freckle

'Black humour meets black noir crime' Books Life and Everything

'Edgy, slightly surreal, witty … This kind of comedy writing, that still has that darkness, is very difficult to pull off and Tuomainen does it with aplomb' Nudge Books

'Absurd, hilarious and thoroughly compelling, Antti Tuomainen has given us another fantastic slice of Finnish fiction that should be at home on as many book shelves as possible' Mumbling About

ABOUT THE AUTHOR

Finnish Antti Tuomainen was an award-winning copywriter when he made his literary debut in 2007 as a suspense author. In 2011, Tuomainen's third novel, *The Healer*, was awarded the Clue Award for 'Best Finnish Crime Novel of 2011' and was shortlisted for the Glass Key Award. In 2013, the Finnish press crowned Tuomainen the 'King of Helsinki Noir' when *Dark as My Heart* was published. With a piercing and evocative style, Tuomainen was one of the first to challenge the Scandinavian crime genre formula, and his poignant, dark and hilarious *The Man Who Died* became an international bestseller, shortlisting for the Petrona and Last Laugh Awards. *Palm Beach Finland* was an immense success, with Marcel Berlins (*The Times*) calling Tuomainen 'the funniest writer in Europe'.

Follow Antti on Twitter *@antti_tuomainen* and Facebook: *www.facebook.com/AnttiTuomainenAuthor/*

ABOUT THE TRANSLATOR

David Hackston is a British translator of Finnish and Swedish literature and drama. Notable recent publications include Kati Hiekkapelto's Anna Fekete series (published by Orenda Books), Katja Kettu's wartime epic *The Midwife*, Pajtim Statovci's enigmatic debut *My Cat Yugoslavia* and its follow-up, *Crossing*, and Maria Peura's coming-of-age novel *At the Edge of Light*. He has also translated Antti Tuomainen's *The Mine*, *The Man Who Died* and *Palm Beach, Finland* (published by Orenda Books). In 2007 he was awarded the Finnish State Prize for Translation. David is also a professional countertenor and a founding member of the English Vocal Consort of Helsinki.

Follow David on Twitter *@Countertenorist*.

Dedicated with warmth and gratitude to
Aino Järvinen, my high-school Finnish teacher.

Thank you for the fails as well as the passes, and particularly the time thirty years ago when you said writing might be my thing.

I promise I'll try my best.

Midway upon the journey of our life
I found myself within a forest dark,
For the straightforward pathway had been lost.

(Dante, *The Divine Comedy*, trans. H. W. Longfellow, 1867)

PROLOGUE

Warm Koskenkorva vodka scours the inside of his mouth, sets his throat ablaze. But he controls the sideways swerve, and the car comes out of the bend at almost the same speed as it went in.

He takes his right hand from the steering wheel, changes gear, glances at the speedometer. A shade over 130. For winter driving, this speed is excellent, especially in freezing conditions along a winding road across the eastern side of Hurmevaara. You also have to factor in that visibility is limited at this time of night – despite the brightness of the stars.

His left foot touches the clutch and his right presses down on the accelerator. He raises his left hand again and swallows a sliver from the bottle.

This is how you should drink Koskenkorva. First a big gulp to fill the mouth, so strong it lights up like a ball of fire and feels as though it could knock your teeth out. Then a smaller sip, a thin gauze of liquor that barely wets the lips but that's enough to extinguish the fire and helps you to swallow the first proper mouthful.

And this is how you drive a car.

He arrives at a long, gentle downward slope, which slowly veers to the right, but so slowly and smoothly that the curve is deceptive. At first it looks as though all you need to do is keep the car straight and your foot on the gas, pedal to the metal. But no. The road then slopes slightly to the left, and the faster you drive the more it feels as though the road wants to buck the car from its back. He grips the steering wheel; he knows he's going about 165 kilometres an hour. It's the speed of champions. He knows that too, and the knowledge hurts.

On his right he catches a brief glimpse of the ice stretching across

Lake Hurmevaara. Fishermen's flags jut out from the surface, marking their fishing holes and nets. He sometimes looks at these flags when he takes this route, because glanced at quickly they almost seem like rows of cheering crowds. But tonight he doesn't need applause.

He keeps the steering wheel angled a fraction to the right to correct the slope of the road surface. As another bend comes into view up ahead, he begins an engine brake. This requires the utmost coordination of hands and feet, the seamless collaboration of clutch and gearstick. He sets the bottle firmly between his thighs, casts his left hand up to the steering wheel, moves the right down to the gearstick, presses down on the clutch and with the accelerator gives just enough gas. He controls the car by harnessing its own power. The brake pedal is for amateurs – guys like the one who'd lent him this car.

After a short, even stretch of road, the car arrives at the foot of a hill with two ridges. He can feel the burning at the bottom of his stomach.

This isn't the Koskenkorva. This is fate.

He uses all the power the car can muster. It requires the utmost control of both the Audi and the situation. You can't just put your foot on the gas. If you do that, the vehicle will be impossible to steer. And at a speed of over 180 km/h, that means careering into the heaps of snow along the road's verges and after that the car would spin on its roof a couple of times – if you're lucky. If you're not and you hesitate even slightly, the car will plough right into the thick spruce forest, where it would twist itself like a gift wrapper round a frosted, metre-thick tree trunk.

He doesn't believe in luck. He believes in speed, sufficient speed.

Especially now, as everything is approaching its conclusion. A conclusion that suits him fine.

The Audi reaches the top of the hill travelling at around 200 km/h. And when it gets there the car launches into flight. As it takes off, he raises the bottle to his lips. This requires as much precision as driving. His left hand is firm but relaxed. Cold Koskenkorva floods his mouth as the car flies through the frozen night. Sweet flames tingle across his lips as one and a half tonnes of steel, aluminium, roaring engine and new studded tyres obey his command.

The Audi flies far and long. It touches down at the very moment the bottle returns to its rightful place between the driver's thighs.

He slips down to a lower gear, accelerates, changes gear again. A downhill slope, a tiny stretch of flat ground, then another hill. And another flight. He catches a glimpse of the flashing red dials on the dashboard and the glinting bottle. The speedometer shows 200, the bottle contains only a few more gulps. When the studs of his tyres once again strike the surface of the road like machine-gun fire, he smiles – as much as a face gnawed with booze possibly can.

He is in his element. Those who turned their backs on him will live to regret it. He's been shunned, ostracised, taken for a fool. He might die, but by dying on his own terms he will rise above everything and everybody. He will achieve something, pass them by, waving to the slower cars as he goes. The thought is a potent one, strong and warm. It burns his mind like the liquor in his mouth.

He slurps from the bottle until it is empty.

The last stretch. The Audi howls.

He opens the window. His face freezes, his eyes stream. He throws the bottle out into the snow.

An open stretch of road. At the end of it, a T-junction. He is not turning either way. He is heading right for the rockface in front of him.

Maximum speed always depends on the driver. People never talk about this. They just say, such-and-such a car's top speed is this or that. Nonsense.

He checks the dial: 240 – in a car that is supposed to stall at 225.

He looks at the road ahead. The last kilometre. Ever.

This is how it's all going to end, he thinks as the car explodes.

He can feel the explosion around him.

What he sees in that split second: the world is engulfed by a huge flash of light, followed by a shadow just as immense; light and shadow both arriving vertically from above. His heart stops and starts again, now throbbing in heavy, hollow beats, like hammer blows against metal. His senses, all five of them, seem to sharpen and come into focus in a way he has never experienced before. He can smell the tear in the car roof, taste the strange, pliable material inside the seat, feel the pressure wave push against his hands. At first he can hear everything, then, as his ears become blocked, he hears the explosion continue inside his head.

He acts instinctively. He shifts to a lower gear, slams his foot on the clutch, the accelerator and the brake. Engine brake, hand brake – a controlled spin. The car slides into the intersection and comes to a stop.

He isn't quite sure how long the moment of stasis lasts. Maybe a minute, maybe two. He cannot move. When his faculties finally return and he manages to release his grip on the steering wheel and focus his eyes on what is around him, he has no idea what he is looking at.

Of course, he understands the fact that right above the passenger seat there is now a gaping hole in the car's roof. But there's a hole in the seat too. The diameter of the hole in the roof is slightly smaller. He congratulates himself on the liquor. Without that in his system, it would be impossible to remain this calm.

He manages to unclip his seatbelt, then stops for a moment. It seems necessary to go through the facts again. The hole in the roof, the hole in the seat, himself. The holes are right next to him.

He steps out of the car and looks up and down a few times. Endless banks of snow, the frozen night lit only by the bright light of the moon and stars. The snow crunches beneath his driving boots as he paces around the car. The hole in the roof is like a pair of lips set in an inside-out pout. He opens the passenger door. Yes, the pouting lips are kissing the inside of the car. The hole in the seat opens inwards; it looks almost lewd. He peers into the hole. It is black. He deduces two things. There can't be a hole in the bottom of the car; if there were, he'd be able to see snow. Whatever made that hole passed first through the roof, then the seat – then stopped.

He backs away from the car. The snow crackles. His heart is racing.

He was preparing himself to die. Then something happened, and he's still alive.

It's the Monte Carlo rally today. People all around. Alpine liquor. Holes don't just appear in cars. Things don't fall through their roofs from…

The sky.

He looks up like a shot. Of course, he can't see anything. You can rarely see anything in the sky. With the exception of stars and the moon, and, in a few months' time, the sun. Clouds. Aeroplanes. But not…

He's a common-sense kind of guy. There's no such thing as UFOs.

Then he remembers. It was a TV show. The documentary said it's only a matter of time before a comet will strike the Earth. When that happens, it will cause a new Ice Age, because the dust that will be thrown up into the atmosphere will be enough to block out the sun. Everything will die.

Except for him, it seems.

Even so, it's hard to imagine that someone sitting only half a metre west of the impact might survive while everybody further away perishes. Though there are no immediate signs of life, he is convinced that, somewhere in the village of Hurmevaara, someone is tucking in to a cold-meat sandwich right this minute.

So it can't be a comet.

But it has to be something along those lines. He can't remember the word. And it's cold now. Neither the liquor nor the thought of death seem to warm him any longer.

His phone should be in the zipped breast pocket of his jumpsuit, but it isn't there. He set out to die, not to make telephone calls. All of a sudden the full force of his inebriation hits him.

Where is the nearest house?

He remembers.

It's three kilometres away. But that's one house to which he will never return. The next one is a kilometre further.

He sets off on foot. After walking a few hundred metres, he comes to a halt. He digs his hands into the snow, washes his face. It feels necessary. The snow-rinse aches, freezes his fingers, numbs his face. But it cleanses him, purifies him in some important way. He takes another few steps, then stops again.

He turns, looks first at the car, then up at the sky.

What *was* that?

PART ONE
THE SKY CAVES IN

1

'And do you know what happens then?'

Throughout my time as pastor in the small parish of Hurmevaara – a year and seven months today – this same man has reserved every conversation slot that has become available. On the reservation slip he even writes that he specifically wants to talk to me, Pastor Joel Huhta. The reason for this is still unclear.

The nature of these pastoral conversations remains the same, however. Only the angle changes.

The man scratches his chin. The stubble is spread unevenly across his cheeks, and in some places is so thick that his fingers come to a halt. His eyes are blue and bright, but with no hint of joy. This is perhaps unsurprising, given the nature of the topics he raises, session after session.

'I'm not a very good fortune-teller,' I tell him.

The man nods.

'But the UN is,' he says. 'I've looked at their most recent report on population growth. The human population of the Earth is around 7.6 billion. By 2030 – so basically in no time at all – it'll be 8.5 billion. In the middle of the century it will already have grown to 9.7 billion. And by the end of the century – what do you know? – there will be 11.2 billion of us. And this is only what they call a medium variant. "So what?" you might say…'

I don't say anything. Silence sighs through the parish building. We are in the south-eastern corner of the building, in a room with Venetian blinds drawn across the windows. Without looking outside I know that the late afternoon beyond the blinds is dark, and that there's finally plenty of snow. The late arrival of winter and the as-yet-unfrozen waters of Lake Hurmevaara made me only a moment ago doubt my ability to read my diary. The room's interior is austere, its low tables and thick rugs lending it an almost Japanese feel. Naturally we are sitting on chairs and not rugs, but there are only two of them and the room is about twenty square metres in size.

'And what happens then?' the man continues, his voice as bright and joyless as his eyes. 'In Finland there might still be five and a half million of us, but what if there isn't? The population of Africa is set to quadruple by the end of the century. Right now there are just over a billion people in Africa, and by the end of the century there will be four point five billion. That's four times as many as now. At the same time there's less water and not enough food to go round. Are people going to wait around until their hunger and thirst get even worse? The average African woman gives birth to about five children. Let's imagine that by the end of the century one in five of them decides they've had enough of hunger, poverty, war and drought. One in five decides to up sticks or is sent away to make a living in better conditions. Let's assume there's an element of natural depletion and only one in ten leaves, then let's assume only one in twenty makes it all the way. That's a modest estimate. But still. If we take a slightly longer timeframe, let's say until the end of the century, to bring in new generations, then we drop the number that make it all the way to Europe, by this point we're only talking about two and a half percent of the four point five billion. How many people do you think that makes? One hundred and twelve and a half million. Where are we going to put them? Where will they settle? In what kind of conditions? And who's going to agree to it all? That's the equivalent of the 2015 immigrant crisis times a hundred and twelve. And that's a low estimate, because it doesn't factor in the millions and billions of people who will be born and die during that timeframe. It's just a figure at a random point in the future, four point five billion. Plenty of things will happen along the way, as history tells us and as the future will show. People are always being born, dying, moving on, having children. Gifts from God.'

The man looks me in the eye. He couldn't possibly know. Of course he couldn't. I haven't told anybody. Anybody at all.

'The Lord alone knows,' he continues, 'I've done my bit – before my divorce, mind. But that's another story. I'm an engineer and I've got a thing for mathematics. I don't daydream; I don't make things up – I couldn't. I make calculations. Every one of them shows that the world is going to end.'

Yes, apparently at the same time almost every afternoon, I think.

'And,' he continues, 'if we live in a world that, according to all the demonstrable facts, is going to end – and pretty soon – then, well, there's no hope.'

I don't know why the man visits me. One possibility is that he simply wants to bring me over to his point of view. It's understandable; it's human nature. Surrendering to the certain destruction awaiting us must be more pleasant in good company. By yourself everything seems bleaker and more difficult, and it appears the same applies to the end of the world. And when no one else will listen to you, the local pastor has a duty of care.

'You can learn to hope,' I say.

'But why?'

'One answer might be that we can use hope to help us do our best for others and ourselves.'

'One answer?'

'I don't have all the answers.'

'Soon I guess you'll tell me God has all the answers.'

'That depends a lot on how you see things. Our time here is almost up.'

'That's what I've been trying to tell you.'

'I mean our session. It's almost four o'clock.'

'I was only just getting started.'

'Everybody has the same amount of time,' I say. 'At these sessions,' I add, to avoid confusion.

The minute hand of the clock above the door edges across the number twelve, shudders, seems almost to flinch at the straightness of its own back. The hour hand is pointing to four. The man doesn't move. There's a question on his lips. I can see it before he opens his mouth.

'What do you think about the meteorite?' he asks.

Six days. Six meteorite-filled days. Six days and nights during which the people in the village have spoken of nothing else. Meteorite this, meteorite that.

'I haven't given it much thought,' I say.

It's true, even though I am a member of the village committee, which will take responsibility for security at the War Museum while the meteorite is stored there for a few more days. The rock will then travel to Helsinki and from there onwards to London, where it will be taken to a laboratory to be examined. Security at the museum is being overseen by a group of volunteers, because the village cannot afford to hire a private security company and the nearest police station is ninety kilometres away in Joensuu. I have spent one night on watch at the museum, but even then I didn't really think about the meteorite. I spent half an hour reading the Bible, and the rest of the night with James Ellroy.

'It fell out of the sky,' the man says.

'That's where they normally come from.'

'The sky.'

'Up there.'

'From God.'

'I'm guessing it's more from outer space.'

'I can't make you out.'

Evolution made me like this, I think, but I don't say it aloud. I don't want to prolong the situation.

'It's four o'clock.'

'Tarvainen says the meteorite belongs to him.'

Half the village thinks the meteorite belongs to them. Tarvainen was driving a car that technically belongs to Jokinen, on land that definitely belongs to Koskiranta, with petrol bought at Eskola's garage, then headed to Liesmaa's house where he made a call to Ojanperä, who arrived at the scene with Vihinen, whose delivery company, Vihinen & Laitakari, is in fact run by Mr Laitakari but half owned by Mr Paavola. And so on and so forth.

'Well, it really is already four, so…'

'They say it's worth a million.'

'It might be,' I say. 'If it turns out to be as rare as people have been speculating.'

The man stands up. His steps towards the door are so hesitant that I find myself holding my breath. He reaches the doorway, manages to pull down the handle.

'I didn't even get round to talking about second-stage Ebola.'

'Godspeed,' I say.

Once I am alone, I open the blinds. The darkness behind the window looks almost like water, so thick that you could dive into it. I've been listening to people all day, and every one of them has mentioned their children. For a while – until today – I've managed to forget about the subject, and find a bit of peace and quiet.

My big secret.

'Conflicted emotions' doesn't seem to cover it.

I listen to other people's secrets as part of my work, but all the while I'm carrying the greatest secret I can imagine. And still I haven't been able to tell Krista the true nature of the situation. It's not as if either of us has forgotten that I stepped on a mine, a homemade nail bomb, during my deployment to Afghanistan. What I haven't told Krista is that by doing so, I lost the ability to have children. That while everything looks and works the way it should, while the surgeons successfully put everything back together, I was left with a blackspot. One that is permanent, incurable, unfixable.

Krista.

Seven shared years.

Right from the beginning, Krista took, and continues to take, such good care of me in so many different ways.

And Krista's most solemn wish? To start a family with me as soon as I returned from my secondment as a military chaplain.

At first I avoided telling her, because it felt like yet another explosion. I'd already survived one, but I didn't know if I'd be so lucky second time round. And now time has passed, and the longer I leave it, the more difficult setting off another bombshell seems. My wounds from the previous one were superficial – I've largely forgotten about them in my day-to-day life. Another explosion would send us back to square one. And probably further still – perhaps to a situation I thought I'd put behind me: a life without Krista.

I don't want to think about a life like that.

And, of course, I'm carrying another secret too. Doubt. For what kind of God thinks this is good and acceptable, yet allows all the evils I have seen? I have asked God these questions, and I realise the paradoxical nature of my actions.

God, meanwhile, has remained silent.

I swap my trainers for a pair of winter boots, shrug on my eiderdown jacket, a thick red scarf, pull on my woolly hat and gloves, and leave. The crisp snow crunches beneath my feet as I walk through the centre of the village: Pipsa's Motel, Mini-Mart, the Teboil garage, the Golden Moon Night Club, Mega-Mart, Hurme Gear, Lasse's Bar, the Co-op Bank, Hirvonen's Auto Repairs, and the Pleasure Island Thai massage parlour. Then, at the end of the perpetually deserted main street, the Town Hall and the War Museum. In the museum car park, cars with their motors running, red rear lights gleaming like pairs of sleep-deprived eyes. Villagers filled with meteor-mania. And, of course, members of the village committee.

I am about to turn onto the street where we live when I recall the confusion regarding yesterday's security shifts.

I walk towards the museum. A large SUV with two men sitting inside is driving towards me. The driver is short and not wearing a hat. In the passenger seat is a man who can only be described as a giant. He fills half of the vehicle. The car has Russian plates. This afternoon's fresh snow billows up and dampens my right cheek.

Four men are having a meeting in the car park. I recognise each of them even from this distance. Jokinen: a storekeeper whose acquisition methods remain unclear. Sometimes I get the sense that his yoghurts come from somewhere other than the wholesalers, and the meat he sells tastes fresher than anything I've ever bought at the meat counter in the local supermarket. Turunmaa: a farmer who deals mostly in potatoes and swedes, who dabbles in a bit of sprat fishing, and who owns so much forest he could form his own country. Räystäinen: mechanic and owner of the village gym, a man with a passion for bodybuilding, who insists that I too should take out membership of his gym and start working out properly. I have natural shoulders, apparently, and almost no fat to burn off. Then there's Himanka: a pensioner, a man who looks so old and fragile that I wonder whether he should be out in temperatures this cold.

The four men notice my arrival. The conversation instantly dies down.

'Joel,' says Turunmaa by way of a greeting. He is wearing a furry cap and a leather jacket. The others are wrapped in quilted jackets and woolly hats.

As usual, Turunmaa seems to be leading the conversation. 'We're having a bit of a pow-wow.'

'About what?'

'Tonight's guard duty,' says Räystäinen.

They fall silent. I look first at Jokinen.

'I have to Skype my daughter in America,' he says.

'What?' asks Himanka, shivering with cold.

I look at Turunmaa.

'I want to watch the match,' he says. 'I've got a tenner on it.'

'That time of the month, I'm afraid,' says Räystäinen. He has a frankly astonishingly young wife, and they are doing exactly what Krista wishes we were doing: making vigorous attempts to start a family. I know this because Räystäinen has regaled me with the fine details.

I don't even consider Himanka an option.
'I'll stand guard tonight,' I say.

Houses line the street at irregular intervals, and the lights are on in almost all of them. Round here people go home early. In Helsinki the lights go on around six o'clock in the evening; here they flicker into life after three. Another car drives past, and this time I recognise the driver. The dark-haired lady often sings at the Golden Moon. She gives me the same look she always does. It's not especially warm. In fact, it seems to say more than simply, *you're in my way*. She is smoking a cigarette and talking to the man sitting next to her. They pass me and continue driving towards the museum.

I turn at the junction, and I can already see the lights. I walk for another four minutes or so, then step into the garden.

I knock the snow from my shoes against the concrete steps of our rented detached house. Opening the front door, I can already smell the cabbage rolls. I slip off my shoes, take off my outdoor clothes and walk inside.

Krista is in the kitchen, standing with her back to me, cooking dinner, just as she has done innumerable times before. The love of my life, I think automatically. What would I have if I didn't have you? The familiar thought echoes through my mind, curling and swirling; it's done that a lot recently.

I give her a hug, press my nose into her thick chestnut hair and draw the smell deep into my lungs. I see her long, thin fingers on the chopping board, in her left hand a plump red tomato, in her right a shining kitchen knife.

'I'm going to be on guard duty tonight,' I tell her.

'I'm pregnant,' she says.

2

Perhaps the nocturnal War Museum, devoid of people, is the right place for me right now. Old weapons, uniforms, recoilless rifles, helmets, grenades, a cannon. Historical maps and demarcation lines. Images of famous local battles.

I'm not in the best spiritual place, as they say. I'm about halfway through the night's guard duty.

I walk around because I simply can't sit still, and I can't concentrate enough to read. The Bible seems to be accusing me of something, and in some inexplicable way I feel it should be the other way round. And the stifling heat of Ellroy's Los Angeles seems too far removed from where I find myself right now: Eastern Finland, in the centre of the remote village of Hurmevaara. Only twenty or so kilometres from the Russian border. It's –23°C outside and it's the middle of the night, the time approaching 2:30 a.m. I realise I'm thinking that if God had a back, he turned it on me some time ago.

I arrive at what's called the Long Hall and come to a halt by the meteorite – a chunk of black rock that has come hurtling through space, and that's exactly what it looks like.

I remember the facts listed in the local paper. Initial tests suggest that it might be an example of the extremely rare iron meteorite; and the thing weighs about four kilos. It contains large amounts of platinum metals. Only a handful of similar meteorites have ever been found. Of those, one – a lump of rock that came crashing through the roof of a sports hall in the United States – was auctioned off in small pieces. The price per gram of meteoric rock can reach 250 euros. The fact box at the bottom of the article calculated that, if the Hurmevaara meteorite were to be sold off by the gram, it could be worth up to a million euros.

Only a few more nights in Hurmevaara, I think as I stare at the black lump.

As for me…

I left the house as soon as was feasible. I absorbed Krista's news, hugged her, gave her a kiss. I listened as she told me a thousand times how much she loved me and gushed that finally we would be a family together. When I finally regained my composure, and when Krista specifically asked me, I assured her I was so very, very happy.

Krista is pregnant. She is sure, she tells me, because she's taken three separate pregnancy tests. I'm sure too. I've been through dozens of clinical tests with numerous specialist surgeons, and I cannot have children. And because I find it hard to believe in the virgin birth, the only option left on the table is that someone else has put the bun in her proverbial oven. And that someone must be a person capable of producing viable sperm.

A man.

This fact is even harder to understand than the pregnancy itself. When was Krista ever anything but good to me? When had she ever told or showed me she was unsatisfied? When was the last time even half a day went by without her saying (and, through the little details of her behaviour, demonstrating) that she loved me and me alone? And had a single night gone by without us falling asleep in each other's arms, she curled in the crook of my arm, her left leg over my legs and her left arm across my chest?

A man.

My throat feels tight. There's a gnawing feeling at the bottom of my stomach. Black electricity courses through my head.

Of course, I could hardly say congratulations, then ask who's the father. I couldn't. I simply … couldn't. If I did that, what would happen? Would Krista run off with said man? Raise the child alone? On top of that, I would have to admit that for two years and four months I've been keeping a secret that would have had an inevitable and irreparable effect on our relationship.

Whatever the outcome, I would lose her.

And life without Krista – I still don't want to imagine such a thing.

The meteorite is displayed at waist height in a glass cabinet. It has been travelling for billions of years and crossed billions of miles – and here it is.

I look up. Identical glass cabinets run the length of the long, rectangular space. The faint night-time light casts a dim glow across the room; it seems the museum is saving electricity as well as security costs. Movement makes me feel slightly better, remaining on the spot is stifling, so I walk along the row of cabinets and stare into the vitrines without really registering what is inside them. Of course, I know without looking; my military background means I feel an almost personal attachment to each of these items.

At the end of the row I come to a halt; I'm not sure what I've just heard.

It's hard to say anything specific about the sound, or whether I really heard it in the first place. It is very faint – vague and distant, bringing with it echoes of a distant thud, the sound of something smashing. I wait for a moment and try to make out what it might have been. I can hear nothing.

I move to the doorway of the Long Hall, switch off the lights and listen closely. It's as though some sort of sound is coming from the other end of the museum. Two or three rapid steps, perhaps. The other end of the museum is kept dark all night. I move quietly, slowly, and arrive in the lobby. The lobby is set slightly higher than the exhibition rooms, and in the middle of the ceiling sits a glass pyramid skylight, which lets in water and isn't strong enough to hold the weight of the snow. As I try to listen more closely, I smell something.

A scent, new and powerful, surrounds me. Here in the museum at this time of night the sensation is so unexpected that it takes me a moment to understand what it is.

Perfume.

A woman's perfume. In the middle of the nocturnal lobby. It seems impossible.

I look towards the entrance. The table and chair set out for the security guard are in their rightful places, as are the Bible and Ellroy, there on the table. Next to them is my phone. The floor lamp, which I've moved near the table, makes the surface of the table gleam and casts a golden semi-circle on the laminate flooring. Again I hear a sound at the other end of the museum.

This time I can clearly make out footsteps. Then I sigh. Of course. The cleaner.

We've been having problems with the museum's cleanliness and we've hired someone who cleans in addition to her own shifts at a paper factory near Joensuu. She cleans at the museum whenever she gets a chance, so it seems she's made it here in the early hours. But there's still something surprising about the perfume. That, and the fact that she is working in the dark.

I hear the footsteps again and walk towards her. I arrive at the doorway, and I am about to enter the room when something heavy strikes the side of my head just above the ear. I stumble, almost fall over, but it's only after the second blow that I lose consciousness. I collapse on the floor.

I hear the sound of smashing glass, running feet. More glass smashing. I was only fully unconscious for a brief moment. Someone runs past me. It's not the first time in my life I've experienced something like this. It feels much like being caught in an ambush. And it's not hard to guess what the intruders are after; the museum is currently home to a meteorite worth a million euros.

It sounds like the running feet are making their way to the far end of the museum. I stagger to my feet and run after them. I can see a beam of torchlight up ahead. My head hurts; I can feel blood trickling past my ear.

I see someone clambering through a broken window and out into the starlit night. Arriving at the window, I see two figures dressed in black trudging through the snow under the gleam of the stars. I jump after them and immediately fall to my knees in the cold snow. My head is still reeling from the blow. The two make their way through the snow. Again the smell of perfume.

I am already running through the snow when I become aware of two things: my own inadequate attire and the direction of the pair of intruders. They are heading towards the edge of the woods, and behind the half-kilometre strip of woodland runs a highway. There's no way the pair are going to hide away in the small woodland; they must have left their get-away car near the highway. I turn and run towards the car park, pulling the keys from my pocket. If I turn back now, the thieves will almost certainly get away. The only option is to catch up with them, see what they look like. Perhaps even more. I've been in worse situations. I can't help but think that this had to happen on my watch.

Their plan is a shrewd one. In order to reach the section of the highway, where I assume their car is waiting, I'll have to drive the long way round. I'm going well over the speed limit. Our small, economical Škoda isn't used to this kind of speed. I let out a frustrated roar as I realise my phone is back at the museum, next to my books, illuminated by the lamp.

It's now even more vital I catch up with this pair of crooks.

I turn onto the highway and put my foot down on the accelerator. Almost nothing happens. The Škoda's acceleration is slow at the best of times, so perhaps it's too much to expect a record-breaking performance at this precise moment. I arrive at the spot where I guess their car must be parked. This is the most probable location: from here, there's a path leading through the woods directly to the museum. I see damage in the snow verges, footprints. I continue driving. So far they haven't come towards me, so the only option is to continue straight ahead. I can't remember how far this road stretches before the next turn off. Far enough.

I take a tissue and wipe the blood from around my ear, and as I do I see a set of red lights ahead of me. I keep the accelerator pressed to the floor and catch up with the car in front one metre at a time. It disappears round a bend, but soon comes back into view. The car appears to be travelling at quite a speed – and why wouldn't it? There are no police round here. The only risk is encountering an elk on the road, but if an elk crashes across your windscreen it doesn't matter whether you're driving at eighty km/h or at 130; the effect is the same.

We drive like this for twenty minutes. Then I lose sight of the lights altogether. I come out of a bend and the road straightens up ahead, and I find myself alone in the nocturnal emptiness. The road ahead is so long, the car in front simply cannot have reached the end and disappeared.

There is only one small lane leading off the main road. I turn and see the tyre tracks. The narrow lane soon turns into nothing but a trail. It's hard going for the little Škoda. I assume I'm nearing my destination. I turn off the headlights and steer the car onto an even narrower pathway. Judging by the depth of the snow, it must have been ploughed about a week ago. A moment later I stop the car, switch off the motor. Then I step out and listen.

The sound of an engine. Light flickering between the trees.

3

The car is parked in front of a cottage, its engine still running. The headlights illuminate the front of the cottage like a set of spotlights. The cottage is small and run-down. It looks like so many of the old houses round here. The original occupants die and their descendants or distant relatives now spend a week or two at most in the house in the summer – for a couple of years. Then even that comes to an end, and, overwhelmed by the weather and the passing of time, the house starts to subside, like someone losing their grip on a lifebuoy.

I watch the cottage, the car and the two people from the side, like a theatre performance.

The pair are wrestling in the snow between the car and the cottage. No. It's not really wrestling. One is punching the other, and the other is unable to fight back. The thuds of the punches and the possible shouts that follow are drowned by the sound of the engine. I creep a short distance forwards through the snow between the tree trunks, and from there I'm able to walk along the tracks left by the tyres. I've had close combat training, and I know more than just the basics of self-defence. I try to recall everything I've learned as I approach the pair.

At the same time I remember why I've come out here. I've been humiliated enough for one day.

Jeans, a jumper and a flannel shirt are, of course, relatively light attire for such biting cold, but I don't plan to hang about. I approach the light-blue Nissan Micra; the smell of exhaust fumes is heavy in the calm, starlit night. Rust has eaten away at the rims of the bodywork. I look at the registration number and commit it to memory. I creep behind the car and look for a suitable route. One of the thieves is lying face-down in the snow. I can deal with him later. The other one walks up to the cottage door, unlocks it and steps inside.

I wait for a moment then step out from behind the car and trudge through the snow towards the cottage. I pass the guy lying in the snow on his right side, still keeping my distance. I keep well out of the light, just in case the guy inside glances out through the window. For a split second, I think I see the thief in the snow moving, but perhaps not. The car's headlights are so bright that I can see a long tear in the right sleeve of his jacket, and in that tear is something dark and wet. Maybe he cut his arm climbing through the broken window at the museum. Beside his left arm is a torch standing almost upright in the snow. I can't help thinking that this is the object that caused the lump above my ear.

The car's lights have been left on for a reason – I assume there is no electricity out here. There are two windows at the front of the cottage. In the left-hand one I see a human shadow passing between the floral curtains. I step nearer the door. I know what I've come to find. I reach out towards the handle.

Then the world suddenly bursts into flame.

And the door comes flying towards me.

If the snow beneath you feels soft and good, it usually means it's too late. I know this, but still I enjoy the sensation. Lord knows I need some rest. Or does He? Is there a Lord at all? I open my mouth, snow falls inside. I realise I'm not on a couch or in bed, not discussing what you might call life's bigger questions. I'm lying in the snow, and I have to get to my feet. I must get up, otherwise I'll freeze. I have to get inside. Then I remember where I am.

I was about to go inside…

The cottage…

Smoke and dust are billowing from what used to be the windows. The remaining shreds of the curtains dangle round the window frames.

All this I see in the light of the moon and the stars. The Nissan

Micra has disappeared. So has the thief who was lying in the snow. I finally haul myself to my feet. I look around, shivering with cold. Beside me, a few metres from the doorway, is the cottage door. I can't hear anything. I can't see anyone. There is a trail in the snow, drag marks. And there's a torch propped upright. I pick up the torch and stand in front of the cottage.

I take a cautious step inside, flick the torch into life and allow the beam of light to wash across the interior of the cottage. I have seen many rooms, apartments and houses just like this. I look in front of me, stepping carefully through the debris. This space was clearly once a combined kitchen and living room.

The fridge seems to have spun round on its axis. The chairs and dining table are spread across the room in different-sized splinters. The shelves have fallen from the walls and collapsed into the middle of the floor. Crockery and various items have smashed, flown through the air and are now strewn in a chaotic mess. And everything – literally everything – seems to have ended up on the floor.

Everything except...

I raise the light from the torch to the walls. Something dark and wet. Small damp blotches, larger ones too. Chunks and strips of solid matter.

I reach the middle of the room and stop. I aim the torch at the floor.

Right in front of the window, where presumably there was once a dining table, is a pair of men's winter boots. Or, more specifically, a pair of boots and a pair of legs. The legs look like they might belong to a mannequin. The large boots seem to be stepping in opposite directions.

Again I look at the walls. The owner of the legs is smeared evenly across the walls and the ceiling. On the ceiling, right above the feet, is a larger, hairy blob the size of a hotplate on the cooker. Given its colour and the length of the hairs I assume this is a scalp. I look back at the boots. Even without my military training, I know this man doesn't need an ambulance. He's not in any danger now.

I feel a deep-rooted sense of gratitude for the German engineer who must have stood up for himself at a car-factory design meeting and demanded that seat heaters should reach such high temperatures, that in normal circumstances they would roast your backside. Now the seat heater is like an open fire that I could curl up beside. Except, of course, there's no time to curl up. I'm driving at break-neck speed back to Hurmevaara and the museum.

My head throbs with the bleak thoughts running through my mind, not just about the evening's events but about the situation at home. I'll soon be a man with no family, I think, and my wife has had to make do with the village stud. I try to prevent the theft of the meteorite and end up witnessing an unfathomable series of events that culminates in an unfortunate soul blowing himself up, leaving his body spattered across the panelled ceiling of a remote cottage. And I didn't even find the meteorite. What have I done wrong? I might ask right now, if I could muster any belief in the power of such questions.

I jump out of the car and in a few seconds I am at the front door. I take out my set of keys, open the door, and with that I am in the War Museum once again.

My phone is where I left it, between the Bible and the crime novel. I pick it up and run into the hall where the meteorite is being kept. I key in the number for the police in Joensuu and am about to report the meteorite stolen when…

…I realise that it hasn't been stolen.

There it is in its glass cabinet.

I stop. There is broken glass on both sides of the meteorite. Then I see what is missing. A grenade. These artefacts shouldn't be active any longer, but that's cold comfort to Puss in Boots at the cottage.

I breathe steadily, the phone in my hand. I hear the voice of the police at the other end. I look at the meteorite. It might have set off on its journey at the beginning of time. It has hurtled through space at immeasurable speed and has struck the Earth at this precise time and place. I raise the phone to my ear.

'Hello? Anybody there?' the officer asks again.

'I'd like to report a robbery,' I begin. 'Someone has broken into the Hurmevaara War Museum. I was battered unconscious. The intruder seems to have made off with a wartime grenade. That's all I know.'

4

It's come to this.

People often use this phrase, though I assume most are either joking or say it in situations in which things could still go in a variety of directions. I only know one direction I want to take. It's the direction that's been given me.

It's another few hours until daybreak. I give the police a statement, tell them what happened at the museum, show them the broken window, the smashed display cabinets. The police pass the case on almost immediately, handing it over to the local army brigade in Kainuu. The missing hand grenade is a matter for the army, the police officer explains, especially since it wasn't supposed to contain live ammunition. I look up at the officer and think how reality seems to escape our assumptions with increasing regularity, but I don't say it out loud. I call the cleaner, who is doing the night shift at the paper factory. She promises to come and clean up when she's finished work in three hours.

After this I call Turunmaa, tell him the news and ask him who can come and replace the window. Turunmaa says he knows a guy who fixes windows at a decent price and promises to call him. Then I get to the main reason I called. I tell him I'll gladly take on all the remaining night shifts at the museum. He doesn't make a fuss about it; it's fine by him, they can all get on with other things and Himanka can carry on sleeping in his own bed.

After I hang up, another police officer reminds me that there was a break-in at the museum three or four years ago. Back then thieves took a map allegedly showing war-time attack strategies, and there was some minimal vandalism to the toilet facilities. From his tone of voice it's clear he doesn't consider either break-in the most exciting case of his career.

Nobody says anything about the meteorite.

And relatively quickly I'm alone again, waiting until the morning staff arrive.

By now a reddish glow taints the eastern horizon. The winter sun is low in the sky, its beams making bright slashes through a frozen world. I know perfectly well that the thieves were after the meteorite. Nobody breaks in to a museum in order to steal a thousand euros of loot when they could have a million. Something must have gone wrong. The grenade was about the same size and weight as the meteorite. Maybe the thieves were in a hurry, or they mistook the grenade for the meteorite for some other reason. It was dark in the room – I'd turned off all the lights at the timer switch. Maybe the person who smashed the display cabinet was different from the one who struck me with the torch. I don't know.

But what I do know is that one of the robbers is still out there. Somewhere. The meteorite will be here for another four days. Nobody is going to take it on my watch.

They can try, I think to myself.

But you have to draw a line in the sand.

And that line runs right here, right through me.

Krista is asleep. I take some ibuprofen to soothe my headache then have a hot shower. But the chill isn't just on my skin; it's somewhere deeper, complete with the usual faint tremors. They seem to come from deep inside me, from the places where the muscles are attached to the bones, and almost flinch away from one another. I'll freely admit that I don't see the meteorite as simply a meteorite. The stupid, inanimate rock could be worth many millions of euros, but that doesn't interest me. It's the integrity of that rock that interests me. And it's an integrity upon which I can have a real effect.

I look at Krista's bottles of shampoo, conditioner, shower gel. Jealousy whispers to me about when and why they have been used.

I feel as if it's inside me – like five litres of rancid, lumpy milk that I can't seem to vomit up from my stomach.

Water drums against my head and neck. For a moment I close my eyes, then open them again. The reddened water swirls round my feet and disappears down the drain. The burglars were prepared to use violence. And they did.

I won't be turning the other cheek.

And that's the main reason why I didn't tell the police about the cottage, the explosion or the missing accomplice. In the course of the last twenty-four hours I've already taken a battering without being able to respond. That's what Krista's news felt like. I'm not planning on waiting for more people to walk all over me. I plan to find and, if necessary, stop the burglar myself. Either when I'm on guard duty or not. It might not be the right thing to do, but it's got to be done. Besides, if years of theology studies have taught me anything, it's that the quest for perfection is futile; perfection simply doesn't exist. Someone else can try to find it, but not me.

I brush my teeth. I'm out of my mind. I understand why. Hard times lie ahead.

5

Krista wakes me. She is sitting on top of me, her slender hips pressing down against my own. Cotton pyjamas separate our bodies. I look up at her.

'Why didn't you tell me?' she asks.

She has opened the curtains. Judging by the amount of light spreading through the room, I guess I must have slept for a few hours. I should be on my way to work. Krista's thick brown hair falls on both sides of her face. Her grey-green eyes are unique; they always seem to reflect the light even when it's dim. My wife is a beautiful woman. She is still a beautiful woman, I think.

'What?' I ask.

'Minna said someone broke in to the museum last night.'

Minna is married to Jokinen, the local storekeeper. Turunmaa must have called Jokinen, who then told his wife all about it. Minna and Krista are good friends. I know she wishes I could be friends with Mr Hannu Jokinen, but for one reason or another I'm not. I know most of the villagers like him. He chats with all the customers in his store, remembers people's special orders, even their birthdays, and even has groceries delivered if the customer wishes.

'It was … just a break-in,' I say and rub my bleary eyes.

Anything that happens in a small village is common knowledge in a matter of seconds. It's a striking phenomenon. Sometimes I think that, were I to stub my toe while alone in my house, someone would call within fifteen minutes to ask how my foot was.

'Just a break-in?' asks Krista. 'Darling. Nothing happened to you, did it? Was it terrifying? Are you all right? Why didn't you wake me up when you got home?'

I don't know which question to answer first. I tell her I was taken by surprise and that the intruders made off with an ancient grenade. I tell her the police visited the scene and passed the case on to the army.

'I'm fine,' I say eventually.

'That's the most important thing,' she says and strokes my head. Her slender hand touches the bump on the back of my head. 'Oh, sweetheart. It'll all be fine. Things always work themselves out. You just have to be careful. You're going to be a father soon. You can't just—'

'I've signed up for all the remaining night shifts. All four of them.'

Krista's hand stops. 'What about us?'

What *us*, I think, quicker than I even notice. I look at Krista and something almost sinister flashes through my mind.

'What do you mean?' I ask, though I guess I already know what she means.

'It would be nice to talk about it, think about things, together. Names, even,' she says eventually and touches her abdomen. 'But we've got plenty of time to talk about all that, I suppose.'

'Names?'

'People generally give their baby a name.'

'Of course,' I say, though this is the first time the matter has crossed my mind, and even then it's not of my own volition. A cold wave of jealousy heaves within me. 'I'll try and think of something suitable.'

Krista looks at me long and hard. 'We can do it together,' she says. 'That's the whole point. After all, it's not just your baby…'

A phone somewhere gives a text-message beep. Krista glances at hers, on the table on her side of the bed. It's only a quick glance, but it catches my attention. Krista's phone is like a broken doorbell, chiming constantly. I, meanwhile, can leave my phone in my jacket pocket, forget all about it, and assume the following morning that nobody needed to contact me. If you'd asked me the day before yesterday to think of something negative about my wife, I would probably have said she's a bit too attached to her phone. Now I might mention something else.

Krista turns her head. 'What about Saturday night?' she asks.

The winter fête in the neighbouring village. I'd been vaguely aware of the fête until last night, the events of which erased it from my mind. Hardly surprising.

'I don't want to go by myself,' she says. 'And I don't like the idea of you sitting all by yourself in that museum while the rest of us are dancing and having fun.'

Isn't that exactly what you've been doing all this time, I think to myself.

'I want you to be there,' she continues. 'And I want to go too. You know how much I like karaoke. Why can't someone else take care of the night shift? Why do you have to do it?'

Because one humiliation and one near-miss are quite enough, I think. Because you, my dear, you have…

'You'll be fine without me. And you can't put just anyone on watch at the museum. I have special training, remember. It's only a few more nights.'

Krista flicks her hair behind her shoulders. Her face is lit from the side. I can see the small, pretty crow's feet at the corners of her eyes.

'It just doesn't feel nice,' she says. 'I'm a bit worried about you – in general I mean. You don't seem very happy or enthusiastic, even though our lives are about to change so much.'

'I am, of course I am,' I assure her. 'It's just that yesterday … The break-in and everything. The lack of sleep.'

'Surely the other men understand that people need to have time for their families. Tell them something has come up. Something unexpected.'

That's one way of putting it. So many times I've stood in front of people and said that there's no way of knowing God's greater plan. Right this minute, it feels as though not even He knows it. Perhaps the difference between providence and freefall isn't as great as I'd once thought.

'You know these guys,' I say eventually. 'It's a done deal. Once you agree a plan, it's best to stick to it or everything falls apart.'

Krista doesn't look particularly satisfied with this response. It's as though she wants to say something else but stops herself. Eventually she sighs and leans over me. She kisses me on the mouth, between my eyes, on my forehead.

'It might help,' she says, 'if you eat some breakfast.'

She stands up, fetches her phone from the table and walks out of the room.

I don't want breakfast. Instead I decide to find out who owns that Nissan Micra.

Typing the registration number into the app on my phone is easy enough. The results appear just as easily. It seems that the vehicle with this registration number has been deleted from the national register. Before that happened, it had a string of owners, the last of which seems to be a company named Eastern Finland Summer Camping Ltd. The vehicle itself is a red Ford Transit van, a Ford designed for professional use, the model dating from 2006. The description is a far cry from the light-blue Nissan Micra SUV that I saw last night.

If I ever had doubts about whether the break-in was premeditated, this anomaly has swept them away in an instant.

6

I need more information. The snow crunches beneath my winter boots as I walk. The centre of the village of Hurmevaara looks smaller than usual this morning. Of course, this is because I'm looking at everything through a gauze of double suspicion: someone must have made Krista pregnant; someone wants to steal the meteorite. Hurmevaara has a total of 1,280 inhabitants. Both the intruder and the impregnator may be closer than I think – or than I know.

Jealousy stops me eating. It's impossible to feel hungry; my stomach is continuously full and knotted. In fact, my entire chest feels tense. Part of the reason for this jealousy is the uncertainty. The snake with two poisonous heads.

I plan to identify the father of the child. It's a matter of utmost necessity. I don't yet know what I'll do with that information, but I'll do something. Knowledge will give me direction. In my case it won't increase my agony, I think; if anything it might alleviate it.

A few cars drive in both directions along the main street. It's about twenty degrees below freezing, but the air is dry and there's no wind. This is one of the things about this place that confused me at first. In Helsinki, by the sea, I was used to a different kind of sub-zero temperature. In Helsinki it could be as little as –4°C, but if there was enough wind and moisture in the air, just waiting for the bus felt cold enough to bring all your bodily functions to a halt, no matter how thick your eider jacket. Out here I could easily spend an hour and a half skiing in a thin ski suit in –15°C, opening my collar and wiping away the sweat as I went.

Depending on the weather, it's a ten or fifteen-minute walk to the church hall. I pass a bar and a clothes shop. Neither have opened yet. The kiosk, however, has already opened its doors, and in its window is a sign that makes me think of something that caught my attention earlier this morning.

The kiosk owner is slightly older than me, a man yet to find his calling in life. He stands behind the counter like a prisoner. He constantly looks outside as though searching for an escape route and seems thrilled at every customer who walks in, as though they were bringing him a file he could use to saw through the bars of his cell. He greets me as though I was the first person in years to step foot on his desert island. This morning I feel as though I understand the man better than usual. I too feel as though I have lost a vital connection to something, and that I'll have to do something decisive if I want to re-establish that connection.

But this time we talk about a different kind of connection. The man with the thick beard seems over the moon to help me. I feel a strange sense of brotherhood with this man, this prisoner of his day-to-day routines, as I listen to him explain the various prepaid phone-card packages on offer. Not that I need any particular information or that I really care what kind of package I should get. There's only one number I will be contacting with this phone, and I don't think I'll be needing talk time. In fact, talking is the very last thing I plan to do with this phone card.

I know what I am about to do is wrong. Nonetheless it takes me a mere thousandth of a second to justify it to myself. This is a fact-finding operation, and I have a right to know. We agree on a package with free text messages, and I pull out my wallet.

Midway through the purchase another customer walks into the kiosk. I know him the way you know someone you've read about in the papers and seen interviewed on television. Timo Tarvainen is a former rally driver who lives a few kilometres away, by the shores of Lake Hurmevaara. I know his career was cut short by an accident and by the various improprieties that followed it, of which I have only a blurry understanding.

His hair is pure white – so white it could be bleached – and he wears a jacket bearing, at a quick glance, the logos of at least thirty corporate sponsors. The jacket is not new. He is sporting a pair of sunglasses too. He nods both at me and the assistant. At least that's what it looks like. His sunglasses are the darkest shade imaginable, so it's hard to say exactly where the former hot-shot driver's eyes are focussed. He places a twelve-pack of beer on the counter just as I slip the phone card into my pocket. I bid the owner a pleasant day, though I can see in his eyes that his daily sentence is far from over.

At the door I stop, pull on my woolly hat and mittens, and step out into the bright, frozen day. I manage only a few steps before I hear a voice behind me.

'What the hell does God think he's playing at?'

I turn around. The rally driver is standing with his back to the low, glaring sun, the twelve-pack tucked under his arm. I look around and assume he must have intended his words for me. I can't see anyone else nearby. Or further off, for that matter. I guess the question must stem from genuine theological concern.

'I don't know,' is my honest answer.

The rally driver rips open the plastic packaging and grabs one of the cans. He takes a few steps towards me and places the rest of the pack on the hood of his car. There's a similarity between the car and the jacket: both are covered in stickers; neither are the newest models on the market.

'I don't know whether you've heard,' Tarvainen begins, snapping open his can, 'but that meteorite fell on my car.'

I tell him I was aware of that. Tarvainen gulps his beer. It's a long gulp, at a guess almost long enough to down the entire contents of the can.

'My old man used to say the Lord works in mysterious ways, but nothing ever happens by chance,' he says, and I catch the smell not only of fresh beer but of a prolonged bout of drinking. 'And it's got me thinking. You know, that thing comes shooting out of nowhere and finds me. Then along comes some bloke from the museum who says it belongs to him. What does it mean? That the Lord gives and the Lord takes right away again?'

'The probability of a meteor strike is—'

'The probability is so small that it almost doesn't exist. I've read a bit about astronomy, watched a video about it on YouTube. The universe and all that shit. Made me really angry, it did.'

There's nothing I can say to this. In me, astronomy prompts quite the opposite emotions. That said, I'm beginning to understand feelings of anger, bitterness and disappointment, of how claustrophobic the universe can feel.

'You know what God's up to, right?' Tarvainen asks with a belch. 'For a moment everything looked great. I contacted an old mate, said we should start a new rally team, world class. I'll drive, he can take care of the business side of things. You see, for a moment it looked like we were sitting pretty on a million euros that just fell from the sky. Then before you know it, it turns out it's not just any old lump of rock, it's something freakishly rare that needs to be researched. My old mate turns up at the house, at my invitation, and I have to tell him the rock is under lock and key at the museum.'

Tarvainen drains his can. I'm listening with increased interest.

'A mate?' I ask.

Tarvainen wipes his mouth with the back of his hand, then waves his hand through the air.

'Doesn't matter,' he says. 'All I'm asking is, what does God think about all this?'

I decide not to tell him there has been some degree of uncertainty about what God thinks for a few thousand years. I want to continue the conversation.

'You were going to start up a new rally team, you say?' I ask.

Tarvainen looks at me more closely. At least, his sunglasses seem to focus on my face. For a moment he is silent.

'Does that meteorite mean something or not?' he asks eventually. 'It's a simple question.'

It's clear this man wants to get his hands on the meteorite. But I'm not sure he's burglar material, and there's nothing to suggest he is the man who was lying in the snowdrift outside the cottage. The mate he mentioned, on the other hand … This business associate sounds interesting.

'I'm not sure it is such a simple question,' I reply. 'If you take it slightly further, it becomes the fundamental question of whether the universe is a tightly, carefully organised system, like a gigantic Swiss clock, or whether it is a random, collapsing cluster of junk – in other words, chaos.'

'I was asking for God's opinion,' says Tarvainen. 'You're paid to know this stuff.'

Despite what people who make this statement think, they are not the first people to put this thought into words. I must have heard at least a few thousand versions of this particular adage.

'I'm paid to serve the community,' I say. 'Is it a problem that the meteorite is being held at the museum?'

The rally driver's hand stops, the can in mid-air. His head shifts position ever so slightly. The reaction is like a sudden realisation of something. Then he appears to notice the empty beer can in his hand. Tarvainen returns to his car, pulls another can from the plastic packaging. He cracks it open; in the frozen morning air the sound is like a branch snapping in two. He takes a gulp and opens the car door, then stops and looks up towards me.

'I guess God is on my side after all,' he says.

I look on as Tarvainen reverses, turns the car and ambles out of the parking lot and into the street. He's clearly over the limit. I could always make another call to the police in Joensuu. They would be here in an hour.

7

'Ash, a metre thick.'

The man doesn't appear to want to make eye contact. His pained blue eyes stare at the floor as though the layer of cinders were right there in front of him. I glance outside. It is a bright, sunny day. The snowdrift, a metre and a half deep, ripples towards the edge of the forest. I don't understand how the man has managed to get an appointment for today. But I remember: he's always checking the diary for cancellations, always calling the office at the church hall. He was sitting opposite me only yesterday, and now he's the first arrival of the day.

'Seismologists and volcanologists all agree on the matter,' the man prattles on. 'The supervolcano beneath Yellowstone National Park – the caldera – erupts regularly. The next catastrophic eruption is only a matter of time. The last time it erupted, the ash cloud caused waves of extinction and climatic changes. The volcano is fifty kilometres by seventy kilometres in size. Half of North America would be instantly covered in a layer of ash a metre thick. The ash cloud would block out the sun. This would cause a nuclear winter – a new ice age. After the last eruption, the ensuing winter, complete with acid rain, lasted a thousand years. And there was no prior warning. You can't predict when a supervolcano will erupt. The lights across the world would go out in an hour, two at most. You'll probably say it won't erupt in our lifetime.'

I'm not about to say anything at all. Not now. If things in Yellowstone are quietly simmering, inside me they've already reached boiling point. I think about Krista, last night, the grenade, the meteorite, the explosion, the pair of criminals. Less than twenty-four hours have passed, and nothing in my life will be the same again.

'The surface of the caldera rises and falls all the time,' he continues. 'There are hundreds of subterranean earthquakes measured every year. Then there's the fundamental question: do you think they'd tell us if they thought the supervolcano was going to erupt in the next four or five years? Of course they wouldn't. If people learned that the world was going to end in three years' time, there would be anarchy. Nothing would matter anymore.'

I don't hear the question in the man's monologue, but he stares at me as though he expects at least some sort of comment.

'Life can sometimes feel quite unpredictable,' I say.

The man puffs out air, agitatedly shifts position in his chair. The chair legs creak, the white brick walls respond with an echo.

'You know what?' he says. 'I know everybody in this village. Judging by what you and I have talked about over the last two years, I would say every single one of them, even the most fervent communist atheists, seems to have more faith than you do.'

I look at the man and see him more clearly than at any time before. Those anguished eyes, his stubble rough like a bear's tongue. The top button of his flannel shirt is done up. It must be hot beneath his cardigan. I hear his words again.

'You know everyone in the village?'

'Of course I do,' he says with a shrug of the shoulders. 'I've lived here all my life – that's forty-nine years. I've gone to school here, worked here. My ex-wife is from here. Both our extended families. I'm involved in all kinds of community activities. The sports club, fixing people's motors, the deer-hunting club. There's nobody here I don't know.'

I think about this for a moment.

'In a small village, word gets round quickly,' I say.

'It certainly does,' the man nods, relieved. 'Which brings me to why I think an eruption is imminent. Nobody has mentioned this subject in the last few years. What happened before that? The papers were full of articles, there was exploratory drilling going on down to a depth of several kilometres inside the supervolcano. At first they told us about the results; now there's silence. What do you think that means?'

I wait for a few seconds, then say, 'If someone did something that might be considered, let's say, inappropriate, word would get round the village quite quickly, yes?'

'What's that got to do with the Yellowstone caldera?' he asks.

'It would be an eruption of sorts,' I say, and gauge from the man's expression that I need to get straight to the point. 'It's to do with what you said earlier. If someone in the village had … dalliances … then people would know about it, right?'

'Dalliances?'

'If they, say, coveted their neighbour's property.'

'You mean stealing?'

'Something like that,' I say. 'Something that would get tongues wagging, that people would talk about in whispers.'

The man turns his head; I follow the movement. A tall, gleaming snowdrift always looks more durable than it really is.

'This is a nice place,' he says. 'Honest people. We're fair to one another. We uphold law and order…'

I wait.

He turns to look at me. 'You've taken a vow of confidentiality?'

'Yes.'

The man leans forwards in his chair.

'People brew their own moonshine. They bring cigarettes across the border. Rattle their fists at people – maybe even take out a knife. Not that they'd kill anybody, mind. Not straight away. They might stab the arm or the thigh first, the chest only if it's a more serious matter. You rarely see axes. Or chainsaws. There was this one time. Rami Kärkönen took a few too many of those steroids he'd brought from Russia. The chainsaw felt so light, and it cut like a knife through butter. It was an accident, sort of. Rami works at the florist these days. People drive around drunk – otherwise they'd never get home. That's about it.'

There's nothing in his words that I didn't know already. Despite what the average Joe seems to think, pastors don't live outside the real world. We are not unaware of people's capacity to do anything imaginable, and plenty of things you couldn't begin to imagine until you heard about it. Sometimes it's hard to appreciate why anyone would cause such injuries to themselves or others.

'Like I said, it's a nice place,' he adds. 'Decent, upright folk.'

We sit in silence. I haven't discovered any new information with regards to Krista. And then I see another way of approaching the subject: the meteorite. My encounter with the rally driver is still fresh in my mind, as are the events of the previous night. The thought, which I slightly adapt to the situation, is a bit nonconformist. Perhaps it goes against the fundamental idea of the pastoral care I'm supposed to be providing, but this is an exceptional situation in every respect.

'I'm looking for something,' I say.

'Me too,' the man nods. 'There are so many things that threaten our—'

'I thought you might be able to help me. Confidentially. Just like our conversations here.'

The man squints as though he were trying to see something very far away. 'Me? Help you?'

'Yes,' I say. 'How does that sound?'

He hesitates, glances to one side then the other. 'What … or how … would I…?'

I'll help you see end-of-the-world scenarios you can hardly even imagine … I stop myself from suggesting that.

'How about we find you a regular slot?' I say. 'You could come here without queuing, without checking for cancellations. You would have your own mark in the calendar, just like at school.'

'And how can I…?'

'I'm looking for a particular perfume.'

In all the hours the man has spent at my surgery, this is the first time he is lost for words. This would be a welcome exception at any time, but especially so now.

'This is a small village,' I say. 'I guess you've been face to face with all the adults round here many times, and, without noticing, breathed in the air around them. You've smelled everything. Because we all have our unique scent. It could be something very faint, discreet or almost overwhelming.'

'It's true,' he says, still hesitating profoundly.

'I'm looking for a perfume that's strong but not too heavy. Not one of those dark, robust evening perfumes, but something much lighter. The person in question wears a lot of it. It hangs in the air when this person walks past. There are undertones of citrus, but the primary ingredient is something else. I believe that once you've smelled it, you'll easily recognise it in the future.'

'You're looking for someone in particular?'

'First and foremost I'm looking for the perfume.'

The man gives this some thought. 'A regular slot, you say?'

'We can look at the diary right away.'

8

It's payback time. Actions have consequences. No one rides for free.

The latter isn't exactly a Biblical reference. I remember it from years back – a sticker in a public toilet. There's a ring of truth about it, unlike many of the other things flooding my mind at the moment. I don't know why my head is so full of things it doesn't need right now – things that only cause me more unnecessary grief – and so few of the things I actually do need. This, of course, is one of the central conundrums of humanity, one that most certainly doesn't apply to me alone; but right now, in some exhausting fashion, everything feels like a profound personal insult.

The room is quiet, I am alone, and on the wall the Redeemer sends me a message. The message is that all is already forgiven. It is hard to square that thought with reality, here on a freezing day in a small village in eastern Finland, a day when I have slept badly and lost sight of the meaning of life.

I regret my actions, and yet I do not.

I have embarked on a path, the end of which I do not know.

And if I do what I have planned to do, nothing will be the same again. That said, nothing is the same any longer.

I take out my old phone and insert the prepaid SIM card. The new card starts to work immediately. I don't yet know the number off by heart, so consult the piece of paper. I notice that as my right thumb keys in the number, the scrap of paper in my left hand is trembling slightly.

The trembling is barely perceptible, but it clearly stems from somewhere deep within. Of course it does. I remember only too well the sensation the first time I typed that number into my phone at the time. It felt like mercy, a victory, a promise. Like life.

The message field glows a bright white, like snow or a bedsheet. Or, it suddenly occurs to me, like a coffin.

I'm not well. I decide that once I have done this I will have some kind of rest, a long one. I haven't eaten anything. Jealousy no longer feels like jealousy. It has consumed me entirely. I *am* it. Blackness, bitterness.

I go through the list of risks involved in the first phase of my plan. Those I can see and that I am able to list without feeling nauseous.

So:

If Krista and the unknown philanderer are the type of lovers who are constantly in touch with each other, my plan will not work. But for a number of reasons I find it hard to imagine she is having a long-term, sustained affair. I'm certain I would have noticed something. Besides, the size and population of this village isn't exactly conducive to keeping things secret for long. It's far more probable that something simply happened and the pregnancy is the result. Who knows? Perhaps Krista found herself in a situation from which, one way or another, there was no way out…

Gambling. Risk-taking. That's what this is about. But so many of the facts suggest that, for whatever reason, Krista and the mystery man have already gone their separate ways.

I base this belief on the facts at hand: only two hours ago Krista told me she loved me. She has been affectionate with me, in her words, her gestures, her touch. She has been her own, warm, funny self. She suggested I eat a bowl of her homemade granola for breakfast. (I avoided this by telling her the break-in had taken away my appetite. In a way this is true. And I have never lied to Krista, not literally anyway.) More facts: Krista wants me to join her at the village fête, in the shower, she wants me to think about baby names with her. How many people would do that while they were still fooling around in the neighbour's bedroom?

I tell myself once again that knowledge will heal the pain.

My fingers feel frozen against the buttons of the phone, though the air in the room is warm. I remind myself that sometimes the things you have to do don't always make you feel good. I force myself to type.

> Hi, I had to get a new number.
> You Know Who

I look at the message. Instantly I realise this is going to be far more demanding than I'd thought. I'm going to have to put myself in the role of the lover. I'll have to act like a desperate, horny hunter. My messages should exude passion, pent-up lust.

Another difficulty, one that I appreciate right now, is a textual one. I have literally no idea of the mystery man's reading and writing skills. How could I? What if he is one of this modern breed of texters who doesn't care for spelling or punctuation? I ask myself whether Krista, a literary translator, would fall for someone barely literate. Desire does funny things to us. Man is but flesh. Lust pays spelling conventions no heed.

I don't quite know why, but the idea of Krista having intimate relations with someone who RITES IN ALL CAPS and has a less-than-adequate ability to deploy them in a sensible order is all the more crushing. I quickly decide that Krista must have found a villager with a flawless grasp of written Finnish. This too feels bad and inexplicable, but it makes it easier to finish my message.

> Krista, I had no option but to shut down my old number and get this new one. At the same time I feel like I'm on the cusp of something completely new. I don't know why. Do you feel like that too? I miss you and I think about you a lot. Just the thought of you drives me crazy. So crazy that I don't even know who I am. Sometimes I imagine you at my place, but I guess that's impossible. I hope to hear from you soon. Yours. 'Maybe still in your affections?'

Ultimately I don't know which is worse. Writing the message or sending it. One press of the button. The world will either come to an end or it won't. I can hardly breathe as the message is sent on its way.

I stand up from my chair, which now feels too hot, walk to the window and stand almost tight against it. All in a day's work, I think to myself. *What did you get up to at work? Oh, nothing much. I pretended to be my wife's lover, that's all. And that was preceded by a joyride through the woods with an old grenade and the small matter of her adultery. See you tomorrow.*

The winter sun casts a cold light against the trunks of the pine trees – not enough to wake the trees from their winter sleep; it doesn't bathe them in soft, gold invigorating warmth. At this time of year everything is covered in such a thick layer of snow that winter feels as endless as the Ice Age. I feel the cold sheen of the windowpane. There's something magnetic about it, something alluring. You want to touch it. As if you can hardly believe that the difference between two worlds, between life and death, is so close, right there in front of you.

The phone beeps.

The journey back to the desk feels interminable. I want to read the message, yet I am afraid to open it. The phone is lying on the desk. I sit down and pick up the phone. The new message gleams on the screen.

We should meet. K

9

I need to move, get some fresh air. Primarily some oxygen.

And I need food too. It's the first time I've been hungry since yesterday lunchtime. The maelstrom whirling inside me dispels hunger with such ease that it could be considered an effective natural weight-loss technique. Want to lose weight? Find yourself a duplicitous partner.

Liisa's Café serves up hearty homemade food, the kind of stuff Krista thinks is unhealthy. I rarely eat at Liisa's Café, not because it's unhealthy, but because I prefer to eat lunch at my workplace, alone. I enjoy eating in peace and quiet; I can keep my thoughts focussed on the day's work, and after lunch my concentration continues unperturbed. I don't have to wonder where I was, what I was doing.

Now, however, the idea of concentration seems like a distant utopia. Besides – and this thought I manage to crystallise as the cold refreshes my body and the frozen air makes me catch my breath – it is only by meeting other people that I can continue my investigation. On the other hand, the sinister truth is that both the impregnator and burglar might be watching me as I spoon down my creamy salmon soup and tuck in to Liisa's famous Karelian hotpot.

The thought makes me feel nauseous. For a moment. Then I begin to see the opportunities in all this. The fact that I am out in the open might encourage one or both of them to act, to do something.

Liisa's Café is almost full, as it usually is at this time of day. It is situated in what used to be the foyer of the local bank; there are eight four-seater tables and three two-seaters. If necessary the kitchen can be sealed off with steel shutters, and the former safe is used to store dry foodstuffs. I order lunch at the counter and turn to choose a table. The clientele is mostly men; I recognise almost all of them.

None of them looks like they have spent the last few weeks knocking around with my wife. And none of them looks particularly like a burglar either.

I hear someone call my name. Räystäinen's tanned, sinewy arm waves at me from across the room. I walk up to his table and he gestures towards the chair opposite him. He only arrived a moment ago. The two-seater table is small and wobbly.

Räystäinen is full of questions. He has heard almost everything there is to know about the break-in, everything that's public knowledge. Now he wants some meat on the bones.

I begin to speak, spreading butter on a slice of rye bread as I do. I have to watch my words, keep strictly to the official version of events. Dressed in only a T-shirt, Räystäinen listens intently, but once I've finished, his solarium-tanned face doesn't look at all satisfied. He crosses his bare arms over his chest; his veins and tendons stretch and bulge. I can see he was clearly expecting more. His eyes only leave me for a moment, then return like a hungry animal to a bowl of food. All I can do is shrug my shoulders and munch on my rye bread.

'Everything happened so quickly.'

Räystäinen leans back in his chair.

'And you can't even say what they looked like?'

I shake my head.

'You didn't hear them talking?'

I continue eating my bread and again shake my head. Räystäinen seems to be thinking about something. I don't know much about him, except for a few well-known facts and what he and his young wife get up to – and how often.

'But you'd recognise them all the same?'

I look at him. I think about the perfume, how powerful it was. I know I'd recognise that smell again.

'Maybe,' I reply.

'From what?'

The question comes so quickly that it completely cuts off what I was about to say next. Just then our dishes arrive at the table. I've ordered macaroni cheese, Räystäinen the chicken breast.

'From what?' he repeats, once the waitress has left.

I hesitate. I decide quickly, and in a purely instinctive way, that that perfume is my private property, with a few provisos. Moreover it is an inseparable part of my task, inextricably linked to the very thing I have undertaken to protect. Räystäinen holds his knife and fork in the air.

'I don't know,' I say eventually. 'I suppose, because the whole event was so shocking, I'm sure it'll stick in my mind. I might be completely wrong.'

'So, you wouldn't recognise them after all?'

This is classic Räystäinen. He asks more and more questions until all your answers have dried up. But why is he fixating on this particular detail?

'I've only had a few hours' sleep,' I say. 'I can't really say what happened. Maybe I need more rest before I start to see things clearly again.'

Räystäinen lowers his eyes and starts eating, and I too begin cutting up my hearty portion. For a moment we eat in silence, exchanging only a few words about the upcoming meeting of the village action committee. Then Räystäinen repeats that I should come over to his gym one day and try it out. He says he'll prepare a personal workout plan for me free of charge. He's got a free slot this evening.

It's a familiar subject, but now it's as if there is a new, more urgent tone to his voice. Räystäinen lays his knife and fork on the plate. Right now there's nothing further from my mind than getting into shape. I'm about to say so, but first ask him to pass the bottle of ketchup from the table behind him.

Räystäinen spins round in his chair, reaches out his right hand. His arm extends, grips the ketchup bottle. His elbow bends in again, the back of his hand comes into view. There it is: a long, fresh scratch. It reaches from his elbow far up beneath the sleeve of his T-shirt. It looks like the kind of wound one could get from a broken window.

I shift my eyes from his arm just as Räystäinen spins back into place and looks at me. I take the ketchup bottle from his hand.

'It might just help me sleep better,' I say. 'A little exercise before bed.'

PART TWO
THE SKY'S THE LIMIT

1

I wade through the snow to the other side of the fence. The heavy lunch in my stomach feels so big and hard to digest that I suspect it's pushing me deeper into the snowdrift. The fence's deep-grey slats look bare and frozen; the winter midday sunlight illuminates the world like a small, tired old lantern sitting on the horizon. The smell of the old building and the spruce forest hangs in the air.

I have arranged – and carefully planned – to come to the area around the outdoor museum at Teerilä.

The plan is simple – and appalling in every respect. And while I regret it, I know it is utterly unavoidable.

I have a meeting with my wife.

This part of the plan sounds banal. But after that come the stages that are harder to accept. Posing as my wife's lover, I have invited her to an appointment I have no intention of keeping. Neither as myself nor as anybody else. And then, to crown it all, comes the very heart of the plan – the bit that will happen once my wife arrives and realises nobody else is coming. I'm going to follow her.

I don't know how many laws I am breaking, societal or divine, or how many rules of etiquette I am contravening, ignoring or dismissing; the lies and falsehoods seem to multiply exponentially with every new turn. But necessity and purity don't always make comfortable bedfellows.

And besides, what makes me think this plan will work?

Krista is someone who doesn't do things by halves. She is strong-willed and always wants to find out everything as soon as possible. Or, to put it bluntly, immediately. At least in that regard, I know her well. I'm convinced that once she realises nobody is coming and when she can't contact the mystery man behind the text message, somehow she will try and sort the matter out in person. She has behaved like this many times before. When Krista gets something into her head, it's hard to stop her.

That's why I chose the outdoor museum at Teerilä. The courtyard formed by the main building, two fences and a barn is outside the centre of Hurmevaara, only a short walk away, at the top of a small hill, beside an intersection of four roads, each leading to villages with a finite number of virile adult males.

The main building of the Teerilä museum isn't exactly a manor house, and it's not even very big. It is a log cabin that has stood on the same spot for a hundred and fifty years, and in the summer it serves as a local-history museum. The walls are red, the window frames white. During the winter months the courtyard is regularly ploughed to keep it free of snow as the house is often rented out for private functions, and the village action committee has held meetings there too.

It is almost our agreed time. I am in position. I can see the courtyard, but nobody in the courtyard could see me. The spruce forest stands silently about thirty metres away. A little more preparation, then…

My phone rings.

I pull the thing from my pocket and answer. Pirkko from the church office. I waste no time in getting to the point.

'I'm on my lunch break,' I say. 'I'll be back in an hour.'

'We need to put in the order for the new hymnals today,' she says.

'We can do it this afternoon.'

'There are so many options for the cover and they're all just marvellous. I think this dark one is particularly thrilling. "Though I walk through the valley of the shadow of death…"'

'"I fear no evil". Yes, it's very atmospheric.'

'Then there's the one with a brook trickling between the rocks. "He lets me lie down in green pastures; he leads me beside quiet waters…"'

'"He restores my soul",' I continue. 'Yes, but right now I'm—'

'Leather,' says Pirkko. 'Black leather.'

I peer between the logs and into the courtyard. Was that movement? I wait a while longer. Then…

Krista.

Approaching.

'Black leather is very stylish,' I whisper into the phone after a long pause. 'But I'm in the—'

'Soft and yet … strong,' Pirkko whispers in return.

I don't know what's going on in the church office, but that whisper has the distinct tone of misunderstanding. Then I realise things all at once: the way Pirkko has started sitting closer to me with every meeting, bringing home-made pastries into the staffroom more and more often, visiting me in my office when she could have asked something by email.

'I really must…' I whisper again.

'Must what?' Pirkko whispers.

Krista is approaching fast; I must put my phone away. She stops in the middle of the courtyard and looks around.

My mind is a blur. This is all I need. What kind of signals have I been giving Pirkko? I realise I've indulged in jokes with her – risqué jokes – and now we finish one another's sentences without a second thought. People can easily misconstrue things like that. Everyone construes everything in their own way. At times the two come close together and produce … something like this. I sigh.

It is a few minutes past our agreed meeting time. Krista takes a couple of steps towards the main building, pushes her hands into the pockets of her down jacket. Her breath steams up in the air. I feel horrific. Surely I can't get lower than this; surely this day can't get any worse…

Krista raises a hand to her ear. It's astonishing how little thought I give this before the phone rings in my pocket. Naturally, I have both phones with me, and the one that rings belongs to the mystery texter. I was supposed to switch it to silent, but just then Pirkko called my work phone and distracted me. I reach into my pocket and peer between the slats of the fence.

Krista has heard the phone.

I look up at the blue sky and curse.

I run.

The spruce forest in front of me draws nearer with every step. The snow is deep, crisp and even.

'Hello?' I hear from the courtyard, which is now beyond the fence. Krista is shouting out: 'Hello?'

I run, pushing forwards, one foot after the other.

'Hello?' I hear again. Each utterance of the word sounds more puzzled than the previous one.

The fence will shelter me for a while, I know that. But will I reach the cover of the spruces before Krista appears at the other side?

The thick sea of spruce seems to be waiting for me, ready to take me in its arms. I dive into it as if it were water. Branches scratch at my coat as I press deeper inside. I hold my gloves in front of my face.

'Hello?' I hear, closer now.

Krista has walked round the fence, and now she is approaching, moving much quicker than me because she can walk in my footsteps. For some reason I assumed she wouldn't follow me into the forest, but she does. And now she's asking why I won't stop, why I don't want to talk about it.

The forest is spread across a sloping hill. The angle of the slope begins to steepen. I know where the ridge comes to an end. At the foot of the ridge is a road, a very straight road, and it's a long way to either end.

I stumble downhill, keeping close to the tree trunks. From further up the ridge I hear questions that are, by and large, perfectly understandable. Why can't I face her? What am I afraid of? Where's the sense in tricking someone into suggesting a meeting, then running away? Now Krista's determination is working against me. Of course, I fully understand her. You don't have to have an Olympic gold in empathy to realise what it must feel like to turn up for a rendezvous only to find the other party legging it in the opposite direction.

Everything that then takes place is horrible, grotesque. We were happy only a moment ago. Now we are both fleeing, chasing each other through the forest.

By the time I arrive at the road, my thighs are stiff with lactic acid. There are no other pedestrians on the road – thank God. I don't know what I'd say if I ran into any of the villagers, especially seeing as my wife is shouting for me through the trees. At its western end the road intersects with a smaller lane that leads back to the village; the eastern end might lead all the way to Siberia for all I know. On the other side of the road another steep ridge awaits; at the foot of the embankment is a stream and beyond that a field. I'll reach hiding quicker if I head west. I am about to spring into a run when I hear Krista scream out.

After the scream, silence.

2

Our relationship is based on trust, on mutual respect, on the natural balance of give and take. We have a shared direction, shared objectives. We are spouses, lovers, best friends. We know each other, comfort each other, we experience happiness and elation on each other's behalf. In a word, we are wedded.

But…

Perhaps all this is being measured on this bright, chilled afternoon in a remote Finnish forest into which I have deceitfully driven my wife, who is carrying another man's child. My wife, to whom something terrible has clearly happened. But what can I do? I cannot return to the spruce forest and reveal my plot. I ponder this for a moment until I think I've come up with a solution. I begin running again. Once I am far enough away, I take my own phone from my pocket. Eventually Krista answers.

'Hi,' she says.

'Hello, my love,' I begin. 'I was just calling to ask if you want me to pick anything up at the shop on my way home. I can't remember if we're out of anything, but we definitely need more bread, yoghurt and eggs.'

Silence.

'Fish,' she says eventually. 'Salmon, maybe.'

'Right. Salmon soup might be nice. We'll be needing some potatoes then, too. What else?'

'Salad,' she says, and from the tone of her voice I can tell her heart isn't in putting together this evening's shopping list. 'A few tomatoes.'

I remain silent for the length of time it would take me to write these things down. It works.

'Joel … I think I've sprained my ankle.'

I need to sound surprised. I try my best: 'Where? I mean … how?' Perhaps there's more interrogation in my voice than pure surprise.

'I don't know whether I've broken it or just sprained it,' Krista says, and I can hear that she's truly in pain. 'I can't step on it, can't really walk.'

'Are you at home?'

A short pause.

'No.'

'Where are you?'

'In the woods.'

'The woods?'

'That's right,' she says. 'There's a spruce forest behind the Teerilä Outdoor Museum. I'm on the hillside. The place with the stream running below it. You remember? The place we watched together back in the autumn because it was flowing so strongly.'

'Like a little river,' I say. 'I remember.'

And how could I forget? It was a beautiful day. We were walking together, hand in hand. The trees were resplendent, their colours glowing for perhaps the last time that autumn – there was already a faint sense of frost in the air. I know the next question is unavoidable.

'What are you doing out there?'

Krista is ready for the question. She too knew it was coming. 'I was having a walk.'

'A walk?'

'I needed some fresh air.'

'In thick snow in the middle of the forest?'

Am I doing this on purpose? Asking her questions, though I know the answers. And her answers are irrelevant; the questions themselves are enough – enough to show my superiority. The situation reminds me of the rare occasions when we've had an argument. Krista is silent. Eventually she speaks.

'It's cold out here.'

Krista is sitting in the passenger seat, staring straight ahead. I am driving. We are lying to each other. It is shocking, but it's surprisingly easy. It feels neither good nor right, but my mouth moves as though it were attached to someone else's face. It's a forty-minute drive to the doctor's surgery.

And lying isn't even the worst of it. Every time Krista lets out a yelp or a moan, it feels like someone clutches my stomach in an enormous fist and squeezes. This is all my fault. There's no point trying to deny it or wriggle my way round it. I don't know if we've looked each other in the eye once throughout the journey.

On top of that, I get the sense that Krista sees I'm not as shocked or worried as I probably should be. Of course, in one way I am very shocked and worried, very much so indeed. But my shock and worry have nothing to do with her accident.

I know the question I should be asking myself and everyone around me. Krista is pregnant, so what would have happened if she'd knocked herself unconscious; would she have frozen to death in the woods? I have to carry on asking myself these things. I try to find a suitable way of looking at this, an angle that might provide surprising answers. Eventually I come up with one.

'I couldn't help noticing…' I begin, '…there was another set of footprints in the snow, along the embankment.'

I don't quite glance to the side, but I focus on what I see out of the corner of my eye. Krista seems to turn her face towards the passenger window.

'My leg was so sore I didn't really look around.'

'What about before that? Did you see anyone out there in the forest?'

'Did I see anyone?'

'It's just … if there was someone there you could have called for help. Was there someone else around? The prints looked quite fresh.'

'I didn't see anybody,' she says, and I can tell from her voice that she's thought about this. 'Not a soul on my walk. Well, I mean while I was in the woods. It was spur-of-the-moment, the whole thing. I thought I could take a shortcut through the forest down to the road, then from there I'd make my way back to the village. Something like that. But then my foot got caught in something and I fell.'

'Right – down to the road.'

I see movement in the corner of my eye. Krista turns to look at me. 'To the stream. Our stream.'

Our stream, I think to myself. The thought was sullied the moment it was born. The stream flows with black water. Krista is silent. Maybe she's expecting me to say something.

'Well, you're here now; that's the main thing,' I say. 'And thank goodness nothing worse happened.'

Krista lays a hand on mine. 'When I'm with you, only good things happen.'

Krista's ankle is badly sprained. The good news is she won't need an operation. She is given a strong bandage and a plastic brace around her ankle, and a set of crutches, which help her get around.

We drive home again.

We lie to each other even more.

The afternoon darkens, shades of golden brown, violet and blood red slowly shift across the sky. Then the day finally loses its power altogether. It slumps behind the trees along the side of the road, leaving me behind just as it has done around thirteen thousand times before, to be replaced with a growing darkness that soon engulfs everything.

Suddenly I find myself living the worst time of my life. But I guess that's what happens; surely nobody decides that on a Wednesday afternoon in a month's time they're going to screw everything up. It just happens, then you're right in the middle of it, regardless of what you do or don't believe.

I remember that happy spring afternoon when we packed up the van and left Helsinki for Hurmevaara. We told each other this would be the beginning of another shared adventure. We didn't say, 'Let's take the sofa, the lamps, the books, the tables and drive straight to Hell.'

But that's exactly what we've done.

The studded tyres grind against the road, and the very presence of the woman I love breaks my heart in two.

3

Krista sits down on the living-room sofa. I put on the kettle, bring her a blanket and something to eat, make sure everything she wants and needs is within easy reach. I sense that she wants to be alone, that for one reason or another she doesn't feel like socialising. It doesn't feel particularly nice or homely, but right now it suits me fine. I pack a bag, pull on my outdoor clothes and leave the house. The temperature has dropped even further. The centre of the village is deserted, and I head north along the empty high street. There's a loneliness I haven't felt in years.

It makes me think of where this all began.

Afghanistan.

One sweltering day I stepped on a mine.

Our convoy left the old base at sunrise. We had reserved all the hours of daylight to undertake the journey. The sun was glowing, the journey was slow. The road network in Afghanistan was in terrible condition and much of the journey took us across unpaved roads. We were on a stretch of uninhabited territory between two villages when we noticed a problem with the personnel truck. The steering wheel kept veering to the right, and the problem was getting worse. We were forced to stop and disembark.

It was midday, the air hot and still. We tried to sit in the shadow cast by the truck but it was futile. The sun looked larger than I'd ever seen it. It was directly above us like a round, yellow inferno. The heat started as an unbearable itch, then in the space of a few minutes started to tighten our skin and singe it. Eventually it felt as if the heat was enough to tear the skin from our bodies.

Bringing the convoy to a halt was extremely dangerous. Roadside bombs, mines, snipers and ambushes were a risk even while we were moving quickly. But if we were forced or decided to stop, spontaneous attacks could be added to the list of dangers. Often these were combinations of various forms of attack – by one individual, maybe a few – and they were almost impossible to prevent, either with normal intelligence or by carefully planning the route in advance. These were crude attacks, born solely of opportunity.

As we disembarked from the vehicle, we tried to position ourselves to maximise our view of the surrounding area. We knew we were sitting ducks. We were surrounded by mountains and boulders, but they didn't provide us with any cover.

The commander of our convoy made a quick decision: the rest of the convoy would continue on its way; the broken transporter would remain there along with its crew. We agreed, of course, though it meant we were left alone. Keeping the entire company there for hours would be far too dangerous.

Repairing the vehicle took a long time. The mechanics were working under extreme pressure. I kept my eyes on the shadowy blackspots between the mountains.

The first bullet split the chief mechanic's skull. The shot came from almost directly in front of us – the direction in which we were heading. It came from high on one of the mountain ridges.

We returned fire. The mountain didn't care for our bullets. But there was another purpose to our firing: we had to protect the remaining mechanic and allow him to work. That was our only hope. Our other hope was that this was a lone gunman. The shots came at fairly regular intervals, all from the same direction; and they were precise.

One soldier was hit in the arm. The wound wasn't life-threatening. But it affected another of the soldiers in what was to be a fateful way.

He jumped out from behind the truck and began running towards the mountainside. Perhaps he wanted to reach a narrow gulley in the rock face; perhaps he saw a possible escape route.

The shooter picked up the pace. Bullets rained into the ground around the running soldier. I hurtled after him. It was an instinctive reaction. Or rather, as I came to think later on, it was a matter of faith. I had set off to Afghanistan to provide others with the support, comfort and security that I had to offer.

I was running fast and managed to catch up with the soldier. He wasn't running in a straight line so his forward momentum wasn't the most effective. I knocked him to the ground, said I'd take him back to safety. The soldier put up a fight. He tried to punch me, but his hands were just flailing in the air. Angry but imprecise. I hit him very precisely and with a rush of adrenalin.

I began carrying the unconscious soldier back to the truck. He was like an ungainly sack round my shoulders. The others were all firing at the mountainside as though they were trying to reduce it to rubble. The sustained barrage of bullets affected the sniper. He wasn't as accurate now as before. But bullets still hit the ground ahead of me and, presumably, behind me too.

The embankment was steep, so I threw the soldier further up the verge. Another soldier darted out from beside the truck, snuck towards us, grabbed the unconscious man's hands and began pulling him to safety. I was on all fours. A bullet struck the ground only a few centimetres from my right flank. I stood up, propelled myself forwards.

I don't remember anything about the explosion.

My next memory is from inside the truck. I can't hear anything, all I can see is a blur. I'm soaked in blood. Someone is tying something round my left leg. Then I lose consciousness again.

I was given a bravery award for saving the soldier's life. He came to thank me in person at the field hospital. I was ambivalent about this; everything about my situation seemed temporary, transient – the kind of thing we can quickly get over and forget about.

The soldier I saved was considerably younger than me, and he was about to be sent home. I noticed he found it hard to look me in the eye. He couldn't sit still. I guessed it had something to do with what had happened. He had panicked, done something stupid, and somebody else ended up paying the price. I told him I only did what he would have done if things had been the other way round. He stared at a spot next to the bed and asked if all the medications on the table were mine.

I had saved a pill popper.

I park the car outside Hurme Gym and step outside; Afghanistan quickly disappears from my mind. It's a cold evening. Hurme Gym is situated in an industrial area on the outskirts of Hurmevaara. It's a small area, but there's plenty going on. You can find everything, from spare tractor parts to dried sauna whisks. The latter are naturally shipped to Helsinki, along with other items designed for the hapless millennial generation. The gym is housed in a former slaughterhouse.

I step inside, and the darkness outside is replaced by a fluorescent glare.

Räystäinen is waiting for me. Apart from him, the space is empty.

The large space is open-plan in every respect: there is plenty of room between the machines and barbell stations. Räystäinen is kitted out in white gym shoes, a black training jacket and a pair of grey tracksuit bottoms. Across his chest is the embroidered image of a heavy-laden barbell, bending at each end as though lifted by an invisible power.

Räystäinen is clearly nervous, and I guess I'm not at my most relaxed either. I remember the long scratch on his arm, the pain around my temples, the intruder lying in the snow.

'Quiet evening,' I comment and look around.

The gym is well equipped. There are countless machines of various types. Dumbbells are neatly stacked in their stands. Something about the empty barbells and motionless machines seems to heighten the sense of abandonment. I notice there's no music either. I hear Räystäinen crack his knuckles. More than that, I hear the phone in his pocket beep as a text message arrives. Räystäinen casts his eyes over the high ceiling as he sticks his hand in his pocket.

'Cardio day,' he says as if to explain the lack of clientele. 'People plan their workouts like that.'

Räystäinen glances at his phone. He doesn't seem pleased at the message. I doubt whether his claim about cardio workouts holds water; it's hard to imagine that yesterday the gym was full and today every client is out skiing or running.

'This is perfect for us, though. We can do your assessment in peace and quiet. See what kind of shape you're in and decide what direction to take.'

'Precisely,' I say, but Räystäinen has already turned his back and asks me to follow him.

We start with some deadlifting. It used to be my favourite exercise, back in the days when I did a lot of weightlifting. It's a few years ago now, but I've still got the technique. Räystäinen seems impressed. Naturally he gives me advice, but I can hear in his voice that he had hoped to take a firmer grip on the proceedings, so to speak. The atmosphere lightens up when we start sharing our weightlifting experiences. He is still wearing his training jacket. And his phone is still beeping as messages keep arriving. Eventually he puts the thing on silent.

'I didn't expect you to be so familiar with this,' he says as we move on to bench presses. 'I always took you for a man of the spirit. You know, like you forget all about your body and concentrate only on what's in the soul or whatever it is.'

He says this as though he were talking about Jesus. At the same time he sounds somewhat disappointed at the thought that I've come to his gym – in my own car – just like any other man, and haven't, say, walked effortlessly across the snowdrifts or turned protein shakes into wine. I won't be telling him how sinful I have been only this afternoon.

We spend a moment warming up, talk about the basic technique of the bench press.

I lie down on the bench and grip the bar. Räystäinen is standing behind my head to spot me, to give me some help should I need it. The idea is to establish your maximum lift. I position my palms along the bar and lift it from the stand. I balance the weight with my arms. Just then Räystäinen begins to speak.

'That meteorite is worth a million, you know.'

He is right above me, upside down. In a second the atmosphere changes.

'I mean, it's hardly surprising somebody tried to break into the museum. That million euros is reason enough.'

Räystäinen brings his own hands nearer the bar and raises them upwards, preventing me from returning the bar to the stand.

'Even if you split it into a couple of parts, there's plenty to go round,' he says. 'You said there were two intruders, but by my counting even if there were three or four, you're still talking about a nice sum of money.'

I lower the bar to my chest and try to lift it again. I know instantly that it's too heavy.

'It makes you think, you know, about family … I mean, starting a family is a difficult and expensive business. The Holy Spirit just won't cut it.'

'What?' I gasp.

The bar will not move.

'Well, I understand you – you two – are having a go.'

I put all my strength into trying to lift the bar.

'I can't…' I almost bellow.

'I know, we're having trouble too…'

'The weight,' I say through clenched teeth.

'If you combine your…'

'No.'

'If…'

'No,' I say, this time very loudly. 'No, no to everything. No. Now lift it off.'

Räystäinen places his palms beneath the bar, but he doesn't lift it.

By now my muscles are stiff. Why won't he lift the bar? It's almost as if he's wondering whether to help me at all. Slowly the bar begins to rise.

I have to push it all the way up. Räystäinen gives only minimal help. I get up from the bench, turn and look at him, trying to steady my breathing. Räystäinen's expression has changed. I can't read it. He just stares at me. There's a metallic taste in my mouth, as though I'd bitten into the bar.

How much can I tell him?

If I let on straight away that I know where he got that scratch on his arm, he will know it was me at the cottage and that I failed to tell the police about it – assuming the scratch on his arm *is* from the museum window. And what did he just suggest to me? Nothing concrete, of course. He was just talking, thinking out loud maybe. But he very nearly left me lying there with the bar across my chest. That's what it felt like, though it would be impossible to prove.

Just then he takes a quick step forwards, right towards me. I instinctively grab a five-kilo weight from the stand beside me. I'm not sure quite what I expect to happen next, but hearing Pirkko's shrill voice is not high on my list.

'Joel,' she chirps. 'I didn't know you came here too.'

I turn quickly, the five-kilo weight still in my hand. Pirkko looks first at it, then at me.

'Ah, you're working out,' she says, genuinely surprised. 'And with dumbbells too!'

For the next half-hour we all stick to our respective roles. Räystäinen plays the part of the enthusiastic personal trainer. I play the student with a renewed interest in keeping fit. Pirkko plays at being interested only in her own workout and studiously pretends not to see us or listen to us.

As a teacher Räystäinen is both overly tense and completely

vacant. Either he wants to continue our conversation about the meteorite or he would rather be somewhere else altogether. Or – and this occurs to me as I grip the cable pulley and see him watching the piles of weights moving up and down – maybe he is thinking of how best to get me stuck beneath a hundred-kilo weight again. I could be wrong. I'm tired, exhausted. The last twenty-four hours has sapped my energy, and on top of that, here I am, lifting weights.

Pirkko's performance is almost as bad. The large, empty room serves only to heighten the sense of her presence, and I can't help noticing how experienced she is in the gym. She is slightly older than me and she's worked in the church office for years. She is divorced, and her adult son is studying in Helsinki. She is very pleasant, she's good at her job, and I know I should apologise to her. My communication with her has been misleading. I've been selfish and thoughtless. The thought doesn't do anything to alleviate my general sense of unease.

We reach the end of the session.

Räystäinen has been taking notes in a small jotter. In a loud voice he says he will put together a thorough personalised workout programme for me. The effective completion of the programme will involve me joining his gym and working out three times a week. I thank him but stop short of signing on the dotted line. Räystäinen's expression reveals his disappointment. He is agitated too; you can hear it in the way he taps the computer keyboard next to the cash register. It's me that should be agitated, I think. I'm thoroughly exhausted. I turn to Pirkko. She is nearby, busy doing abdominal exercises on the floor, and doesn't see me.

'See you tomorrow, Pirkko,' I call out.

She stops her movement, remains on all fours and looks up at me. 'Great,' she says. 'I'm doing legs tomorrow.'

I haven't a clue what she means, I realise, and shake my head. 'No … No, not here.'

'Somewhere else?'

'What?' I ask before again realising her misunderstanding. 'I mean see you at work.'

'Oh, of course,' she says. 'We need to look at those hymnals.'

And with that, she winks at me. It's an impressive wink too. She's upside down, her eyes large and brown. Instinctively I look away towards Räystäinen, now standing beside me. He hands me a sheet of printed paper, presumably my personalised workout routine. I'm convinced he saw that wink, and I get the impression he's waiting for an answer. I don't have one.

I fold the piece of paper, place it in my pocket and thank him for everything. I glance at the barbell resting on its stand above the bench and leave.

4

The inside of the car is refreshingly cool. The chill of the seat feels like opening the curtains on a bright morning. It simultaneously wakes me up and calms me down. I reverse and turn the car around, shift into first gear and look over towards the gym. Next to the door is a large window. In the window stands Räystäinen; the light coming from behind him makes him look even bigger and blurs his facial features. He raises his hand in what looks like a goodbye. I raise a hand too and drive out of the car park.

I think about what just happened, about Räystäinen's words. Naturally, I've never before taken part in such a surreal workout. It's hard to say whether I know more or less than I did before. Räystäinen might be one of the intruders, or he might just be an irritable gym owner. I'm fairly sure he's not Krista's lover. Or could he be after all?

I think of all those text messages pinging on his phone. The timing is almost too good to be true. I left the house and went straight to the gym. Krista is by herself for the first time since sustaining her injuries, and as we know, she likes to sort things out straight away. His phone was beeping like there was no tomorrow.

Was Krista trying to contact her lover's 'old' number and not the one I offered her earlier today? Has Räystäinen expanded his attempts to start a family beyond his own wife? He is a brawny man, and in his own very peculiar way he is tough, relentless. Maybe…

Black poison flows through everything to do with Krista and her current situation. I grip the steering wheel.

The village has settled down for another winter's night. Smoke rises from the chimneys; the high street is virtually empty. The layer of fresh snow a few millimetres thick, which fell earlier in the afternoon, has made everything white again. I drink the protein shake I bought at the gym; essence of chemical mango fills the car as I glug it down. I pull my phone from my pocket. I've received a call from a number not in my contact list.

I call the number and recognise the voice immediately. The man wants to talk about the subject he knows best: the impending end of the world. I tell him we haven't got time for that. To be precise, he says, we won't need time, because when the world stops there will be no time. I can't face getting into an existential debate with him. Perhaps he can hear in my voice that I'd prefer he got straight to the point. I must admit, it takes me slightly aback when, for perhaps the first time ever, he does just that.

He thinks he has identified the perfume I'm looking for.

I pull over outside the petrol station. I need to fill the tank anyway. And I'm more alert now than five seconds ago.

'I'm not sure about it,' he says and begins to hesitate.

'You're not sure it's the right perfume?' I ask.

'I'm sure of that, but I don't know whose it is.'

Then we have the same problem.

'Can you say where you smelled it?' I ask him.

'That's why I'm calling,' he says. 'I was having a beer. We should talk about that too one day. I try to take comfort in the Lord, but sometimes alcohol does the job a bit quicker.'

'We are all only human,' I say.

The petrol station is quiet. I park the car by the petrol tanks; nobody will complain at this time of night. In Helsinki people would already be blowing their horns and reaching for the nearest crowbar. The light beneath the roofing is yellow, making the snow look like fibreglass.

'Once I've had five pints, the world loosens its half-nelson,' the man continues. 'I know it's wrong, that sort of escapism…'

'I'm not sure I'd say it's *wrong*,' I say, and I know I'm interrupting his train of thought. 'Ultimately, human existence is a pretty complicated matter. Jesus thought God had abandoned him. John of the

Cross spoke of the "dark night" of the soul. Luther descended into despair and anti-Semitism.'

The man is silent.

'I can't make you out,' he says for the second time today.

'Perhaps we should simply trust in the Lord's mercy. After all, it is everything,' I say. 'So, you were saying you smelled the perfume?'

'Yes,' he says, snapping back to the moment. 'When I was in the Golden Moon.'

'When?'

The man pauses before answering. 'I left about an hour ago. I think I might still be under the influence. Maybe the effects are wearing off. It's the most wretched feeling in the world. It's the Devil's curse.'

'Something like that,' I concede.

The call comes to an end. I get out of the car, unscrew the fuel cap, pick up the icy pump and fill the tank. It seems to take longer than usual, and the frosted air no longer feels as refreshing as before. I return the pump to its holder and step inside to pay. There are a few people in the café. The owner of the petrol station is leafing through a tattered tabloid; according to the headline, a singer of yesteryear has apparently squandered all his money.

The owner barely raises his eyes from the paper as I pick up a bottle of windscreen fluid, take out my card and pay. This suits me fine. My thoughts are already in bars and nightclubs. I realise people often use perfumes and aftershaves before going out on the town, but still. Maybe there's something I can latch on to here: the Golden Moon Night Club.

I go home and take a shower.

It takes a while to explain to Krista why I had to start my workout routine today of all days. I don't lie; I tell her I've had enough of

Räystäinen harping on about it. This is true in one sense, in the sense that people are truthful to one another at all. We choose what we say, cherry-picking certain details, scrupulously omitting others.

Jealousy is corroding me, inching its way forwards like rust, swelling and blistering. When the agony becomes unbearable, it feels as though the only way to survive is to play a role, to step aside from myself and what is happening to me. If I don't, it feels as though I might shatter into pieces, or implode.

After my shower I feel marginally better. For a moment. Then I catch sight of the shelf in the bathroom cabinet where Krista keeps her perfumes. I look at them. I know the thought is mind-boggling. But I have to be sure. I pick up each bottle in turn and sniff them. None of them resembles the scent I am looking for.

I close the cabinet door and see my face in the mirror. I sigh and think about what I am about to do next. I pick out a clean shirt and pull on my best pair of jeans, run some gel through my hair. I try to look like my normal self. I've got my work cut out.

Krista is lying on the living-room sofa, her right leg propped up. My stomach lurches every time I see her injured ankle and the bandages around it. What I did was wrong, I know that. Immediately after that a small, spiteful voice seems to whisper in my ear that Krista isn't exactly without sin either – after all, she started this ball rolling; without her original transgression nobody would have injured their leg. The voice is loathsome. It's a voice that seems to justify acts of evil. It's a very human characteristic, I know that, inherent in our nature. But it doesn't make things right or good. It changes the way I look at Krista, the world, everything.

'Wow,' she says. 'I thought it was a model, but it turns out it's my own wonderful husband.'

She is lying beneath a large red blanket, glowing with warmth and softness. At least, I know that's what I would think under normal circumstances. I know she is my beloved wife, but I can't muster that feeling right now.

The television is switched on. A group of volunteers has been flown out to a paradise island to talk behind one another's backs. The task doesn't seem to cause them too much trouble.

'You're off to keep an eye on the meteorite,' she says, and I recognise the tone of voice. There's more to come.

I think of Räystäinen, the rally driver, and the friends he mentioned. I think of the perfume.

'That's right.'

'You'll be by yourself in the museum, won't you?'

'I hope so,' I say, trying to lighten the mood, but Krista isn't easily fooled. Her expression is genuinely inquisitive.

'Is that why you've dressed up smart and put gel in your hair? To be alone in a remote museum all night?'

I've dressed up smart because I'm going to a karaoke bar. I can't say that, of course. In fact, the whole reason for my going is, in many ways, extremely vague: it might or might not help me work out exactly what I'm doing, and why. But right now I need to look at this from her perspective. I don't have time to answer before she fires more questions.

'Should I be worried?'

'About what?' I ask, genuinely confused.

She pauses before answering.

'In general.'

'Why on earth should you be worried? Like you said, it's a museum in the middle of nowhere.'

Krista looks at me.

'Be careful out there,' she says.

My attention is drawn to the final two words.

'At the museum?'

'Yes,' she says. 'There was a break-in last night, in case you've forgotten.'

'I haven't forgotten. But what makes you think I need to be careful?'

Again, a genuine question.

I'm standing in the middle of the living room. Beneath my feet is a thick rug, but it feels as though the cold is rising from the earth, through the soles of my feet and coursing upwards into my nerves and muscles. Krista takes just slightly too long over her answer.

'There might be other people interested in that meteorite,' she says. She is trying to sound off the cuff, but she doesn't quite nail it. 'I mean, people other than those who broke in last night.'

She straightens the blanket. It didn't look crumpled to me. I wait for a moment.

'There were two intruders,' I say. 'I told you this morning.'

'That's what I mean,' she says. 'So, be careful.'

'I will, I promise,' I say. 'You're right. The thought of a million euros might tempt other people too. It's a lot of money.'

Krista turns to look at the television, the screen is reflected in her eyes. The blue of the sky and sea, the green of the jungle.

'You could pay the mortgage many times over with that,' she says trying to sound light-hearted, again failing. 'And we could get a little cottage in Provence, like we've talked about sometimes.'

I try to resist the thought forcing its way into my mind. It's a terrible one.

This is the thought that I try to resist: there's a link between Krista's surprise pregnancy and the attempt to steal the meteorite. Krista is somehow involved in the web surrounding the meteorite. Nobody is forcing this thought upon me, nobody is suggesting this is the case – not even me. But suddenly the thought seems perfectly logical. This is what might have happened: Krista and her lover have met up. They have developed a relationship of trust. The lover tells her about a way to get rich quick. Krista's interest is piqued, either because she is so entranced by the lover or because she has suddenly discovered a new side to herself.

No.

No, I tell myself. This is jealousy in its purest form. And jealousy is craziness. It thrives that way; craziness is like petrol to its black fire. I'd rather think that Krista is expecting quadruplets and each one of them has a different father. That there has been an eighth wonder, a miracle of biology and physiology, and this is the result: four children fathered by four different villagers. Even that sounds more plausible than suspecting my own wife of attempted robbery.

5

The Golden Moon Night Club is situated in a long, low-rise building along Hurmevaara's high street. The building houses three other occupants: a car-parts warehouse, a physiotherapist and a mushroom exporter. As the name suggests, the Golden Moon Night Club is a night club, though it opens its doors first thing in the morning. Happy hour lasts six hours, from nine in the morning until three in the afternoon. During the summer months I've often passed the beer garden outside during happy hour. The happiness I witnessed was fleeting and somewhat … confused. Then again, who am I to say? As has become painfully clear in recent days, I'm not exactly an expert on happiness.

The evening show starts after seven. This is generally an ever-changing cavalcade of karaoke, the occasional guest artist and events organised by the locals themselves: music, parties, quiz nights.

There are a few cars parked out front; I recognise two of them. The Golden Moon isn't a trendy locale; it isn't minimalist or open-plan. The lighting and the cramped interior most closely resemble a sauna. Lots of dark wooden panelling, dim, yellow lights, booths with high dividing walls. The bar is opposite the front door; at the far end of the room is a small dance floor and a stage. Booths run along both walls like compartments in a train.

I step inside, past the fruit and poker machines crammed beside the door.

The barman is also the local barber. I once asked him if it was hard to combine night shifts at the bar with cutting hair in the mornings. No, the skinny fifty-something man replied; when you've spent all night listening to drunkards you're only too happy to pick up something sharp and hold it near the jugular. I ask him to pour me a pint of local ale. I glance around as I pay him. The air is thick with the smell of electric cigarettes, sweat, alcohol and the hint of a hot dog eaten moments ago. But not with heavy perfume.

A woman croons through the PA system. The stage is empty.

Turunmaa and Jokinen are sitting in the penultimate booth, facing into the room. I saw their cars parked outside. I approach their table and am slightly taken aback. It turns out there are four men in the booth. Turunen, Jokinen, Himanka and Räystäinen. Their greetings are lukewarm. I've interrupted something; I can see it and feel it.

'Joel,' Turunmaa says eventually. 'Pull up a pew.'

I place my pint on the table and look at each of them in turn. I fetch a wobbly metallic chair from beside the dance floor and sit at the end of the table. At a quick glance, this table now houses half of the bar's clientele.

'Shouldn't you be at the museum?' asks Turunmaa.

The men stare at me.

'I'm on my way there,' I say. 'Räystäinen and I just had such a hard workout I thought I needed a beer before my shift.'

This is true.

Räystäinen neither confirms nor denies the matter. Jokinen sips his pint, his corpulent figure stretching every item of clothing he wears, from his jeans to the top button of his flannel shirt. Turunmaa is wearing his leather jacket. His face looks like it was carved from stone, his expression impossible to read, always the same. Himanka is rolling a cigarette, his fingers surprisingly nimble. He is beyond elderly but apparently not in every respect. None of them looks like they are about to start a conversation.

'Making a night of it then, are we?' I ask. 'Or is there something going on that…?'

'Just having a pint,' says Turunmaa and looks at the others.

'Right,' I say.

We sit in silence.

'Shouldn't you be at the museum?' asks Himanka. I don't know what he heard when I explained why I was here only a moment ago.

I raise my voice. 'I'm on my way.'

Himanka nods. His cigarette is ready. He props it between his lips.

'Why did you take on all the night shifts?' Jokinen asks out of the blue.

Turunmaa and Räystäinen glance at him. This is what they were talking about before I arrived. I can see it.

'You were all busy. Skype, football, hobbies…' Time of the month, I think, but decide not to say it out loud.

'That was yesterday,' says Räystäinen. He looks like he's going through some kind of internal struggle. His face is taut, his gaze agitated.

'And tonight you're having a pint,' I say. 'I don't mind being at the museum. Besides, I don't think I'd get much sleep anyway.'

'What's keeping you up?' asks Turunmaa. 'The break-in?'

I look at him. The forester with vast tracts of land is unreadable.

'Stress, I suppose,' I say, trying to steer the conversation away from the break-in.

'What's stressing you out?' asks Himanka. So now he can hear.

'It might be something personal,' Jokinen interrupts; he directs his words at Himanka but he's clearly speaking to me too.

Jokinen's comment is so unexpected, I have no time to prepare for it. I react quickly, move my hand away from the bottom of my pint glass. 'No, nothing like that,' I say, and realise that my tone is a bit too acerbic.

Jokinen shrugs his shoulders. In his tight shirt it looks as though his whole upper body lurches.

'Wives and mothers-in-law,' says Turunmaa. 'They're the worst.'

'That's not really my experience,' I insist.

'Me neither,' says Turunmaa. 'Not any more. My wife upped and left, and my mother-in-law died. Everybody got something out of it.'

'That's not quite what I meant.'

'On guard duty all alone,' says Turunmaa, bringing us back to the original subject. 'That'll cause you stress. You've probably been thinking of tactics to get you through the night.'

'Tactics?'

'You can sleep on duty, if you know what you're doing and how to do it,' says Himanka. It seems he can always hear when he wants to. The unlit cigarette is between his fingers, and he uses it like a pointer. 'Quite a few times there were too many men in those trenches. You had to keep watch and sleep at the same time. The Russians could have come over the defence lines at any minute. You learn to sleep with your eyes open. Sometimes they're shut, but you're still wide awake. Still, once you've been doing it for a few months your head starts to go funny. I forgot my own first name. No matter, mind; in the middle of a war a name's no help to anyone.'

I look more closely at Himanka. The skin on his face is like paper, almost translucent. Across the deep wrinkles on his face is a fluffy gauze, almost like a web. It's about seventy-five years since the end of the trench-warfare campaigns. Assuming Himanka was twenty when he was at the front, he must now be well over ninety, if not closing in on a hundred. That would explain his hearing problems, but not the agility of his fingers or the smoking.

'I wouldn't compare this to the trenches,' I say. 'At least I hope not.'

'You'll need food,' Jokinen says.

'We didn't have food back then,' says Himanka.

'I could bring you a bite to eat,' Jokinen says with a nod.

'The soup was nothing but water,' says Himanka. 'A few potatoes to feed an entire troop.'

'And if you need a pal,' Turunmaa interrupts, 'I've got nothing on this evening. Barcelona is playing tomorrow; I've got a couple of grand on Messi.'

'I'll bring you some sandwiches,' says Jokinen. 'We've just had a delivery of cured meat…'

'After a workout you need rest,' says Räystäinen. This is the first time he's spoken. The others fall silent. I don't know if he's told them about our workout together, about the nature of that workout or how I almost lashed out with a five-kilo weight. 'Your muscles need rest to grow properly.'

'What?' asks Himanka.

'Protein,' Jokinen nods. 'I've got fresh natural yoghurt, straight from a local dairy. I'll bring some of that too. They make their own quark…'

'No,' I say. The word comes out so forcefully that the conversation comes to an abrupt halt.

The men look at me.

'Thank you … for everything. Everything's fine. I'm happy to take the night shift.'

Himanka places his cigarette back between his lips. Turunmaa looks the way he always looks. Räystäinen moves his pint glass across the surface of the table. Jokinen shrugs his shoulders again, takes a gulp of his pint.

'So, it's just you and a million euros,' says Turunmaa. 'All night. You keeping watch, stressed out of your mind and your muscles knackered from the gym.' There's no sympathy in his voice. There's a sense of promise.

I notice I still haven't taken a sip of my beer. I pick up the glass. My hand is trembling, and I can't control it. The trembling seems like a culmination of many things: the weight lifting, this conversation, my general state of mind.

'Are you going to sit at that table in the foyer all night?' asks Räystäinen, his voice taking me by surprise.

'Why?' I ask and manage to swallow a drop of cold beer.

Räystäinen looks at me from beneath his furrowed brow. 'Sitting is a bad idea after doing back exercises.'

'I'll walk.'

'At regular intervals?' asks Turunmaa. 'Once an hour, wouldn't you say?'

'That would be best,' Räystäinen nods in agreement. 'You should stretch your muscles every fifty minutes.'

'It should take you by surprise; it should be regular but irregular,' says Himanka. He can hear again, and now I realise quite how selective he is with his hearing.

The conversation has taken a new direction, one that causes me considerable restlessness. It awakens doubts that weren't there ten minutes ago. I lower my pint to the table, praying that I can find the right words, when I hear rapid footsteps behind me.

Someone has come in from the back room and is walking across the dance floor in high heels, right behind my back. I can feel a shift in the flow of air. I am about to open my mouth to speak. I breathe in through my nose. And suddenly I cannot say anything.

The perfume. I would recognise it anywhere.

The men look at me, clearly waiting for me to say something. I must leave. If those high heels and perfume leave the building, I will have to follow them.

'I think I've left my credit card at the bar,' I say.

I stand up and look towards the front door. Nobody is walking that way. I turn and look at the men again. I think about their questions, their advice and insinuations.

'There will be no break-in at the museum tonight,' I say. This time my words sound exactly the way I intend them to. This is a promise.

The men do not answer. I turn and head towards the bar.

On the way I bump into the village barber. It seems his stint as barman has come to an end. I approach the counter and see a dark-haired woman reading the evening paper.

I sit down on a barstool so that I can't be seen from the main part of the room. I know it's a risk. If those four see me chasing young women round the village, it'll only raise more unwanted questions. And plenty of spurious insinuations to boot. There's that perfume again. I already have an almost full pint, and I'm not planning on ordering more to drink. I look at her.

Did she really clobber me with a torch?

Was she lying face down in the snow in front of the cabin?

She is sitting on a high barstool, her right leg crossed over the left.

She seems slim, sinewy. There's something about her that reminds me of a formerly great athlete now past her prime. She is wearing a red, long-sleeved, tight-fitting sweater. Her long, almost black hair shades her face, and I can't see whether there are any bruises from the punches that I witnessed. On her legs are a shiny pair of fake-leather trousers and on her feet black ankle boots with high heels. Within arm's reach on the counter is an opened pack of white Marlboros and a cup of coffee. She is approximately my age. If I'm right, she wants to get her hands on the meteorite, and I am standing in her way.

She glances up from the paper, looks towards the windows, and only then notices there is someone at the bar. She looks at me. I try to follow her expression, how she reacts to seeing me.

Her reaction is entirely self-explanatory. 'Drink?'

I shake my head, raise my pint glass, which is still half full. 'No, thanks.'

And that's it. She returns to her newspaper. It's perfectly possible that she doesn't realise it was *me* she hit. It's also possible that she hasn't hit anyone at all. She might be the one who smashed the glass cabinets, who took the grenade, which someone else subsequently took from her before inadvertently blowing himself to smithereens. Perhaps she doesn't even know I was the one on night watch.

But there's no mistaking that scent. It is the same, right down to the undertones, the way it hangs in the air, the way it envelops me.

I order a whisky.

The woman stands up, moves fluidly behind the bar. Her body is slender and there's definition in her thighs. The whisky slowly fills a shot glass. She brings it to me and tells me the price. I hand her my bank card and see her face. There might be a bruise beneath all the heavy make-up around the left eye. Her lips might be swollen, though that's a matter of interpretation. She is wearing a thick layer of red lip gloss. She places my card and receipt on the counter.

'Anything interesting in the paper?' I ask.

Now she looks up at me. Her eyes are green, the liberal quantities of mascara bring out their brightness.

'What paper?' she asks. The question sounds sincere.

'That paper, the one you're reading,' I say and point to the tabloid folded on the counter.

She doesn't look at the paper but keeps her eyes on me.

'No,' she replies. She pauses for a few seconds before continuing. 'I didn't know priests went to bars.'

So she does recognise me. She is only a metre away; her voice is soft with a note of tobacco. That might even be a hint of a smile. Before the smile disappears altogether, I reach my hand over the counter.

'I'm Joel.'

'Karoliina.'

We shake hands. I try to sneak a glance at her hand and check for any scratches. She quickly pulls her hand away again.

'We moved to Hurmevaara just over two years ago,' I say. 'I've been here a few times for local events. Tonight I thought I'd pop in for a pint. And a whisky too, apparently.'

'Special night tonight?'

Yes, it is, I think. We meet at last. You hit me over the head, and I know what you want.

'Sleepless night ahead, that's for sure.'

She is listening, I can see it.

'I'm keeping guard over the meteorite,' I add.

Her expression remains unchanged.

'A lump of rock worth a million euros,' I say.

'Sounds exciting,' she replies. 'Didn't someone try to break in there?'

'Yes,' I nod. 'But the clowns took a grenade instead. There was a million euros right beside it, but these guys wanted an old grenade.'

Karoliina says nothing.

'Can you believe it? There's a million euros on offer, and someone would rather have a smelly old…'

'No, it was a proper idiot,' she says. Her voice is steady, without a hint of speculation. She glances to the side. At the end of the bar there's a hatch, through which she can doubtless see the four men sitting in their booth.

'That's all there is round here,' she says and turns towards me. 'Village idiots.'

'Have you always…?'

'Lived here? Yes, so I know what I'm talking about. It's Cretins Anonymous round here. This place has the highest density of dunces in eastern Finland. Welcome!'

'Thanks. I've been enjoying it.'

Karoliina gives a smile; she is clearly thinking about something. 'Why are you here?'

'I'm a pastor,' I reply. 'I go where I'm needed.'

'Do they need you round here?'

'I try to believe in providence, that there's a reason why I am where I am.'

'And is there?'

'Sometimes you only realise it afterwards, that things were supposed to pan out a certain way so that something else could happen.'

'You say you *try* to believe. Doesn't it come to you lot naturally, believing all kinds of things?'

'I don't believe everything.'

'I mean, God and all that jazz?'

'I'm not sure what "all that jazz" means, so I'm not sure I believe in it.'

'Jesus and his mates. Aren't you supposed to believe in them?'

'I'm not *supposed* to any more than you are. It's all voluntary.'

'You don't sound much like a pastor.'

'What's a pastor supposed to sound like?'

'The previous pastor used to turn every conversation back to God and Jesus,' says Karoliina. 'If I bumped into him in the shop, I'd say good afternoon, the liver bake is on special offer, and he would say God has given us this wonderful afternoon and thanks be to Jesus that today we can have liver bake at a knock-down price.'

'I guess that was the end of the conversation.'

'It wasn't really a conversation. Thank Christ. Did he really walk on water?' There's an electricity now about Karoliina's expression, a sense of interest in her eyes.

'So they say,' I answer.

'Is it true?'

'I wasn't there.'

'Right,' she says. 'You're way too young.'

I take a sip from my glass. I swallow slowly, cautiously, the whisky pleasantly burning the inside of my mouth. Karoliina follows the glass from my lips to the countertop.

'So you're keeping an eye on the meteorite in the museum?'

I lick a drop of whisky from my upper lip. 'By myself,' I say. 'Until it continues on its way to London.'

We look each other in the eye.

'Maybe it has a purpose after all,' she says.

'Maybe.'

'Another whisky?' she asks.

My glass is empty.

'It's not a good idea. Long night ahead.'

Karoliina opens her mouth, glances towards the windows. Something about her posture shimmers, something in her expression changes. A large SUV is pulling up in the yard outside; it's a vehicle I've seen before. It's a German model, new. The car stops with its boot towards the windows. The doors open. I see the passenger. He is the largest human being I have ever seen.

Karoliina picks up my empty whisky glass and takes it to the sink. I find myself thinking that I would have enjoyed continuing our conversation – even if it meant talking about theology. I immediately tell myself I'm only thinking that because of the break-in and trying to get to the bottom thereof. I'm not sure I even believe myself.

Karoliina looks outside again, then turns to me. 'You should come in more often,' she says. 'Or will it be a case of when they roll the stone away, there will be no one there?'

'I'm not in holy shrouds yet,' I reply. 'And unlike Him, I'll definitely be back.'

Karoliina is standing perhaps five metres away. She smiles. Her hair is black, her eyes green. Shadows dance across her face, perhaps because of the distance and her heavy make-up.

'When?' she asks.

I don't get a chance to answer.

The front door opens.

The new arrivals are speaking Russian to each other. Their voices are low. They walk behind me and come to a stop in front of Karoliina.

The gigantic man leans across the bar, kisses Karoliina on the cheek, and just when I think he is about to draw his head away, he places his lips on hers. By both Russian and European standards, it's a lingering kiss.

I can't see Karoliina's face, but I can see the man's. His expression is one of joy and undeniable lust. It's the kind of expression you normally see only on the faces of younger men. His hands reach for Karoliina's body, but she has already extricated herself from his clutches and taken an almost imperceptible but decisive step backwards.

The man's hair is brown and tightly curled, the skin of his face very pale. He is wearing a black down jacket, which makes him seem all the larger. Judging by his shape and height he must be a former basketball player. With the emphasis on the former, because he is at least my age or perhaps a few years older.

The man's friend is noticeably older. Silver hair; the bags beneath his eyes acquired through years of office work no doubt; his skin loose and wrinkled. A suit and tie, exaggerated posture. At first glance he could be a CEO, an ice-hockey coach or a news anchor. If I had to offer an opinion on the dynamic between the two men, I would say this man made the decisions while the giant carried them out. Pure speculation, of course.

Karoliina brings them glasses of the same whisky she gave me.

The giant speaks to her in English; I can make out a word here and there: 'beautiful', 'you', 'me'. I can't hear Karoliina's replies. Her body language suggests she is trying to keep a respectable distance, though half of her lipstick is now smeared on the man's cheek.

I can't help noticing that the elder of the two men doesn't speak at all. He seems to be pretending not to follow what is happening around him, but he's a bad actor. His gaze moves from one spot to the next, and briefly alights on me.

I glance outside. It's started snowing again. I drink the rest of my beer and place my glass on the counter. I'm about to leave, when Turunmaa appears at the bar, seemingly in need of a top-up. He is bewildered to see me.

'Joel,' he says for the second time this evening. 'I thought you'd gone to the museum.'

His voice is loud and resonant. It's not normally this loud, and I doubt Turunmaa is trying to reach a large audience. And yet his voice carries, cutting through the hubbub of conversation. His final sentence silences all chatter the length of the counter.

The Russians look first at Turunmaa, then at me. Karoliina glances at me, then the Russians, then at me again. Turunmaa looks at me, then Karoliina, then the Russians, and finally at me again. Eventually they all end up looking at me in silence.

If I were even slightly predisposed to paranoia, I would see in this set-up at least a hundred different scenarios, a hundred ulterior motives, a hundred secrets. I'm not paranoid, but I see them all the same.

6

Snow falls from the sky as vertically as I think is possible. There is not the faintest breeze. I can still taste the whisky on my palette. I walk along the pavement running parallel to the main street in the crisp minus-twenty air, the fresh snow providing a soft layer of padding on top of the old, hardened, compacted ice. Karoliina's image refuses to leave my mind, and I have to remind myself that I am a happily married man. But am I? I ask myself a moment later. Am I really happily married? How happy can I be when I'm married to a woman who is suddenly a stranger, a woman carrying another man's child?

Fragments of my visit to the Golden Moon still flash though my mind. At times it feels as though all the conversations, everything that was spoken out loud, blends into one. And sometimes it's just chaos, one red herring after another. On the other hand, I think, there's always more to a conversation than what is said out loud.

It's not easy to separate everything I know for certain and things I'm still unsure of into neat categories. What's clear is that everything revolves around two fulcrums: Krista and the meteorite. Which, in certain ways, almost combine into one.

I walk at a fair pace through the village, and on the way I happen to glance into an empty shop window. I see the snowfall, a few metres of snow-covered path, and myself. Something about what I see makes me stop – the reflection of myself in the windowpane, a blurred image, fragmented here and there.

For some reason I think of my father. He was a pastor too, and that's why I became one. This is true in its own way. But it's not the whole truth.

My father was certain about everything. Everything about his profession he proclaimed as final, definitive truth. The other world was as real as the city of Tampere. Scripture was the literal truth – with the exception, perhaps, of the most brutal stonings, burnings and mutilations. But even they had a hidden truth of their own. Hidden, that is, for others, but not for him. For him, everything was perfectly clear. And it was with this attitude that he approached the rest of his life too. He knew everything about driving a car, about ice hockey, building a house, human relations. He was never wrong; he was always right. It was easy for him, because he knew he knew everything, and in that way he knew he was right. I can't remember at what point it all became a bit unbearable for me – all that certainty.

And there was another reason my father appeared in my thoughts too. His certainty was automatically linked to the belief that everything good that ever happened was down to him and the God on his side, whereas everything bad that happened was always someone else's fault. Other people were a long series of disappointments to him. His life was a constant stream of complaint, agony and blaming other people's evil and wrongdoing. He would come home from work and bemoan the things people do. He would watch television and scoff at people's stupidity. He would spend time with family members and correct their words and deeds. He suffered. It was a suffering that stemmed from constant, incontrovertible certainty. I found it off-putting. It led to his despair.

Meanwhile, I always doubted things. And that's why I became a pastor.

It was my father's certainty that eventually killed him. He was certain he knew how long the ice would bear his weight. One spring morning he set off onto the sea ice to fish, and his body was washed ashore the following summer.

I look at the reflection in the window. The unfocussed image with all its missing parts looks almost like him. Of course, there is a part of him in me, I think, but what…?

I hear a car approaching. Before long I see the reflection of an

SUV in the shop window. It slows and comes to a stop behind me. I recognise the car and turn around.

I cannot see inside. The car is alone on the road running through the village, and it has come to a stop in the shadows between two streetlamps. Neither of them can quite light it.

And there we remain for a moment. My breath steams in the air; the car churns out exhaust fumes.

The window on the driver's side begins to slide down. It seems the driver is alone in the car. This is the older of the two Russian men I saw in the bar.

He beckons to me. I glance in both directions but cannot see anybody, cannot hear a single vehicle, not a car, moped or snow mobile. In Hurmevaara this is not exactly out of the ordinary. At times the silence is so profound that you start to question your own senses. I step towards the car. I keep my body's centre of gravity low to the ground, ready to act quickly. The driver is sitting behind the wheel, wearing a trench coat over his suit, his hands clasped in his lap.

'Good evening,' he says in perfect English.

'Evening,' I reply.

'Nice winter's night. Can I offer you a ride?'

It's all of five hundred metres to the museum.

'Thank you,' I say. 'I think I'll walk. I'm almost there.'

In the glare of the dashboard and the faint, yellowish light from the lampposts the man's face looks even more wrinkled, more officious than before. I can't help thinking of an exhausted news anchor. The inside of the car gives off the smell of aftershave and stale tobacco, though at this moment the man isn't smoking.

'You're a priest, right?'

All I can see of the man's eyes is their gleam; I can't see their colour.

'Yes.'

'You listen to people? To what's on their minds?'

'Sometimes.'

'I've got something on my mind,' he says.

Don't we all? I feel like saying. That's what makes us human. A person with no worries is a person without a conscience.

'You can book a slot at the church reception…'

'Now.'

I shake my head. 'My office hours start tomorrow morning at—'

He shakes his head. 'I mean, I need to talk right now.'

Again I glance in both directions. Nobody. Then I remember what I was thinking about a moment ago. My father and myself – what I am, and why. I have to help people. That's my calling. Besides, it's only half a kilometre. I can enjoy the heated seat for that distance. I grip the door handle, lower myself into the passenger seat and pull the door shut. The car begins to move immediately.

'Towards the museum.'

'I know,' the man replies.

In only a moment the car has accelerated quite considerably, and we are well over the speed limit. The man holds out his right hand.

'Grigori,' he says.

'Joel.'

We shake hands without any problems; the car is an automatic. Grigori doesn't need his right hand. Perhaps that's why his handshake feels unnecessarily long.

'Okay if we talk somewhere quieter?'

Grigori steers the car off the main road before I can answer.

'Well, what's on your mind?' I ask him.

Grigori seems to think about this.

'I feel it's just a small worry,' he begins. 'But it's a shared one too.'

I say nothing. The houses become further and further apart. We pass a solitary runner. Grigori is driving fast. Perhaps he knows the nearest police station is miles away, in Joensuu. We arrive at an intersection. Grigori doesn't slow at all on approach but swerves the car to the left. The turning is a familiar one. The car starts up a steep hill. Eventually Grigori guides the car into the yard at the Teerilä Outdoor Museum.

And he's right. This is certainly somewhere quieter. Near the village but far away from it. You can drive here in a matter of minutes, but you can be here in peace and nobody lives nearby.

Grigori stops the car, the motor dies down. He clasps his hands in his lap again, then turns to face me. All this he does very slowly – clearly an attempt to show me how calm he is.

'A priest,' he says. 'That's great.'

I don't know his profession, so I can't return the compliment. Though for some reason I doubt he needs my approval.

'It's valuable work,' he continues. 'In many ways. So much anguish. These days people's souls get torn to shreds.'

'I don't know if it's just these days,' I say. 'I guess tearing people's souls began when…'

'When Adam and Eve were expelled from Paradise.'

I say nothing.

'That's right', Grigori nods. He must surely register the expression of mild confusion on my face. 'And that's appropriate to this situation in more ways than you can imagine. God gave them everything, and all they had to do was recognise their gift, accept it and take care of it. Nothing else. Everything was provided for them. Accept it, that's all – accept what was given them. But no. The moral of the story – one of the morals of the story, because, you see, there are many – is of course that sometimes it's wiser to do nothing than to run headlong into an apple tree.'

The contradiction between his monologue and his physical appearance is striking. An ice-hockey coach contemplating scripture.

When I'm certain he has stopped, I speak. 'Is this what's worrying you?' I ask. 'A fall from grace?'

He moves slightly in his seat, turns his upper body towards me. 'In a way,' he says. 'My friend, I wish to offer you Paradise.'

'Really?'

'Yes,' he says. 'By that I mean an earthly Paradise. You don't even have to do anything. In fact, this Paradise is conditional on you not doing anything. You have to do … nothing at all.'

We sit in silence. The air in the car has become stuffy. Grigori looks me in the eye. His eyes are blue and moist.

'Tonight, at the museum,' he says in a soft, pleasant voice. 'All you have to do is leave the door open when you go for a cigarette.'

I return his gaze. 'I don't smoke,' I say, trying to keep my voice friendly and neutral.

'Ten thousand euros,' says Grigori. 'One cigarette. Anyone can smoke one cigarette. And how many people are paid ten thousand euros to smoke that single cigarette?'

'Ten thousand euros?'

Grigori smiles. It doesn't flatter him. The smile reveals a set of large, yellowed teeth, and doesn't seem to suit his face in any way.

'That's right,' he says. 'Right now. I have here…' He raises a hand to his jacket pocket.

I interrupt the movement with a question. 'And what if it leads to addiction?'

'Excuse me?'

'Say I smoke one cigarette. I realise I quite like it. I smoke another one. A third. I get hooked. Before long I'm smoking a packet a day. One packet costs ten euros. At that rate I'll have smoked my reward in less than three years. In the worst scenario I'll have a problem with my lungs and be in a spiral of debt.'

Grigori clacks his jaw, purses his lips, clearly thinking. 'You want more money? Isn't poverty supposed to be a virtue? Just ask yourself, what would Jesus do?'

'I can't really see him having a cigarette outside the War Museum,' I say. 'He performs miracles, but to be honest I think this one would be far-fetched even by his standards.'

Grigori's hand remains in his jacket pocket. He's not smiling now.

'If it's all the same,' I say. 'I was just on my way to the museum. I can walk, if you're not going that way. You can drop me where you picked me up. It's fine.'

Grigori is silent.

'You don't want more money,' he says eventually. It's not a question, just a statement of fact.

'I don't want any money at all.'

He doesn't look disappointed *per se*, but something about his expression seems to indicate he's been misunderstood.

'So you don't want Paradise either,' he says. Again, a statement, not a question.

'Maybe I don't want to believe the snake.'

Grigori leans back in his seat. The shift in position changes the way he looks at me.

'You're a pastor in a remote village,' he says, his voice now less pleasant than before.

'That is true,' I say.

'You have no power whatsoever.'

'I don't need power.'

'I don't need to pay you,' he says. 'I could simply take what I want. If I want that meteorite, I'll take it.'

'I don't believe that.'

Grigori looks at me. 'And who's going to stop me?'

'A pastor from a remote village,' I say.

Grigori turns his head, looks straight ahead. The snowfall has paused. Large, individual snowflakes lie on the car bonnet.

Grigori's speed takes me by surprise.

The pistol is made of gleaming steel, probably a Smith & Wesson .375 Magnum. Grigori pulls it out of his jacket pocket, the same pocket from which he was supposedly going to produce his wallet. Which, of course, begs the question as to whether the wallet existed in the first place. I don't have time to give the matter much thought. The barrel of the pistol is at my temple, Grigori's hand pressing it against my skull. I can sense the weight of the metal, sense the strength and determination behind Grigori's movements.

'Out,' he says. 'Slowly.'

I slide my right hand towards the handle. My movements are slow. I open the door, push it wide. With my left hand I unlock the seatbelt and it rolls back into its holder. The air inside the car lightens, the temperature plummets. Grigori continues to press the pistol against my head, the barrel almost boring through my skin.

'Down on the ground, slowly,' he says. 'Take one step forwards.'

I do as he says. I slowly lower myself to the ground, move one step closer to the main building of the Teerilä museum. A solitary lamp high on a pillar lights the yard.

And now I realise what Grigori has in mind. He is watching me closely; he slides over onto the passenger seat and steps out of the car behind me, keeping the pistol tight against my head all the while. It isn't the first time he's done this.

I'm standing in the freezing night with a gun at my back.

'Forwards,' he says.

I take a few steps away from the car, then Grigori tells me to stop. He is still very close to me, but now not touching.

'Turn around.'

I begin turning to the right. When I have rotated almost ninety degrees, I pretend to stumble, as though I were about to fall on my right flank. I spin round to the left, drop down and dive towards him.

The trick works.

Grigori fires a shot at the spot where my chest should have been. I almost reach him, but he has moved a fraction further back. I grip his gun hand just as he starts spinning round. We turn 180 degrees – and the gun goes off again.

The bullet would have hit me in the chest if I hadn't tackled him and grabbed his arm. The movement that follows my lunge and the gripping of his arm continues. And when the bullet exits the barrel of the gun, the gun is pointing at Grigori's chest.

A long, black-and-red flare bursts from the back of Grigori's jacket and sprays across the fresh snow.

Grigori dies instantly. He falls to the ground silently, and the gun slides half a metre across the snow. Grigori is lying on his back, staring up at the sky. His blue eyes are as open as they could possibly be. The scent of gunfire is strong in the pure winter air.

I try Grigori's pulse. It's gone. I pull back his trench coat. There's a bullet hole in his suit jacket. There's surprisingly little blood. The bullet has travelled through his heart, which has stopped pumping blood instantly. I stand up.

My thoughts are whirling, swirling. Most emphatically – and to my great surprise – I find myself thinking of Krista, of how much I love her, how, above everything else, she is the most important thing. She is what really matters.

I take a deep breath.

I raise my eyes from Grigori to the stars. They are so bright that it almost looks as though they are connected with strands of filament. I blink my eyes, the filaments disappear. The universe expands at an ever-increasing rate. I am clearly in shock. I lower my eyes. Around me is the nocturnal forest, the undulating, snow-covered landscape…

And further in the distance, a figure walking along one of the paths leading to the museum yard.

7

I think about things for a second, a second and a half at most.

In my mind I see Krista's face. She is everything. The thought is as bright as the brightest stars above.

I grip Grigori beneath the armpits, haul him almost upright and pull him towards the car. The door is still open, and I manage to drag him inside. Once Grigori is in the seat I zip up his trench coat and attach the seatbelt. He sits there staring ahead, his eyes wide open. I wrap a dark scarf a few times round the headrest to keep him upright. Grigori is in the passenger seat and looks like a passenger – not someone who's just shot himself through the heart. I fetch the gun from the ground and kick some snow over the bloodstains, then press the gun into Grigori's pocket. His fingerprints are all over it, it's been in his hand, it belongs to him, and fortunately, I'm wearing a pair of black gloves.

Something on the dashboard begins to flash. A phone; a text message has arrived. In the upper corner of the large screen a blue bar glows brightly: the phone is sharing its location data.

Again I glance down to the pathway. Yes, the person I saw has chosen the trail leading towards the yard. Thankfully the path dips slightly before leading up to the museum. The rolling hills give me some cover. I guess I still have a few seconds to get round to the driver's side, slip into the car, start the engine and drive off, albeit with Grigori in the passenger seat. Then I'll have time to think about things…

But no. There is no time, not even a few seconds. I can already see the woolly hat bobbing beyond the ridge. Whoever this is, is walking at quite a pace. I dive inside the SUV, pull the door shut. I am about to jump behind the wheel but glance up to the path once more. I see the top of the head, then the face. I last saw that face this morning. There's no way I could drive towards him without him recognising me. I jump into the backseat and curl up in the footwell.

And not a moment too soon. I can hear the steps; they are heavy and determined. There is a tap on the window on the passenger side. Grigori, naturally, doesn't answer. The steps move round the car. A moment passes. I can't see what is happening outside. Then the door on the driver's side opens. I hear a familiar voice.

'Grigori,' says Tarvainen. 'My friend, I saw your car heading up this way. Stroke of luck I ran into you, eh?'

Tarvainen's voice and the rhythm of his English reveals that his state of inebriation is profound, acquired over an extended period of time. He climbs into the car. I see a slice of the back of his head. He sits down in the driver's seat.

'I've been thinking,' he says. 'A lot. I invite you out here, promise you a million euros. Together we start up a rally team. I get back to the top of the profession. Then you decide you don't want to. I think about what went wrong. Then I understand. You don't believe in me, and I wonder how I can make you believe in me. And I've got a solution. I'll show you. I'll show you how I can drive.'

I hear Tarvainen opening a screw-top bottle, hear him taking great gulps. He grunts, puffs. I can smell the alcohol. His general scent is a mixture of petrol station and a bucketful of garlic.

'Koskenkorva?' he asks.

I knew it. He offers the bottle to Grigori.

Grigori needs to answer.

I reach my right hand as far as I can between the seat and the door, careful to keep it out of sight behind the headrest. I find the end of the scarf round Grigori's neck and grip it. Thankfully the scarf is made of flexible material. I gently pull the scarf to the side, once, twice, trying to make the movement look as much like the shake of a head as possible.

'You don't talk,' says Tarvainen. 'I know that. Leonid does the talking. You make decisions.'

Tarvainen screws the top back on. The bottle rattles against the dashboard. The engine starts. The back of Tarvainen's head disappears from view.

'I'll show you,' he says. He is speaking so loudly that it feels as though he is shouting right next to my ear. 'I'll show you how to drive a car. Then you can decide. That's what we'll do. Is that fair?'

Again I stretch out a hand. I try to think of my options. What if I refuse? I mean, what if Grigori refuses? I don't believe for a moment that Tarvainen will back down. There will only be more discussion, more awkward questions and even more awkward answers. Maybe letting him drive is the lesser of these evils. It's a step forward. It has to be. I'm doing this for Krista, I tell myself. I pull Grigori's scarf lengthways. The stretchy scarf returns his head to its original position. Grigori gives a decisive nod. Twice.

'Yes,' Tarvainen yells, in a voice that resembles the sound a man makes when his favourite team scores a goal. 'Five, four, three, two, one.'

The engine starts to rev as Tarvainen does something with his feet. I hear a thud, then the car leaps forwards.

Tarvainen might well be so drunk that he can't tell the difference between the living and the dead, but he certainly knows how to drive a car. That much is clear within the first minute.

Even to me, lying in the footwell in the back.

I can feel and hear the snow and ice scraping against the bottom of the car and can only assume our speed must be well over the legal limit. At times we seem to slide almost sideways, but our speed remains the same. Then suddenly – we are flying.

The car's tyres release from the surface of the road and the motor howls. I feel a sense of weightlessness. Then the entire chassis rattles as we hit the ground again, and Tarvainen slams his foot on the accelerator. I hear him switching between the accelerator and brake pedals, slamming them to the floor in turn, like he's hitting a punchbag.

I press my feet against the door and hold on to the runners beneath the seat in front, gripping them for dear life.

Tarvainen gives a shout. 'Hold on, Grigori. This is just the beginning. The motor still has to warm up. The driver has to warm up.'

The engine seems to complain, almost scream at the very thought. We pick up speed.

The vehicle begins to shake in a way I've never experienced before. The car must be at the very limits of its abilities. I assume the German SUV's abilities are already quite substantial, and in extracting the last remaining drops of horse power from the engine, the speed along the narrow lanes of Hurmevaara must surely be approaching suicidal dimensions.

'We're halfway there,' shouts Tarvainen. 'Then you can decide.'

So Tarvainen is still planning on asking Grigori questions. The main thing is to avoid hurtling into a rockface or the trees. Down in the footwell, my ears ache from the noise. When I am on the verge of begging for mercy, the car suddenly turns into an aeroplane again. It's a long-haul flight. Tarvainen howls above the sound of the engine.

'Grigori, the meteorite is my million bucks! Another million from you. That's the original plan. Imagine – an international rally team!'

Our return to solid earth feels like an explosion. Tarvainen slams his foot on the accelerator. I guess we must be over halfway now. I can cope with the rest, if the car can cope. If Tarvainen can cope with his state of drunkenness and doesn't make the kind of decisions that a man drunk on the idea of instant riches can make. Again the car takes flight.

'Don't say anything, my friend. A bit more, then we can shake on it…'

The flight is just as long as the previous one. The crash landing hurts me to my kidneys.

'Surprise!' Tarvainen shouts.

So it is possible after all: the car begins to pick up speed. The chassis rattles as the bottom of the car smashes against the snow and ice with such force that I can feel the impact through my body. I hold on. I can't speak. I wouldn't be heard anyway, because I can't get up. The car seems to be floating in a purgatory between sky and earth. For a moment, nothing happens.

Then Tarvainen simultaneously stamps on the accelerator and the brake, does something with his hands – I can hear him rattling the gearstick and thumping his hands on the dashboard. The car launches into a wild spin. I press my legs in one direction and my hands in the other.

The SUV is like a food blender. It spins, the world around it spins. Tarvainen makes the motor wail, revs the engine more and more, letting it drop, then revving it again. The spinning seems endless – but somehow we manage to stay on the road.

At last the speed seems to die down. It slows gradually until we are gliding calmly across the ice like a speed skater after crossing the finishing line. And finally, finally we come to a stop. My arms hurt. Though I'm lying down, I feel dizzy; but at least I'm alive. Inside the car it's quiet. After a while I hear the sound of a bottle-top being unscrewed.

Tarvainen stretches his head back, takes a long gulp and finally hisses. 'World champion,' he says.

I'm unsure whether he's referring to what just happened or to what might happen in the future – the future he and Grigori seem to have been planning together. A future in which, for one reason or another, cracks have started to appear. I'm in such a state of shock that I don't comprehend what's happening. Tarvainen says something and, after a moment, repeats himself. Naturally he offers the bottle to Grigori. I reach out my hand, only to pull it back at the last minute.

Grigori's scarf has disappeared.

It must have loosened during the rodeo-ride a moment ago. Of course, Grigori's head is now drooping down towards his chest. My theory is confirmed when I hear Tarvainen scream. It is a scream of terror, and he starts shouting out apologies. A few drunken words confirm the matter. Tarvainen thinks his reckless driving has caused Grigori's death. A heart attack, maybe, or a stroke. To Tarvainen's mind this looks like yet another lethal driving mistake – exactly the kind of misjudgement that sent him and his map-reader hurtling into an Alpine river. The map-reader drowned, but Tarvainen managed to survive – drunkard's luck.

The door opens. Tarvainen clambers out of the car. I hear his feet thudding to the ground; he starts running the moment he is back on *terra firma*. The footsteps disappear into the distance.

I try to climb out of the rear door, but the child lock is on. I have to get up, haul myself between the front seats and crawl out via the driver's door. I don't so much as glance at Grigori. Finally I manage to extricate myself from the car.

I vomit as soon as my feet touch the ground, hurl out everything inside me. I can't remember the last time I felt this terrible, physically and mentally, or when the nausea has been this powerful and lasted this long. Perhaps it was in the field hospital in Afghanistan.

For a moment I support myself against my knees, then take a few steps away from the car and look around. At first I can't work out where I am, then I recognise the T-junction and see the familiar road sign.

We are a few kilometres from the centre of Hurmevaara. Tarvainen is nowhere to be seen. He has disappeared into the frozen night.

The car has come to a stop in the middle of the deserted intersection. Behind us is a steep rockface. A set of deep skid marks reveals which direction we slid from. Tarvainen brought the car to a standstill about a metre and a half from the rocks. Admittedly a *tour de force*. But that's as far as my respect goes. I vomit again.

I don't know what to do. I have no plan. In fairness, I didn't have one before either. I realise that until now I haven't needed one. All I had to do was trust in life and divine providence, whatever that means in my case. But in this situation, in this situation right now, I need a clear plan of action. There doesn't appear to be one. Nothing can prepare you for something like this. Not to mention…

Krista.

She is the one I should be thinking about. She is the one I'm afraid of losing. Everything else seems to be in flux, in doubt – but not her. I love her. I want to live my life with her.

The thought is, at the very least, conflicting, because it doesn't change the fact that she is still carrying another man's baby and I am in the middle of an intersection with a dead man in the passenger seat.

8

The site is located slightly above the rest of the terrain, the rockface provides shelter from the eastern winds. But a cold wind has started gusting from the north, and at this particular location and at this time of night it is biting cold. My hat and gloves have disappeared. I take the thick, red scarf from around my neck and wrap it round my head and across my face, leaving a narrow slit for my eyes.

This is Hurmevaara on a frozen January night: it will take the police at least three quarters of an hour to get here from Joensuu, and I don't much like the thought of sitting in the car and keeping Grigori company.

I take my phone from my pocket. I don't know what I'm about to say or where to start. Maybe I should just inform them of the situation, of what I see in front of me: an SUV, a dead man. Then once the police arrived I could start taking the story to pieces and tell them about the events leading up to this: Grigori's self-assassination, the rally driving, Tarvainen. It doesn't take military training to know it doesn't look too good when two people have a disagreement and one of them ends up shot to death – even when the one left alive is a man of the church.

The idea that the deceased shot himself won't be the first thing that comes to any police officer's mind.

But still. It has to be done.

I walk round the car in the freezing cold, tapping the numbers into my phone. I arrive at the passenger side, raise the phone to my ear, sliding it between the layers of scarf. I open the passenger door. Just then I hear the sound of a car and turn. The car is approaching so quickly that I lower the phone from my ear.

A lot can happen in half a second.

I don't recognise the car, can't see the registration number. The headlights are dazzling; they're on full beam. What I can make out is that the only person in the car is the driver. And that driver is a giant. I glance to the side. Grigori has slid from his seat; somehow he has managed to slip free of the seatbelt. He is slumped in an unnatural position, hanging half out of the car, his grey hair almost touching the snowy surface of the road. The lights of the oncoming car are reflected in his open eyes and awaken a strange sensation in me, somewhere between life and death.

The half-second is over quickly.

The giant leaps from his car. I'm not sure whether the car actually came to a stop or not. The man is shouting his friend's name. I look at Grigori, who by now has slid even further out of the car.

Afghanistan took a lot out of me. But it also taught me to remain focussed in exceptional circumstances. As the giant pulls a knife out of his boot, all my training and everything I have learned crystallises before me. I know exactly what to do.

I run for it.

A field separates this road from another, and the other road leads right back to the village. I hope I have the strength to run faster than this enormous man, who I assume must be even more ungainly than me.

The snow is deep, even in the tracks I find, left by a snowmobile. The giant is on my heels, bellowing, threatening to kill me, to skin me alive.

And he's not ungainly.

The distance between us remains the same, though I increase my speed. In fact, the distance might even be getting shorter. The stars above us are bright and illuminate the snow-covered terrain in such pallid light that it feels like running through a negative image.

The field is broader than I'd thought. Still, there's some benefit from being an active jogger. I know how to breathe correctly, and even once my legs are full of lactic acid I can still carry on.

The large man is propelled forwards with untrammelled rage. At least, that's what it sounds like. He is running hard but still has the energy to shout. It's a good thing too; there's no uncertainty about it. He bellows that I killed his friend and that for every wound on his friend's body I will repay with a hundred.

I finally reach the road. It slopes gently downwards, leading back to the village. I continue running and thank my luck that I wrapped the scarf round my head. If I manage to escape, it will be incognito. Breathing is hard; there's not enough oxygen reaching my lungs. My throat hurts. In addition to my legs, my arms are starting to stiffen. The decline in the road is steeper. The nearest houses are now only a few hundred metres away. I peer over my shoulder to see how far away the man is.

It's a mistake.

I slip.

As my back lands on the ground with a thump, the final remnants of air are knocked from my lungs. My back hurts from top to bottom. I haul myself to my feet and start running again, though I'm out of breath. Pain radiates from my coccyx, and my legs are about as agile as concrete blocks. I hear the giant running behind me. His steps echo, long and heavy.

I just have to reach the…

Through the trees I see the lights of the petrol station. I remember the yard at the back and have an idea, an idea I'll have to put all my hope in. I pass the first house. The windows are dark. Then more houses.

At the next bend in the road, I turn. Snow has turned the hedgerows into walls. I can't extend my lead on my pursuer enough to get behind them and hide, and, besides, my footprints would be visible in the snow. The man is constantly on my heels. He's stopped shouting now. Perhaps he too has finally run out of breath.

We turn again. I pray it'll be for the last time.

The road starts to rise gently, and the houses are behind us. The tall billboard at the petrol station is like a moon I'm desperately trying to reach. We are like two long-distance runners keeping a steady gap between them until they enter the final straight – with the difference that the big man can't possibly know when the final straight will start or what it will be like.

Behind the petrol station is a large collection of assorted junk, a DIY repair area and old buses, snowmobiles, tractors, diggers and other workman's machinery. I might be able to lose the man, gain enough of a head start to escape round the station, back to the road leading into the village, and from there head home.

From the road I jump into some even deeper snow. The billboard is much taller than the main building and casts a yellow light behind the station. I wade through the snow directly towards one of the buses, walk round the front and edge my way along the side of the bus towards the workshop. At the next bus I do the same. I find a route someone has clearly taken before. My footprints mix with those already there. I half run along already trodden pathways in the snow, using the enormous billboard to keep my bearings. Before long I'm behind the workshop. A lamp attached to the wall glows like the sun. I've ended up here so quickly that I haven't given a thought to what happens next.

In the rear of the workshop there are two bay doors and one normal door. Both bay doors are locked, but the normal door opens when I turn the handle and push. I quickly peer inside.

The mechanics' workshop is empty of people and cars. The space is dark. Light seeps through the windows in the bay doors and through the door at the back, which is ajar. This door presumably leads to the other areas of the workshop, right through to the shop front. My back hurts and I cannot run any further. I have to step inside.

Two metres deep and about a metre across, the grease pit between the tracks is like a canyon in the half-lit workshop. To the left of the pit is a platform about a metre wide, and to the right there are a few more metres of space. Behind that is another canyon, another grease pit.

The space is utterly silent. I make my way along the left edge of the pit towards the door at the far end of the workshop. I see another room, a storage space-cum-staffroom, and at the other side of that space another door. That door is wide open, and through it I see the station owner's back. I can see half of his broad, white buttocks too, as he is sitting behind the counter on a tall stool with his back to me, his jeans sagging woefully. I slip away from the doorway; there's no need to count my options.

Back to the rear door.

And as I make my way towards the door, I see it opening. The enormous man steps into the workshop and stops, twisting a knife in his hand. The movement is slick. It's also completely unnecessary, because he's already made a lasting impression on me.

I'm still wearing my thick, black winter coat and the scarf wrapped round my head. There's no way he could recognise me. When I left the Golden Moon I only pulled my coat on once I was outside – and the scarf was tucked up my sleeve.

The man seems to take stock of the situation. It sounds as though he sniffs to himself. Either that or the shadows across his face shift position. The blade of the knife is sleek, the steel glints whenever a flicker of light from outside touches it. I move closer to the space between the two pits. He moves.

And then it hits me.

An awakening.

The workshop seems to change shape, to grow in height and width. It feels as though all my recent thoughts about Krista fill the space with light, as though this oil, petrol and metal-smelling workshop was in fact the most beautiful cathedral, a place that the setting sun filled with soft, golden beams. The cathedral glows with warmth and light. Its metre-thick walls protect us from the wind, from our enemies, and there I will be in perfect safety.

The cathedral is within me.

I can't run away from it anymore.

Here I stand.

My breath begins to steady. My muscles relax. I am filled with a renewed power.

I have nothing to fear. As I know only too well, the opposite of fear is not bravery. The opposite of fear is trust. Trust is faith.

It's a peculiar moment to rediscover my lost faith.

The man steps nearer. He is close enough that I can see his face. He looks confused. We are standing on either side of the grease pit, separated only by a black emptiness a metre wide. I can imagine the situation from his perspective. The prey is no longer running but has turned to face him, his arms relaxed at his sides.

The man attacks. He leaps across the canyon, aiming his knife at my abdomen. His speed is impressive, but he doesn't quite nail his landing. His centre of gravity shifts forwards. I grip the arm with the knife and twist.

The man yells, drops the knife, and does not regain his balance. His shoes fumble for support, but there is none. I twist more, again using his forward momentum to my advantage. He is like a runner who has gained too much speed on a downward slope; the only way to come to a stop is to fall forwards.

He dives forwards, head first, and raises his free hand in preparation for landing on the workshop floor – but there is no floor.

The giant plummets into the grease pit as though it were a lake. His speed is impressive, his descent precipitous. There comes a soft thump, then another. After that I hear nothing. I wait for a moment, walk to the edge of the pit and look down.

The man is lying on his back at the bottom of the pit. I crouch down and hear the sounds of life: breathing, moaning and spluttering that seem to come from the boundaries of consciousness.

I make my way back to the rear door, step outside.

My breath steams in the air. It is silent. The stars twinkle above.

I start walking towards the museum.

9

But why the museum? Because it is the most logical place. Because that is my mission. Because it advances both my investigations.

What I have just experienced in the petrol-station workshop seems to affect everything. Physically I am a wreck, mentally I am in shock. I'm on the edge, but despite this I seem able to think more clearly than in a long time.

Here's how I see it now:

Grigori wanted the meteorite. Grigori and the giant are in Hurmevaara at the invitation of Tarvainen the rally driver. I already knew that Tarvainen wanted the meteorite, and what he told Grigori in the car only confirmed the matter. Judging by what he said, I imagine they must have had a disagreement and have subsequently been trying to further their own interests individually. At least that's what the Russian duo has been doing, as, having met Grigori, I now know. Which probably leaves the big man still trying to get his hands on the meteorite by himself.

I doubt he will lie in the grease pit for long. And he will in all probability want to avenge his friend's death – which is quite another matter. He will come after me. Except he doesn't know who I am. Or does he? Did Grigori tell him in the Golden Moon that he was going after me? It's possible.

On the other hand…

Tarvainen said Grigori doesn't talk much. Maybe Grigori just said he was going outside and might be a while. This sounds logical, especially as Grigori must have thought I was an easy target: if bribery didn't do the trick, he would simply get me out of the picture for good. Another factor that speaks to Grigori's reputation as a man of few words was his professional approach. This was clearly not the first time he had handled a gun. He was a professional, and professionals don't talk; they act. And the big man is doubtless in the same line of work.

But he will not walk all over me.

Whether he wants that meteorite or not, he's not going to get it.

And neither will Turunmaa, Räystäinen, Jokinen or Himanka.

I'm not sure what to think about them. At the gym Räystäinen was either trying to harm me or send me a message. I don't know which. There is a long scratch on his forearm, the same kind as that of the burglar lying in the snow. The four men's furtive questions and insinuations all indicate that my guarding the meteorite is some kind of problem for them. But why? Because I'm in their way? Because I won't go along with their plans? Or I'm messing them up?

And why have they all – directly or indirectly – made reference to my marriage? In one way or another each of them has mentioned Krista in a manner that suggests they have all discussed her on some level. But why would they sit around talking about Krista? Do they know something I don't? Something about Krista's current situation? About the situation in general?

Then there's the most important question: is one of them the man I'm looking for?

There's a certain raw attractiveness about Turunmaa; his voice is low and rasping, and he owns half a million euros' worth of forest. Jokinen knows what Krista likes down to the last fruit, the last slice of cheese and chocolate bar, and brings our shopping to the door. Räystäinen's stomach muscles could break a brick wall, and there's something about his determination: he's like a long-distance skier, pushing forwards all the time. Himanka is the joker in the pack: he's not what he seems; he constantly surprises me with his youthful movements and, when he wants to, the clarity of his thought. With regard to Krista, he is probably the least likely culprit, but what about the meteorite? He has lived through a lot of hardship and might think he deserves a more affluent end to his days.

After going through the four of them, one at a time, I am forced to confront perhaps the most unbearable thought. What if they all know about Krista? More than that, what if these four men and a group of other people know all about the private lives of the village pastor and his pregnant wife? What if the whole village knows?

This is what jealousy does. It knocks your thoughts off kilter. Nothing is in the right proportion. I force myself to think calmly and rationally for a moment; and when I do, I don't imagine many people are interested in my marriage or our current strife. I believe our secret is still a secret.

I eat the food I bought at Maiju's Grill in the museum's small staff-room kitchen. To see me through the night I ordered two meals: grilled sausage and chips and a double cheeseburger. I eat both of them and wash them down with a litre of cold semi-skimmed milk. On the wall there is a clock whose hands begin to tick more and more slowly. I make some coffee, drink two large cups. But the hands of the clock drag worse now than before. Eventually they stop altogether.

Krista and I are walking side by side along the village high street. She has slipped her arm round my elbow. It's baking hot. The sun is high in the sky, searing down from directly above us; there are no shadows anywhere. It's one of the few truly hot days at these northern latitudes. There is something wrong with the asphalt, our steps feel sticky, walking is slow and arduous. For some reason Krista finds it much easier than I do. She walks unhindered, with light, brisk steps. I force myself onwards; I'm startled as I glance to the side.

I realise we are in some sort of marathon; the sides of the road are lined with onlookers. And they all look familiar. People from the village – people I have seen this evening and others I know, faces I have seen around the village but which I can't seem to name. I turn back to Krista, but by now she is well ahead of me. She is walking quickly. At first she is only a few metres in front of me, then ten, then fifteen. But that's not the worst of it. Now I'm startled all the more.

Krista is naked. I try to shout out. She can't hear me, and now my legs won't move at all. The asphalt is like a pot of glue into which I have fallen. I look at my feet and realise I'm naked too. I can't see Krista up ahead any longer; she has disappeared. I don't know where.

The road is straight and the day bright as a pane of glass. The villagers are shouting instructions.

'Raise your left leg!'

'Lean forwards!'

'Walk on your hands!'

Just as I'm about to run out of strength, it starts to rain. Heavily, pouring down, so hard that it presses down on my shoulders like a solid mass. The rain solidifies the asphalt. Now it won't give way. It is hard, unyielding. Walking is easy again.

But only in this respect.

The road has become unfamiliar. I no longer hear people calling instructions from the sidelines. I look right, then left. The villagers have all disappeared. I am alone on the empty road.

The rain becomes cold. It whips me, thrashes me. Suddenly I see a stone building in front of me. It isn't a house, but some sort of warehouse or factory. Its walls gleam from the rain. The road comes to an end at the brick wall. Just then I hear Krista's voice. She is talking to someone. The other voice is low, and I can't make out the words. All I know is it's a man's voice and that his words are directed at Krista. I can't see her anywhere. I try to call her name, but no sound comes out of my throat.

There's a door in the wall. I don't know why I didn't notice it a moment ago. I'm agitated; I pull the handle and dash indoors. Inside the building it is cold. I guess this must be because of the thick stone walls, the rain, the dark. The floor is made of concrete, and now it is covered in a thin layer of water a few millimetres deep. Every step makes a splash. I try to follow Krista's voice. The building is longer than it looks. It feels as though I'm not making any progress at all. The far wall gets further and further away. And the voices of Krista and the unknown man seem to get further away too. As though the man were luring Krista somewhere. I can't work out what they are talking about.

There's something in front of me. I raise my hands. I feel first a chain then a hook. A meat hook. Strange, I think. What is Krista doing in an abattoir?

Then I hear her voice. She is nearby. And there she is, my wife, standing with her back to me. I step forwards. The water splashes and sloshes beneath my feet. Krista is talking to a man. This is the father of the child, that much I understand. I cannot see him; he is standing behind her, moves in time with her, remains invisible. The more I try to reach Krista, the more quickly the man disappears. I am right behind her and I cannot see the man at all. I don't understand how he can have disappeared so quickly.

I raise my hand, and I am about to place it on Krista's shoulder when something whooshes past my ear. The meat hook latches on to Krista and whisks her away. She is gone. I open my mouth but stop myself from shouting out.

In front of me is a pit, a black hole in the concrete floor. At the bottom of the pit lies a large man. He looks dead. I look at his face. Suddenly his eyes open wide. I take fright and turn around.

Only to be startled again.

Standing in front of me is Karoliina, the waitress from the Golden Moon. Her face is impassive; her expression tells me nothing of what she's thinking. She is dressed in the same clothes as before – it's quite a strange outfit for an abattoir, for this cold, stony, damp environment where meat hooks whizz above us and snatch people away.

Is that a bruise on her face? Is the corner of her eye swollen, or is it something else? A little smile, perhaps?

Her lips form a curve, the corners of her mouth rise slightly. I start to smile too. When I am finally about to speak she moves more quickly than anyone I know.

Her hand moves. Her fist is heading towards me; I can see it coming. Behind the fist her arm stretches out, and I can see her face. She says something. I can't hear what, because the fist strikes me right in the middle of the face, I stagger backwards, fall…

From the chair. Slump, at least. I wake up. I manage to put my right leg on the ground, find my balance and stand up just as I realise I am awake and in the small staffroom at the War Museum. There's a coffee cup on the table, the taste of grilled food in my mouth. It's the early hours. The limbo between sleep and consciousness is gone in seconds.

10

I brush the snow from our front step before going inside. The morning is dark and quiet. I can see the lights in the house next door, the lady sitting there eating breakfast. She is at the table, reading the morning paper; the lampshade above her head looks like it is hanging in mid-air. The snow puffs up as I sweep it with the broom, forming small, silent whirls in the air.

I lean the broom against the porch, open the door, step inside. I take off my coat and shoes, hang them in the closet, walk through the inner door, close it behind me and find myself in the hallway. I stop.

I am home.

It feels as though I've been away for years, as though the journey back here has stretched over thousands of kilometres. After all the adversity, I am finally home again. Home, the place where Krista is. This is my destination; this is where I want to be, more than any other place in the world.

For a moment I simply stand in the hallway. The living room is through to the left. On the right-hand side a set of wooden stairs winds its way upwards. Straight in front of me is the kitchen. The smell of home, the house's own, distinctive air. No other place is quite like it. The silence is pristine. Krista is presumably still asleep in our bedroom upstairs. Recent events flash through my mind in a series of images. I survived. Providence allowed me to come home.

I close my eyes, take a deep breath. I do it again. I manage to grasp the gratefulness, the warmth, the brightness and certainty that I experienced in the petrol-station workshop.

I remember that I resolved to hug Krista as soon as I got home, but it can wait. I can simply rest and … be. There will be plenty of time to tell her how much I love her, to let her know that everything is forgiven. I can wait. I am home much earlier than planned, a few hours at least.

I busy myself in the kitchen. I'm hungry again, starving. I fry six eggs, put some bread in the toaster. Then I stack the eggs on two slices of toasted rye bread, sprinkle them with sea salt and black pepper and eat. I make some coffee. It tastes better than last-night's coffee – and it wakes me up more effectively. Still, the coffee, eggs and bread cannot hide the fact that every muscle in my body aches and that so many matters are, to put it mildly, up in the air.

There's a knock at the front door. Someone has rapped against the windowpane in the door, though there's a doorbell right beside it and beneath that a small sign reading DOORBELL. Now whoever it is has started tapping the glass with their fingertips. There's something familiar about it, something friendly. The tapping fingertips feel more intimate than a conventional ring on the doorbell or a simple rap of the knuckles against the glass.

I glance at the wall clock. Half past seven.

Why doesn't whoever this is just ring the doorbell? I can see only a small section of the porch and cannot see the front door, at the right-hand side of the porch. I stand up from the table and move cautiously, walking round the kitchen and taking the other door into the living room. I crouch down, creep towards the window and peer out at the porch.

Looking from the street, our front door is technically at the back of the house, at the end of a short set of steps. At the top of the steps I see a man's back. I recognise him. All the warmth I felt a moment ago disappears in an instant.

I straighten my back, quickly peer through the other living-room window, which looks out onto the street. I can't see anything out of the ordinary: no movement, no other people, only the empty street and houses etched in snow standing along it. Then I walk to the door, my steps creaking on the wooden floorboards. I don't give Jokinen the storekeeper any extra time to prepare for seeing me. I open the door quickly and concentrate on the expression I see on his face. The hiatus lasts perhaps only a few tenths of a second. Then he gives a broad smile, or at least tries to muster a smile.

'Good morning,' he says and holds up the paper carrier bag in his hand. 'Home delivery.'

Jokinen is wearing a blue sporty jacket over his shirt. It's a different shirt from the night before. This one has red stripes around the inside of the collar. Still, it's as tight round him as all his other shirts. He smells of aftershave – lots of aftershave. His short blond hair is combed in a parting and patted down with a fresh layer of gel. His hair gleams; it might even still be damp.

'Come in,' I say.

'What?' he splutters before correcting his expression and posture. 'No, no. I was just bringing…'

'I've just made coffee,' I say.

We look at each other. It's obvious that he wants to be on his way as soon as possible. And that's what makes this little visit so interesting. That and the fact that the bag of shopping he has brought isn't even full but a small paper bag containing only a few items, or that the car outside is his own car and not the shop van usually used for home deliveries. Everything suggests this is no ordinary home delivery. But he can't back out now without a decent reason.

'Well, maybe one cup,' he says eventually.

The paper bag crunches in the morning silence of the house as I show Jokinen to the kitchen table and take a cup and saucer from the cupboard. I am behind his back. The paper bag ends up by his feet. I tell him why I'm home already, though my shift on guard duty only officially ends at nine, as he well knows. I assure him I didn't leave the museum unmanned. The security guard arrived earlier than planned, as did the maintenance man.

'Right,' says Jokinen. The fate of the museum clearly wasn't his primary concern.

'What's in the bag?'

'Where?'

'Your home-delivery bag?'

Jokinen looks down at his feet as if he's just remembered he'd brought something with him. 'Right, this one. Some Belgian chocolates and Italian biscuits.'

'That sounds nice. I always thought home deliveries were a bit bigger and maybe contained more … actual groceries.'

Jokinen says nothing. The coffee is ready. I pick up the pot, sit down at the table and pour us both a cup. Jokinen's eyes flit between the window to his left and the folded newspaper on the table.

'You're out early,' I say.

'Service is everything these days,' he nods as he pours milk into his coffee. His hand is almost steady. I only notice a slight trembling once he's almost finished pouring. 'Customer focus. If you're going to stay afloat, service is what'll do it. Things are tight as it is, we're just scraping by. You need to go to the customer. Like the mountain going to … like Moses … I can't remember which way round it was.'

Jokinen is clearly surprised at his words bursting forth like this. There's something on his mind, on his heart. I've seen and heard the same thing thousands of times.

'The story goes that Mohammed went to the mountain,' I explain. 'How are you doing otherwise? Still ice fishing?'

Jokinen looks at me. It might be a look of surprise. 'Yes,' he says. 'Lake Hurmevaara is full of pike perch at this time of year. We've made a few holes in the ice, put down some nets. A slightly bigger net, you know.'

'I could join you some time.'

'Ice fishing?'

'Ice fishing, net fishing, whatever's going.'

He doesn't look too enthusiastic. And he says nothing, simply raises his coffee cup to his lips.

'I thought it might make your lives easier if I take all the night shifts.'

My words seem to take him off-guard. He looks at me across the brim of his cup, then lowers the cup to the saucer. Nothing is as quiet as a wooden house on a winter's morning. The clink of the cup against the saucer is like an orchestra right next to my ear.

'But last night I got the impression that you find the idea somehow unpleasant. Can you tell me why?'

'I didn't notice.' Jokinen adjusts his legs, positions himself better in the chair.

'I truly hope it's not because you doubt my ability to look after the meteorite,' I say.

'No.' Jokinen shakes his head. Then he nods. 'I mean, yes. We do trust you. I'm sure it's … perfectly safe.'

'That's good to hear,' I say, then prop my elbows against the table and lean towards him. The meteorite is only one matter, and there's no need to talk about it anymore. At the same time I realise a now familiar cold, slimy feeling within me is gaining in strength. Who brings someone chocolates and biscuits before daybreak? And above all, why?

'I always make sure there are staff at the museum before I leave. As I said, today I could leave a bit earlier than planned. Two hours earlier, to be precise. I haven't even woken Krista yet…'

I leave the last sentence hanging. Jokinen is either thinking about how to answer or simply concentrating on stirring the milk into his coffee. He is silent, staring at the swirls in the cup.

'Would you like me to wake her now?' I ask.

Jokinen looks up. 'No need,' he says quickly.

'But you brought her Belgian chocolates and Italian biscuits.' I'm not proud of my cold tone of voice, of the way I stress every single word. It's not normally my style.

'I can leave them here,' he says, nodding at the paper bag. 'They're nothing special, just a little … Something she might like. I didn't mean to disturb you.'

You don't mean to disturb us? Is that why you're drumming on the front door with your goody-bag at seven-thirty in the morning? I need to control myself.

'Shall I give her a message?' I ask.

Jokinen takes a last sip of coffee. He makes to leave; starts to stand up from his chair without actually standing up.

'Greetings…' he stammers, 'from the grocer.'

The foreplay is over. Jokinen gets up.

'What kind?'

By now he is almost upright. 'What?'

'What kind of greetings? She'll know they're from the grocer.'

I'm not in a good mood, far from it. Jokinen doubtless notices it. He seems to hesitate.

'*Tasty* greetings?'

We look at each other.

'Right, I'll give Krista tasty greetings from the grocer,' I say.

Jokinen blinks first. He turns and walks towards the front door. The floor creaks. He doesn't look behind him. I hear him on the front steps, hear his car starting outside, hear it drive away.

11

In Ancient Rome, Christians were routinely tied to four horses by their four limbs. Then the horses were whipped into a trot, and when they reached full speed the ropes began to tighten. It feels as though something similar is happening to me, but instead of horses I have thoughts.

My breath steams up in front of me as I walk towards the Golden Moon Night Club. The snowdrifts glint in the morning half-light. I grip my phone – the phone that only sends a certain type of message to a certain recipient.

It isn't easy to admit.

Jealousy isn't just the loss of our everyday common sense; it's a degenerative disease. That much I understand. Judging by everything that's happened, I have reached the stage where I think – secretly, in the back of my mind, in the deepest, darkest recesses of my soul – that I have the right to look around. Of course I know that when someone sufficiently plagued by jealousy says he is just looking around, he is either planning a murder or heading off in the early hours to play away from home. This logical conclusion begs the self-righteous question: if Krista has, shall we say, made more than a passing acquaintance with one of the villagers, why can't I do the same? This is pure madness, I know that. I recall seeing and hearing hundreds of people whose lives were more or less ruined after they decided to avenge their perceived wrongs at the hands of a wayward partner. It's hardly surprising because more often than not those wrongs are only imaginary. It's hard to cure madness with more insanity.

I pass my workplace.

The church looks as though it has been flung into the snowy woodland, out of reach. It is surrounded by tall pine trees and behind that a row of thick spruces. Situated slightly to the west, the church office is still in shadow. The beams of the rising sun catch the tall, narrow metallic cross on top of the church. I've often wondered at quite how durable that cross is. This morning it looks even flimsier than usual as it reaches up into a new day, alone and vulnerable.

The low stone wall around the graveyard is covered in snow. I can see the car park serving the church, the graveyard and the church hall. There appears to be a car parked in the furthest parking space. I recognise the car and make – a Volkswagen Jetta – but I don't know who it belongs to. The sun is shining into the car windows at such an angle that I can't see if there's anyone inside.

I try to formulate a message. I'm going to try one more time. I know I'm only accruing more things for which I'll eventually have to apologise, but that is certainly not the only matter in which I am conflicted. It feels as though my whole life is a contradiction. The rising sun gleams between the snow-covered trees. Its beams cut through the grey; it tears, giving way. The same can't be said for my state of mind.

Just before reaching the car park at the Golden Moon I stop and look at what I've written:

> My love. I'm sorry I ran away. When I saw you, I panicked. You affect me in so many ways. Meeting you would have been too much right then. I want to ask for another chance. Can you forgive me?

I send the message, drop the phone into my pocket and glance once more at the darkened windows of the night club. Naturally I can't see inside, but I know that the DJ this morning is not the village barber. Mornings are the busiest times at the salon.

And why am I heading back to the Golden Moon?

Because it's an instinctive reaction, the kind that my opponent – for I have one or more of them – isn't expecting. The element of surprise is at the heart of every victorious campaign or battle. But also because I need to retrace my steps, both my own and the steps of the investigation I'm undertaking. And, of course, because of…

The official version, the one I'm telling myself as I open the Golden Moon's door, still stiff with morning, is that meeting this woman again is an essential part of my investigation and the suspicions that have arisen through it. When I see her behind the counter, my heart immediately beats more ardently and there's a current inside me that doesn't just warm me but strengthens the very sense of being alive. I tell myself that it must have something to do with the situation, the stress and the fact that she might be the person who knocked me unconscious.

Karoliina is pouring a pint of weak beer for a middle-aged man leaning against the counter with both arms. The man's dark-brown hair juts in all directions as though a small bomb has gone off in his head. He is wearing a suit that looks not only as though he slept in it but as though he probably had a wrestling match in it too. The man appears to be at the very limits of his capabilities. His tie is astonishingly straight and tightly knotted, as though he had tried to pull himself together but forgotten about everything else. Karoliina places the pint in front of him. The man picks up the glass, raises it to his pouting lips, gulps down half. Karoliina angles her head towards me but keeps her eyes on the cash register.

'What's it to be?' she asks.

'I don't really know, to be honest,' I reply.

Karoliina looks up, turns slightly. 'Pastor,' she says, straightens her posture and brushes a hair from across her face. 'Or am I supposed to call you Reverend Huhta?'

'Joel is fine.'

Karoliina steps closer. I have positioned myself at the same end of the bar as yesterday. Even during the daytime, the Golden Moon isn't a bright place. Here there is a perpetual dusk where people drink beer for breakfast, their hair a tangle. Here works a woman in ripped, holey jeans, a black polo-neck jumper, heavy make-up and dark-red lipstick. Her long hair, darker than dark, covers her face, her lips flicker like a lantern amid the shadows. When she is finally standing in front of me, I can't see any discernible difference in her expression. If she really is somehow involved in the events of the night before last, you'd never know.

'I thought you were joking,' she says.

'About what?'

'That you would come in again.'

'I keep my promises,' I say and look into her green eyes.

The sound of loud conversation is coming from the room, an argument about which cities hosted the Olympics in the fifties and sixties. It seems there are many people in the village who start their day with something other than a yoghurt or a bowl of porridge.

'You haven't slept; you've been at the museum all night,' she says. It isn't a question. 'And now you're here.'

'So are you,' I say.

She doesn't respond. Perhaps she's thinking. 'So, what's it to be?'

Which is the least suspicious option, I wonder? A vicar coming into a bar in the morning for a beer or a vicar coming into a bar in the morning but not ordering anything? It's not a question that needs much thought. When Karoliina brings my beer, I pick up the glass but don't drink.

'How was the museum?' she asks.

'Pretty calm. I felt almost lonely.'

'Almost?'

'Especially compared to the previous night,' I say. 'Then I had company and there was plenty of action.'

'You sound as if you miss the company and the action.'

'It depends on what kind of action we're talking about,' I reply calmly. 'And what kind of company, of course.'

Karoliina takes a packet of cigarettes from behind the bar. 'What does it feel like, being there with a million euros right next to you?' she asks.

'I don't really think about it.'

'So why are you there?'

It's a good question, a justified one.

'Personal reasons.'

'And they are?'

I shrug my shoulders. 'Personal.'

Karoliina takes a cigarette from the packet. She holds it, unlit, between her forefinger and middle finger, as though she were smoking it.

'So it's not as though God spoke to you and told you to look after the thing?'

'I saw a burning bush outside the museum, and that's when I knew what to do.'

Is that a smile? If it is, it's gone quickly.

She looks at me intensely. 'Can I ask you something?'

'Of course.'

'Is this what you want out of life?'

'What exactly?'

Karoliina gestures towards my pint with her cigarette. 'Sitting in a pub in Hurmevaara having a pint at nine in the morning.' She stresses every word individually. I can tell she doesn't like any of them.

'No,' I say. 'It isn't.'

'Nobody drinks beer at nine in the morning if they've got something better to do.'

'I imagine that's true.'

'And nobody spends as much as an extra day in Hurmevaara if they can be somewhere else.'

I say nothing. Karoliina has touched a nerve, one of many nerves, a nerve that I've barely noticed amid the chaos of the last few days. It's true: I don't feel the same admiration I once did for this quaint little village and the nature surrounding it. Of course, there are various reasons for that. The quaintness and fresh air have lost their allure of late.

Karoliina leans towards me. 'Have you ever thought how easy it would be to change things?'

'I'm not sure it would be easy.'

'But you want to change things?'

'Yes.'

'Then it's simple.'

'And why is that?'

'Because I can see that you want to,' she says. 'And because I can help you. The question is…'

The middle-aged man calls over for more beer, giving his empty pint glass a jiggle. In a strange way he seems to have perked up a bit. Karoliina walks to the other end of the bar and glances behind her. We look each other in the eye. She pulls the pint, takes the payment, returns to my end of the counter.

'You can help me,' I say, reminding her where we left off.

She doesn't reply straight away. She leans her hip against the bar, places her hands on the counter top. She is closer to me than ever before. And yes, the perfume is familiar. It is familiar, its scent not at all unpleasant.

'I was saying it's a question of how we can help each other. But I don't know if I can trust you. You're a vicar.'

'Does that make me untrustworthy?'

We are speaking softly, our voices lowered. Any quieter and we'd be whispering.

'"Thou shalt not steal",' says Karoliina. 'Isn't that one of the commandments?'

'The seventh,' I reply.

'How closely does your lot keep to all those rules?'

'I can't speak for others.'

'What about you?' The look in Karoliina's green eyes is either one of playfulness or utter sincerity. I can't tell which.

'What do you suggest?' I ask.

'What's your answer?' Karoliina leans closer still. She is so close that looking into her eyes almost hurts.

'I try to uphold certain tried-and-tested principles,' I say. 'But if I'm going to give you a specific answer, I need to know what we're up to.'

'I like the idea that you think we're up to something.'

We are now so close to one another that I can feel her warmth, feel her face near my own. The moment is significant. The middle-aged man starts shouting again. By now there's a new-found depth in his voice. The beer has redeemed him, has started to soothe him. Before long his tie might even slacken. Karoliina doesn't take her eyes from me. Then she turns her head and shouts at him for a moment.

And when her head turns and her hair swings to the side, I see it.

A bruise.

It's higher up and further back than I'd thought, but there it is all the same. There on her temple, hidden behind the layers of make-up, the skin is still ever so slightly swollen. She turns back and looks me in the eye again. I hear the front door opening and closing behind me; I feel the cold draught of air against my lower back; I hear hearty, male laughter, the sound of winter boots kicking off the snow.

'You know where to find me,' Karoliina whispers, her eyes still fixed on me.

She presses her lips together and blows me a kiss. Then she turns again and walks to the other end of the counter and doesn't look back. She doesn't need to. She knows my eyes are following her.

It's an important part of the play.

12

The sky is glowing, the snow glittering, the sun gilding the world's surface. The gravestones flicker in the corner of my eye as I pass the cemetery. I arrive in the car park and notice that the car that had been in the furthest parking spot has gone.

I wouldn't have given the matter any further thought if I hadn't seen an envelope taped to the glass window in the front door of the church office. It's a brown A5 envelope, half the size of an A4. The upper left-hand corner of the envelope is slightly tattered and there is no stamp. But there is a name on the envelope.

PASTOR JOEL HUHTA

The text is written in stick letters with thick black felt-tip. There is no other text on the envelope. No address, no return address. Only my name and profession.

I turn and look around. The winter's day is devoid of people. A car drives past in the distance. It reminds me of the solitary, unfamiliar car I saw earlier, when it was parked at the edge of the car park. It was a light-blue Volkswagen, either a Passat or a Jetta. Probably.

I peel off the ends of the Sellotape and stick them back on the envelope. I glance behind one more time and make my way inside. The church office is empty, quiet, so I open the envelope right away. It has been sealed carefully, so I have to tear it open. The paper is brittle; the envelope has been used before. Inside there's a sheet of A4 folded in half. I pull it out and open it. The text looks like a computer print-out, the font a perfectly ordinary Times New Roman. The paper contains a short text written in all capitals.

STAY AWAY FROM THE MUSEUM.
THIS IS YOUR FINAL WARNING.
BE TOLD.

I turn the paper over, but there is no more text. It doesn't need any. The message is simple and to the point. I fold the sheet of paper and slip it back inside the envelope. Again I peer out into the yard, but it's futile. The snow is glimmering and there's nobody outside who looks like they've just taped a threatening letter to the door of the church office.

Pirkko is in the secretary's room. She has heard my steps but still looks surprised to see me, almost as though she were out of breath. The work desktop flickers on the screen in front of her. Nobody sits looking at their desktop. She must have just clicked a window closed, out of my sight.

'Has anyone been in here?' I ask.

'What do you mean?'

Still Pirkko seems somewhat … not quite startled but something like that. A soft red colours her cheeks.

'The church office is open,' I say. 'Office hours.'

'Yes, that's right,' she says. 'I mean, no.'

'You haven't seen or heard anyone?'

Pirkko shakes her head. 'No one,' she says and looks as though she really would remember. 'Nothing. And as the next session was cancelled, I imagine it'll be fairly quiet for the next hour or so.'

'Good,' I say and can't think of anything else to ask her. Except of course… 'Pirkko… Is everything all right?'

Her brown eyes look up at me. 'Everything's just wonderful.'

The coffee machine bubbles. I read the letter again. It doesn't tell me anything that wasn't abundantly clear the first time. I don't know what to think of it. But in the light of recent events the letter seems the least of my worries. I leave the envelope on the table and go to the bathroom. I do my business, rinse my face. The warm water refreshes me, soothes me. I turn off the tap, and dry my face and neck with a rough paper towel. I am looking at myself in the mirror when I hear a voice behind the door.

'Joel?'

'Yes?'

'The cancelled session was booked again. There's someone to see you.'

'I'll be out in a minute,' I reply.

I give my face another wipe. I might look like the same man I was two or three days ago. But I'm not. There are some explosions that leave physical traces, and there are explosions that other people cannot see.

'He's waiting in the corridor,' comes Pirkko's voice from behind the door.

'Thank you.'

'He…'

I lean forwards and gulp cold water straight from the tap and don't hear the rest of Pirkko's sentence. I stand up and draw a breath. I'm still wearing my coat, my scarf still wrapped round my neck, my hat pulled over my head. I stuff the hat into my coat pocket, shrug off the coat, pull the scarf into the sleeve, fold the coat over my arm and open the door.

Pirkko has disappeared. The staffroom is empty, and quiet except for the puffing and gurgling of the coffee machine. As I walk along the corridor I feel almost normal.

Until I realise I have reached a dead end. Literally.

Behind me the corridor comes to an end at a window that reaches up to the ceiling. In front of me it continues all the way into the foyer. But that doesn't help me. And none of the numerous doors along the corridor can help me either. They are all too far away. The only door I can use is the door into my own office, the nearest door. Along the right-hand side of the corridor, diagonally across from my office, is a chair. Sitting in that chair is the largest man I have ever seen. For a fleeting moment, I consider jumping through the window and fleeing into the snow. But that wouldn't be a wise course of action. Only in the cinema can you get away with a plan like that without killing yourself.

The man's left arm is in a sling. He is reading a magazine. I look at his profile. I slip the coat from my arm to my hand, hold it near my waist. He turns his head almost in time with my steps. I go through the facts in my mind. He couldn't have seen my face. His eyes focus on mine.

'Pastor,' he says in English.

'That's me,' I say and gesture towards my office. 'Come on in.'

The man stands up and walks in front of me into the office. I step inside after him, close the door and make my way straight to the wardrobe. I hang my coat inside and close the wardrobe door carefully, silently. The man doesn't need instructions; he heads directly for the consultation area.

We sit down.

I've never paid attention to the small armrests on these chairs before. The man fills the space between the armrests. He's not stocky, let alone overweight, but his waist is simply slightly larger than the seat of the chair, and the effect is of someone squeezing himself into a tight spot. He carefully positions his injured arm too. Once it looks as though his arm is in an agreeable position in relation to the chair and the rest of his body, the man sighs, as though his work is done, and looks at me.

Outside, the blue sky and the white snowdrifts reflect each other and the room is filled with light. On the wall behind the man, the Redeemer looks positively radiant.

'You're probably wondering why I'm sitting here,' the man begins. His large, grey eyes look right at me. His face is almost paler than yesterday. His English is impeccable. It has a strong accent, but his speech is very fluent indeed.

'People have different reasons for coming to—'

'I mean, because I am Orthodox.'

'Right, in that sense, yes…'

'I'm not very orthodox Orthodox.'

'Few of us are—'

'And neither are you,' he says. 'And yet we have the same Bible, isn't that right.'

For a moment I wonder how to answer. I'm sure he will interrupt me whatever I say.

'Yes, the Bible is the same.'

'I cannot visit my local church. It's across the border.'

'Exactly.'

'You have a duty of confidentiality, isn't that right?'

I nod.

'Everything I say remains within these four walls?' The man pauses before continuing. 'My friend has died.'

He looks me in the eye, directly, insistently. I try to discern whether there's anything else behind his words. I can't find anything.

'I'm sorry to hear that.'

'He was murdered.'

'No … surely not?'

The man nods again, gently rocks his head back and forth. 'No, it's true,' he says. 'Here. Right here in this village. Somebody murdered him. Brutally. Perhaps you remember my friend?'

I don't have time to reply before he continues.

'He was at the bar last night. Just like you were. He went outside for a moment, or so I assumed. I had other business in the bar and couldn't join him. Besides, I knew where he was. We were always … in contact whenever we were … working together. But he never came back. I sent messages. No reply. It wasn't like him. I went out to see if he was all right. Then I found him.'

The room is bathed in the pale, winter brightness. My breath is shallow, then stops altogether.

'Someone had shot him,' the man continues. 'A single shot. Right through the heart. If you know what you're doing, that's enough. You pierce the heart. Every professional knows that.'

'Professional?'

'Someone who has used a gun before,' he says, turning his head and squinting as he looks outside. Then he returns his focus to me. 'Not the village priest, I assume.'

I can't make out any insinuation in his voice. I wait, slowly filling my lungs with air.

'He's from round here,' says the man. 'The shooter – he's a local.'

'From Hurmevaara?'

'Yes, from this cold, godforsaken backwater,' he nods and lowers his voice. 'This … this place is like Siberia. Nothing works the way it's supposed to. Nothing is certain. This is like … a smaller version of Kamchatka. It's Little Siberia. That's what this is.'

I say nothing. On this day of all days I can relate to the man's sentiments about Hurmevaara.

'I'm going to find him.'

'The shooter?'

'Yes. I'll recognise him. He is … He thinks he's some kind of commando; he'd disguised himself. But I'll recognise him. And when I get my hands on him…'

The man sounds neither threatening nor vengeful; he sounds merely confident.

'And where is your friend…?'

The man shakes his head. 'I buried him in the snow,' he says. 'Temporarily. Once this business is sorted out, I'll take him home.'

'Right,' I nod. I can't exactly ask what kind of business the man is undertaking; that's beyond the purview of pastoral care. 'And this event made you wish to seek the counsel of the church?'

Again the man fixes his grey eyes on me. 'This event made me hungry for revenge.'

'So that's what you want to talk about?'

'I want revenge.'

'So why did you—?'

'Grigori was like a father to me, the father I never had. Of course, there was a man somewhere who fathered me, but that doesn't make you a father. A father is something else. A father protects you, teaches you. Grigori taught me everything. Everything. He was my father, though he was not.'

I say nothing.

'We came here on business,' he continues. 'We were meant to take care of something and go home again. But then I fell in love and Grigori was murdered.'

'You fell in love?'

'Her name is Karoliina. The most beautiful woman I've ever met.'

'Is she involved in your business matters?' The question pops out too quickly. Completely the wrong kind of question.

'Maybe,' the man answers eventually.

His expression is impossible to read. We sit in silence for a moment.

'If someone murdered your father, what would you do?' he asks.

'My father drowned,' I say, deliberately ducking the question, trying to steer the conversation back to more neutral ground. 'It happened years ago.'

'Was he a sailor?'

'He was a pastor.'

The man thinks about this. 'In the Orthodox church, priests don't get married,' he says. 'And they don't have children.'

'I know that. Our practices are slightly different.'

'It's peculiar,' he says. 'But indeed, I see that's a ring on your finger. So priests here can get married and have children?'

'Yes.'

'As many as you like?'

'There's no strict limit.'

'So you have a wife. Any children?'

'No … I mean, we're in the process of…'

'Ah,' the man sighs as though he has tasted something delicious. 'You're working on it. That's the fun part. The final result, not so much – unless you like children. And if you like them, you naturally wouldn't want anything bad to happen, either to them or to yourself. Or to the children's mother.'

From murder to infertility, and from there to a veiled threat. My attempts to steer the conversation haven't turned out quite as I imagined. Not to mention that I'm sitting opposite a man who wants to take revenge on me for the death of his friend.

'I wish to confess to something,' he says. 'I have killed three men.'

The man's expression is like cold, grey steel. I have no intention of telling him my duty of confidentiality doesn't cover homicide.

'Before now,' he continues.

The Redeemer shines on the wall. His right flank reflects the light streaming in from outside, angling the brightness towards me. I can't hear a single sound.

'You understand me,' he says. 'When I catch up with Grigori's killer, I'll ... you know.'

'I think I understand.'

'I want to apologise.'

'What for?'

'For what I am about to do.'

'In advance?'

'Yes,' he says and looks up at the ceiling. 'From up there. From Him.'

'I'm not sure it works like that,' I reply.

'Why not? If we feel remorse and ask for forgiveness of our sins, then we are forgiven. What difference does it make, the order we do things in? If sin is my lot and forgiveness is His, who am I to tell Him what to do?'

I don't know the answer to this, so I remain silent and wait. My heart is racing, like a sledgehammer pummelling a wall, almost breaking my ribs in the process.

'Thank you for this,' the man says suddenly.

Our time is almost up. I struggle to retain my composure.

'You're welcome,' I say.

'This was a good conversation. I think we understand each other.'

The man stands up from the chair, careful not to bash his elbow in its sling. With his other hand he places the strap round his neck.

'I hurt my arm,' he explains. 'Well, I should say I was assaulted. In a most egregious manner.'

'That's not … very nice.'

A small, almost imperceptible smile creeps across the corner of his mouth. 'He was lucky,' says the man. 'I hadn't got serious yet.'

You weren't serious, I think to myself, but you hunted me with a knife, bellowing at the top of your voice. I wait for him to take a step towards the door, allowing the distance between us to grow. The man is almost at the door when he suddenly stops. He turns his head to face the wardrobe, the door of which is standing ajar.

Can he see what I can see? The black sleeve of my coat, the flash of my red scarf sticking out of the cuff?

I act quickly. The man is still standing with his back to me. I take a few sideways steps towards the wall and reach for the copper and brass cross hanging there. It is heavy, sharp at the edges. My fingers clench round the base of the cross, and it rests in my hands like a baseball bat. The man begins to turn; I pull the cross from behind my back.

He is standing by the door, looking at me from across the room. The light is coming from behind me.

'I almost forgot,' he says.

I wait.

'My name is Leonid.'

13

Day slowly wanes behind the trees, eventually freezing on the horizon. The room, which only a moment ago was so bright, has become dim. Nothing looks as focussed, as sharply defined as it did a few hours ago. The gradually descending darkness softens the contours, deepens the shadows.

The Redeemer is on the wall again. He's not glowing now; his flank no longer reflects the fading beams. He looks tired. His face is angled downwards, cast in shadow.

Over the course of the day I have led two pastoral sessions and one meeting, the latter on the telephone. My superior in Joensuu reminded me of our upcoming professional-development seminar – his words, not mine – and encouraged me to consider whether there were any particular challenges or factors in my work that have taken me by surprise. I promised to give it some thought and he asked me to make a list that, with regard to our limited resource dynamics, would help us prioritise our strategy focus. So far I haven't put pen to paper.

My pastoral sessions were fairly routine. People's problems are often very similar, with some small variations; life is hard and sometimes feels senseless. But as I have observed over the years, listening is a privilege. For the duration of our conversations I don't have time to think about my own problems. But after each session I realise I've learned more about myself, and I feel more grateful, either for my life in general or for something specific.

But I mean this in the most general sense.

Today things feel completely different, or, rather, I feel different from how I felt this morning.

The church office is empty. Pirkko has gone home, locking the front door behind her. I sit in an armchair and try to put the jigsaw together.

I can't help looking back at the cross on the wall. When under threat, I'd grabbed it. I wasn't afraid, I was ready – for what, I don't know. Perhaps for anything. I remember my emotions upon returning home early this morning: hope, something clear, bright. Then everything went black, very quickly. I try to make things out, to differentiate things from one another, when I hear a surprising voice in my mind. Leonid's voice.

He was my father, though he was not.

There is Krista and there is the meteorite.

I can't begin to think that Krista is involved with the latter. It's simply not possible. Krista is … just pregnant, that's all. Saying it to myself is perhaps all I can manage right now, and that too feels like a lot. It is a lot. She is carrying a child inside her; she calls me the child's father. And no matter how bleak or paranoid my perspective on the matter is, from Krista's point of view she is giving me the greatest gift imaginable. As I've thought before, 'conflicted' seems the smallest, most inadequate of words. I glance again at the phone from which I sent her a message. No answer.

The room darkens further as the sun finally disappears behind the trees. As though the spruces have grown metres in a matter of minutes. Beneath the cross, the brick wall loses its contours, becomes an even, light surface.

Then there's the meteorite.

The meteorite will be in the War Museum for a further two nights.

The list of people keen to get their hands on it seems to grow as time runs out. As for Leonid, I am in no doubt. He wants the meteorite. Karoliina wants the meteorite and is apparently willing to collaborate with me – the guard on the night shift – to get it. Leonid is in love with Karoliina, a matter that raises a number of questions.

Is Karoliina employing Leonid's help in order to achieve her goal? If she is, why does she want to involve me in her plans? And if she isn't, why has she started a relationship with a man for whom she feels no attraction? I well remember Karoliina trying to avoid his touch, how she quickly and very thoroughly wiped her face after Leonid's kisses. Be that as it may, there's something between them, and both are interested in the heavenly body currently residing in the War Museum.

As for the compiler – or compilers – of the threatening letter, I don't know. I think of the quartet of Jokinen, Turunmaa, Räystäinen and Himanka, and I can imagine each one of them in the museum that night, but I can't get a closer grip on them, and even after reading the letter several times I can't find anything in the writing or the manner of delivery that points directly to any of them. I feel as though I know them too well to think of them as my pursuers, and too little to know what really moves and motivates them. Of course, the same applies to everyone I know, including my own wife. I don't even know the people I know.

Two more nights.

I have been threatened, asked to stay away from the museum. In so many words, I have been guaranteed that the meteorite will be stolen, one way or another. Everything will happen either tonight or tomorrow night. And right there and then a thought enters my mind for the first time: I am about to be a father; I could be in danger. Strictly speaking that was two thoughts, but they are linked, they are one.

I feel something unlike anything I've ever felt before. Perhaps it is mercy. Perhaps it is the gift that Krista is about to give me, to give us. Perhaps they too are one and the same.

The room is almost dark by now. I look up at the cross on the wall. It's almost as though the Son of God has raised his head slightly.

I stand up and I know what it is I have to do.

Hurmevaara.

One main road, a few smaller roads leading off it and dozens of twisting pathways that all lead deeper into the endless forests and stop either at a dead-end or a wall of spruce trees, or become narrower and narrower as they wind their way to the garden of an abandoned cottage somewhere. Inhabitants: just over a thousand. The first snowfall is in November and the snow melts for good in May. Summer always takes people by surprise – almost blinding the eyes, burning the skin, it gleams for a month or two, then disappears. And we return to the darkness. On a dark winter's evening, it can sometimes feel as though summer is an instance of faith. Nothing around us indicates that something like that could ever come into being or has ever existed.

And still we carry on. In the dark, often far away from where we began.

I walk along one of these narrow lanes, and I'm not sure why I've started thinking things like this. Maybe part of the reason is that I've been thinking – perhaps subconsciously, without putting it into words – for the last few days that something like this couldn't possibly happen anywhere else. But it isn't true. We carry ourselves wherever we go, and wherever we end up we carry our deeds – and the consequences of those deeds.

The television is on in the living room. Krista is in the kitchen. In an American legal drama, lawyers are talking to an empty sofa. I take the remote control from the coffee table and switch the TV off. A moment later I hear Krista's voice.

'Hello, love,' she calls through.

'Hello,' I say to my reflection in the living-room window.

Krista has raised her sore leg up and is sitting diagonally at the kitchen table. She is making a lingonberry pie, her fingers gleaming as if they've been dipped in blood. She smiles and, in that way she has, looks up as if about to give a trusting kiss, a warm embrace. Her lips are soft and familiar.

'Good day?' she asks as I walk round the table and pull out a chair.

'Up and down,' I say and sit down. At the other end of the table is a box of Belgian chocolates. 'But I'm still alive. What about you, how's your day been?'

'I translated ten pages,' she says, placing lingonberries evenly at the bottom of a cake tin. 'And went through the editor's comments on another manuscript. I don't envy their work. I can hardly imagine anything worse than having to read the same manuscript – not even a book, but a manuscript with all its flaws and mistakes – four or five times. Whose brain could cope with that?'

'I don't know,' I say. 'We're all different.'

'And when I talk to editors, they say they get sent hundreds of new manuscripts, thousands, and you're supposed to read them all while going through the fifth round of editing with another twenty authors. If I were a publishing editor, I'd end up going through phases of hating all writing, books, literature in general.'

'Maybe sometimes we all hate the things we love the most.'

Krista stops, her hands in the air, lingonberry juice dripping gruesomely from her fingers. Maybe it was the way I spoke, maybe my tone of voice. We look each other in the eyes. It has taken seven years to reach this point, I think, to confront my wife here and now and do what I have to do.

Because this isn't about me. Not even this time.

Despite what some people seem to imagine these days, life and the world don't owe me anything. Quite the opposite; it's my duty to give both of them what I can, to do my best.

'Krista, I need to apologise to you.'

This isn't about feelings; it's about deeds. Feelings don't always tell us how things really are, about what we should do or what would be wisest. Not to mention that we all feel something at any given moment. If Beethoven, Henry Ford and Josephine Cochrane had spent all day thinking about their feelings, we wouldn't have symphonies, cars or dishwashers.

It doesn't matter how jealous I am, how hurt, how angry, how vengeful, how desperate.

This is how I will be judged.

Krista is quiet as I start telling my story from the beginning. Some of it she has already heard, some she has not, but now I am going to tell her everything exactly the way it happened. I begin in the baking heat of Afghanistan. I am admitted to the field hospital and am flown home. On arrival back home I have to spend more time in hospital. I explain that each subsequent operation is both a success and a failure. A success in that they keep me alive and fully mobile. A failure in that…

'Krista, the fact is I cannot have children.'

Those green eyes whose gleam I once fell in love with – they look at me in a way that I couldn't have predicted. For some reason I had prepared myself for a more stereotypical scenario, in which Krista's mouth dropped open, she gasped for breath and her eyes widened to the size of saucers.

But none of that happens.

Krista looks at me steadily, sharply. Instead of her eyes widening, she in fact slightly squints, presumably to see better. Her mouth remains shut, the neutral expression on her face tightens. She leans forwards, tilts her head slightly to one side, looks at me more intensely from beneath her eyelashes. I can't read her expression. It might be one I've never seen before.

The moment is both long and short.

Long if you consider everything that flashes through my mind, though in reality it probably lasts only a few seconds. I have time to think that I have said what I came to say and that now I am free of my burden. I think of the future, which of course is wholly absurd. I don't know what is going to happen, but I imagine I will survive, one way or another – Krista packing her bags and leaving or telling me to pack my bags and move out. I will survive Krista flying into a rage or falling silent or not wanting to believe me. I can easily produce reams of doctor's reports; to me they read more like prison sentences than health assessments.

I think about what I'll do in the event that nothing happens, in a scenario in which Krista just carries on making her lingonberry pie, and we talk about doing the shopping, watching a movie, going skiing or visiting relatives.

Krista's expression darkens further. She looks at me with such weight, such presence, that I have to look away. Her hands have moved slightly, her fingers groping for the edge of the cake tin, holding it in place on the surface of the table. Either that or the tin is keeping her hands steady. The small diamonds in her engagement ring sparkle. Outside it's twenty-three degrees below freezing and already completely dark; I know without looking. The lamp hanging above the kitchen table is reflected in the window.

It seems that the turning points in our lives are always associated with a strange combination of the banal and the extraordinary, like watching a spaceship land in a perfectly everyday landscape. Like this moment right now: a January evening, a lingonberry pie, chit-chat about everyday things and the small matter of a confession that changes everything.

Krista leans slightly forwards. I assume she wants to talk, and I take the movement as a signal, an invitation. I lean towards her, our faces are at most a metre apart. Still she says nothing. On the other hand, only a few seconds have passed since my revelation, my confession that will change the course of our lives. Perhaps she's choosing her words, forming a question. She must have at least one of them.

But she has no questions.

She has an answer.

Krista promptly vomits over the lingonberry pie, quickly, in bubbles, almost like letting a small animal out of a cage. She tries to stand up from the table, but her sore leg thuds against the floor. She winces with pain and another mouthful of sick bubbles up, this time onto the floor. She supports herself against the table. By now I am on my feet, walking round the table. I lift her beneath the arms, tell her I will carry her to the bathroom.

'The pregnancy…' she stammers. 'The pregnancy…'

Of course, I think as I haul us both towards the toilet. Morning sickness. We reach the bathroom door. I open it, and help her to kneel in front of the toilet. From there onwards she's on her own, and that is how she wants it. She gestures me out of the room, letting out a series of deep moans and groans. I back away and watch to make sure she really is fine, the vomiting notwithstanding.

Eventually I close the bathroom door and stand in the hallway for a moment. That's no use to anybody. I return to the kitchen and start cleaning up. In a few minutes the rubbish bin is full, the liner tied up and ready to be taken away. I hear the sound of Krista retching in the bathroom. The sound tears my heart from my breast.

14

After a few star-lit nights, the lights of the sky have once again been switched off. Circles of light appear one lamppost at a time as I walk along the pavement towards the War Museum, pulling my hat tighter over my head. When I asked Krista through the bathroom door if she wanted me to stay home, the answer was a feeble no, there's no need.

Maybe giving her some space was the wisest thing to do right now. I couldn't continue my confession, couldn't tell her about the dead men and the car chases, the threatening letters and the explosions. I don't know if I'll get the opportunity to do so now. I have stepped into the unknown, and never again will I step…

On familiar territory.

The next time my feet press into the snowy surface of the pathway, I concentrate on listening. I was so lost in thought that I didn't realise what I was hearing. My next steps only confirm what I heard but didn't properly register. My steps have an echo. Only it isn't an echo. I continue walking.

The street is badly lit. The lampposts are quite a distance from one another, and between their circles of light are large unlit blackspots. It's about a hundred metres to the next intersection, where I will turn right. As my ears grow more accustomed to the sound, I can hear the steps clearly. Someone is walking in time with me; of that I am certain. To make absolutely sure, I stop, take off a mitten, pull my phone from my pocket and raise it to my ear. I don't call anyone – but I can't hear any steps either.

I set off again, and the two sets of steps again start to echo through the sub-zero night. Someone is following me. As the intersection draws closer, I pick up my pace, and for a few steps I hear a faint disparity in our rhythm, then the person behind adjusts their pace enough to keep up with me and once again we make our way forwards in stereo.

Nearly at the intersection. I am about to turn right, to continue along the lit pathway leading to the War Museum. The other three paths are unlit. A house stands at each corner of the junction. The windows of the house I am nearest to are dark. In the yellowing glow of the streetlights they look like black holes covered in a thin layer of sheer ice. I turn the corner, and as soon as I pass the corner of the house I stop, spin round and peer back in the direction I came from.

And there, there in the blind spot between two street lights, is a figure. The figure has stopped. That's right, I think to myself, this person hears my steps just as well as I can hear theirs. It's hard to say anything definitive about the figure; the distance is too great, the darkness consumes any detail.

But perhaps it is possible to make an informed guess after all. Once I place the figure in the surroundings, a neighbouring house and a car reversing out of a snowdrift across the street help me make a judgement about size, and from that I conclude at least one thing: that the figure cannot be Leonid. This is no giant. My stalker appears to be of average build and wearing dark winter attire. I set off again. Before long I see the front lights of the War Museum through the trees. I hear the steps again, this time further behind me, but now they no longer try to keep up with me. I cross the main road, look in both directions. Once on the other side of the road I set off along the street and see the side street I have just left behind. My pursuer has fallen back slightly. I can still see the figure, though whoever this is is trying to use the darkened areas between the lights for cover.

A few minutes later I unlock the War Museum door and say hello to the evening janitor in the staffroom. By day the man is a local farmer but he is a regular volunteer at the museum. When I ask him how it's gone, he tells me he hasn't seen anything out of the ordinary all day and asks whether I have. I reply that I haven't seen anything suspicious, or *more* suspicious than the events of the last few days.

He yawns, collects the plastic tubs he has washed and left in the cupboard above the sink to dry, packs them one inside the other in order of size, pulls on his coat and leaves. Once I am alone, I return to the foyer, switch off the lights and look outside. I cannot see anyone.

The time is approaching midnight when I hear something near the museum's front door. When it happens, I am in the meteorite room. The nocturnal museum seems to carry sound like the surface of a lake. Even the quietest rustling or knocking sound shimmers to the other side of the building. This is it, I think as I rush to the front door. I arrive at the doorway separating the lobby from the gallery hall and stop.

There is someone at the front door. I hear a banging sound, another. But something about this person says they're not moving the way a burglar would move. At least not an experienced burglar. There's far too much noise. Then I hear a metallic clank, and I am certain I recognise it. I walk into the lobby, make my way towards the front door. Now I can see the crutches that caused the clank, and I recognise Krista, though her face is in shadow.

She has taken our car and driven out here. I open the museum door. The nausea has passed; she tells me she's managed to eat something and that her ankle coped surprisingly well with driving. I can hear from her voice that isn't the main reason for her visit; she hasn't turned up here in the middle of the night to tell me she's able to drive again. Moreover she doesn't seem to need my help – either that or she doesn't want it. She is quick on her feet with the crutches – she swings back and forth in front of me and comes to a stop in the middle of the room.

'Is there anywhere we can talk?'

'If you're up to it, we can go into the gallery over there,' I say and gesture towards the hall. 'There's a sofa at the far end.'

Krista doesn't stand around thinking about it. The sofa is in the meteorite room. It's been positioned so that people can sit down and gaze at the meteorite in its glass cabinet. I don't switch on the main lights, but instead turn on the spotlight aimed at the meteorite. This is also a precaution; with this lighting it's impossible to see the whole gallery from outside. Krista sits down on the sofa. I sit next to her. Not right next to her; I instinctively leave a polite gap between us.

'There it is,' she says, nodding towards the meteorite. 'A million euros.'

'It might be worth that, yes.'

'Many people think it is.'

'That's true,' I say.

'People can believe almost anything.'

'That's true too.'

We sit in silence. Eventually Krista speaks. 'Joel, I love you.'

'I—'

'Wait,' she immediately interrupts. 'Let me speak.'

She turns her eyes to the middle of the room.

'You have been brave,' she continues. 'You're the bravest person I know, Joel. You're not afraid of anyone or anything.'

'I spent over two years being afraid.'

Krista shakes her head. 'I don't know if that's true. But anyway, you stopped.'

I say nothing.

'I'm not that brave,' she continues. 'At least, it doesn't feel that way. But I want to try.'

Krista's voice is quiet and serious. Besides, at night the museum is the quietest place on Earth.

'I've loved you from the very first day and I love you now. To be honest, I love you more every day.'

Again Krista has turned her eyes to the meteorite, but I don't think she's particularly looking at it. She gives a sigh, wipes the corner of her eye.

'I've made one mistake, and it's been weighing on my conscience, in a truly terrible way. I did something ugly. I acted against my better judgement. I betrayed you. I don't know why.'

I wait. It is almost exactly midnight.

'But I must at least try…' she continues. 'To explain, I mean. You were in Helsinki on one of those professional development weekends. I was here. I'd been working all day. It was evening, I stopped working and the house was empty, so I thought I would go to the bar and have a bite to eat. But it wasn't quite what I was expecting. I didn't fancy a hotdog or anything else that was on offer. I ordered a glass of red wine. I hadn't eaten anything, so I guess it went straight to my head. I had another glass, then I bumped into a lively bunch of people, a hunting group, men and women. They were already quite merry; they'd been out in the woods hunting for a week. I sang karaoke. I realised I was getting quite drunk, so I decided to go home…'

Krista shakes her head. There are tears in her eyes.

'This sounds like an excuse,' she says. 'I know that. But I can't keep holding this back. I was about to walk home. It was cold and dark, and a freezing wind was coming in from the north. A man appeared next to me, said he lived out that way too. I know, I know, I shouldn't have taken a ride from him but…' She continues to gaze at the meteorite. 'Then before I knew it, I was in the car. And the car was flying. I've never experienced anything like it. The car was like an aeroplane. Every jump felt like flying. It felt like I was somewhere else, in another world, somewhere up among the stars. I was swept up from the Earth. I recognise that now. It was all over in seconds. I felt ashamed.'

I have to turn to look at her.

'The following day was the worst of my life,' she continues. 'You came home in the evening and I just … loved you so much. I couldn't talk about what had happened. Our life together continued. Then I realised I was pregnant, and I thought…'

She swallows. I can hear it. All I can see is the meteorite.

'I thought I'd been forgiven,' she says, her voice hushed. 'That the child was a sign of forgiveness.'

There follows almost a full minute during which neither of us says anything. I realise that I too have been for a ride very much like the one Krista just described. In me it certainly didn't awaken the desire to go forth and multiply. I think of death, in a variety of different ways. I mull over the next question for a moment, and it's the last thing I want to ask, but it needs to be asked all the same.

'The car *flew*?'

I look at her again. She wipes her eyes.

'Like a spaceship.'

'There's a former world-class rally driver in the village,' I say.

Krista dries her eyes with the sleeve of her white jumper.

'Is he the father of the child?' I ask.

'Yes … I suppose … maybe,' she replies, letting the words drop slowly, one after the other, almost whispering.

'Krista,' I say. 'What do you mean, you suppose or maybe? Are there more candidates?'

'What?' she asks, turning to look at me. She looks shocked and shakes her head. 'No. But, if you can't…'

'I cannot have children.'

Again fresh tears well at the corners of her eyes.

'I'm sorry, Joel. I love you so much. I want to be good to you.'

How's that? By getting yourself pregnant by one of the other villagers? I don't say it out loud. This – this is the boundary between light and dark. I can see that. I recall what I was thinking only a short time ago. This isn't about me. Not everything is about me. I respond in a way that I know is every bit as honest as the anger I feel inside.

'You are good to me.'

She looks at me. Her eyes are moist from weeping, always that beautiful shade of green and grey. I must tell her everything.

'There's something else,' I say. 'I sent you some text messages. In his name.'

She looks as though she has remembered something, as though one thing suddenly connects with another. She wipes her eyes.

'I wondered about those messages,' she says. 'They were so… unexpected.'

'I wasn't sure how poetic or…'

'I didn't mean that,' she says quietly. 'I mean, I'm not sure he remembers anything about it. I don't think he so much as registered the event. I got the impression the only things that matter to him are his car and the bottle.'

We sit for a moment in silence. I can hear her breath, sense her presence next to me.

'I didn't plan things this way,' she says eventually. 'Life, the move out here. All this.'

'I doubt I would have scripted it quite like this either.'

'But there you are,' she says, moving a fraction closer. She takes me by the hand. Her hand is warm.

'Thank you, Joel.'

She presses herself against me, rests her head against my shoulder. I can feel her scalp against my cheek, the roughness of her hair, the warmth of her skin. I close my eyes, open them again, and I can't help thinking the same thing I thought on my first night here in the museum. That meteorite has crossed billions of kilometres over billions of years, only to end up right there in front of me.

'I think it's a boy,' she says after a while.

15

Morning air is always different from that at night. Regardless of whether the temperature is just as low or the dark just as impenetrable, the morning carries with it a renewed freshness, a sense of hope. The air is purer, lighter. That's what it feels like as I finally step out of the museum once the morning staff arrive. For a moment I stand in front of the building, draw the thin, chilled air into my lungs and look around.

Nobody appears to be waiting for me. Whoever was following me last night is either very well hidden or has had enough either of me or of traipsing around after me. Hopefully both. I set off. I feel surprisingly awake, especially given I only slept three and a half hours on the museum sofa between two and six a.m.

Hurmevaara is quietly waiting for a new day to dawn. The streets stand empty, each leading its respective way; the lights in the shop windows look almost bored. I notice my thoughts spinning between my two selves.

My wife loves me. Nobody tried to steal the meteorite.

On the other hand…

My wife is pregnant by the rally driver. The meteorite will be in the museum one more night.

It feels as though every piece of good news in my life also contains some bad news: for every silver lining there's also a cloud. But there are moments in which I am able to push myself and my own needs to one side. And as my horizons widen and I examine things from the right angle, I even feel something approaching a sense of gratitude. Things might not be ideal right now, but they're as good as they can be. From experience, I know that everything could be so much worse.

I seem to perk up the closer I get to home. I see the lit-up windows, villagers waking to a new day: one sweeping snow from the front steps, another peering at the thermometer through the window, a third climbing on the back of a snowmobile.

Things just might turn out for the good, I think; it's entirely possible.

In any case, the grand scheme of things remains a mystery to us. The only thing that's clear is that such a scheme, a plan, really does exist. Either it is based on chance and is shaped by it, a grand cosmic game of roulette, or there is a predefined beginning and an end, and everything in between is simply movement towards that end, and in that movement everything has its own place and meaning. Either by chance or by design, what will be will be.

I realise the extent of my fatigue. It conjures up thoughts like this. Maybe it doesn't matter, I think, and take a deep breath, what's important is that Krista and I have been given another chance.

I brush the snow from the front steps before going inside. It's a cosmetic procedure more than anything, but one that feels important. A fresh start. I pull off my outdoor clothes in the porch, walk through the inner door into the hallway, and stop still.

So many things catch my attention at once.

The lights in the kitchen are still on, and in Krista's office too – that small, cosy space filled with books. The bathroom door is open, the lights are on and the tap is running. I listen for a moment for any other sounds. All I can hear is the gentle trickling of water. I walk into the bathroom.

Krista's toothbrush is at the bottom of the sink. The water is rinsing the brush, on which there's only a small fleck of bright-blue toothpaste. Seeing the toothbrush is like a chilled knife cutting through my stomach, allowing an icy lump to form there. I begin to feel my pulse, to hear the dull thump of my heartbeat in my ear.

'Krista,' I call out. 'I'm home.'

I say it again, this time slightly louder.

I don't like what it sounds like.

A fresh bout of nausea, perhaps, and there's something very frightening in quite how consoling that thought now seems. I leap up the stairs to our bedroom. The bed is still neatly made; nobody has slept there. I look into the guest room, but it too is untouched. I return to the bathroom downstairs, turn off the tap and back out of the room.

I cross the living room and head towards the door to Krista's office. Spinning across the computer screen is a spiral pulling colours into its black depths one at a time: blue, green, red, blue, green…

Next to the computer is the book she is translating, propped up on a stand. Beside the keyboard is her teacup, still half full of tea.

I know Krista; I know her evening routines. She has supper, brushes her teeth, washes her face, then returns to switch off the computer and the lights. And there's a reason for this specific order of events. Krista often says that a translation problem that's been bugging her will sort itself out while she's having supper or brushing her teeth, just before bed. That's why she leaves switching off the computer till last.

Here everything has been left unfinished.

I switch off the lights in the office and retrace my steps to the kitchen, listening all the while. The lamp above the dining table is reflected in both the surface of the table and the window. Even from a distance I can see there's something on the table. A sheet of A4, text on it. Apart from that the table is clear, which only underlines the placement of the paper right in the middle, making the text written in block lettering seem all the more threatening. I reach the edge of the table, the cold sensation in my stomach spreads to the rest of my body and my hands begin to tremble.

JOEL

YOU'RE NOT LISTENING. DO AS I SAY OR
KRISTA WILL NEVER COME HOME AGAIN.
THE METEORITE WILL BE TAKEN TONIGHT.
IF YOU CALL THE POLICE, YOU'LL NEVER SEE

KRISTA AGAIN. IF YOU TELL ANYONE ABOUT THIS, YOU'LL NEVER SEE KRISTA AGAIN. WE'RE WATCHING YOU. TOMORROW YOU'LL RECEIVE INSTRUCTIONS BY PHONE ONCE WE SEE YOU HAVE ARRIVED AT THE MUSEUM – ALONE. CARRY ON AS BEFORE, ACT NORMALLY. AND REMEMBER: WE'RE WATCHING YOU. WE ARE EVERYWHERE.

PART THREE

THE SKIES OPEN

1

'Should we pray?'

It takes a moment before I realise I'm being asked a question. Through the window day is slowly breaking, the horizon behind the trees tinged red. The rough-shaven man is my first customer of the day.

'It's worth a try,' I say.

He looks at me as though he was expecting something else. But right now I have nothing else to give.

'I just wondered, isn't it standard practice?' he asks. 'In your line of work, at a moment like this?'

'A moment like what?'

'At the last trumpet,' he says. 'Exactly what I've been talking about.'

'Right, yes,' I say, and because I'm more than a little unsure, I ask a follow-up question. 'Specifically, which moment are we talking about?'

The man scratches his stubble.

'This is simple cause and effect. There's a nuclear attack in the Middle East. It doesn't matter who was behind it, which side started the game of ping-pong first. Let's say Israel carried out a strike against Iran, or the other way round. It doesn't matter. The other side has to respond. And because the victims of the attack can't respond by themselves, an ally has to do it. Iran has Russia; Israel has the USA. The next strike has to make a real impact. It might be a US military base in Germany, and a handful of Germans will be taken out too. Then it's a medium-sized Russian town. On the ground there's panic. Armies look to see where the borders really run. The Baltic Sea is allocated to one of those superpowers. Finland either rolls over and gets itself a new master or defends its territory. If it chooses the latter, a cyber-attack will switch all the lights out, cut off the water supply and heating. Time passes, and the inevitable upshot is that we're offered an agreement that doesn't really feel fair. All this will take less than twelve months. I've counted.'

We are silent.

'You see, there's nothing to be done,' the man says eventually. 'So, I wonder if praying might help after all.'

Since the early hours of the morning I've been able to think of only one thing.

Krista.

I read the letter a few times, tried to find something in it, something to latch on to, but there was nothing. Since then I've thought of a thousand and one ways to find out what's going on.

'Don't tell me you don't pray?' The man's voice sounds genuinely despairing.

I look at him. I remember something he said on one of his numerous visits.

'You once told me you belong to the local elk-hunting club,' I say. 'Still doing that?'

'What's that got to do with prayer? Does the hunting club pray? Is that what you mean? "Lord, who art in Heaven, hallowed be thy elk? Give us this day, our daily moose"?'

The man has become agitated. It's understandable. I have to backtrack a little. Besides, before I get to the point, I need to make sure the man isn't one of the *we* mentioned in the letter.

'Let us pray,' I say.

I assume a comfortable position in my chair, lean against the backrest, clasp my hands together. I close my eyes. I realise it's been a while since the last time I did this. Once the silence has lasted thirty seconds I half open my left eye. The man has closed his eyes; he is sitting in his chair and at least appears to be deep in prayer. I close my eyes again with the realisation that I don't know how to pray anymore. At least, not for the one thing of which I am guilty.

Without my pride, without my stubbornness, Krista would be at home, blissfully unaware that she could have been the victim of a kidnapping. But because I decided that nobody was going to steal the meteorite on my watch, and because I have behaved intractably in every possible way, they have decided to strike against Krista instead.

They.

My first furious thoughts were aimed specifically at *them*. I thought of Turunmaa, Himanka, Jokinen and Räystäinen – him in particular. I no longer know what to think of the cut on his forearm, his bizarre behaviour, or indeed the bruise on Karoliina's temple. One of them is almost certainly the person I saw lying in the snow. I'm not sure which I suspect more. I thought of Leonid and his possible connections. It's more than possible that Leonid knows many more men in his line of work than simply Grigori. I thought of others who have expressed an interest in the meteorite. I even thought of Tarvainen, but thinking about him at all is a challenge. I then went through various configurations of people, but none of the possible options offered me the certainty I needed. And I don't know what to make of the suggestion that *they* are everywhere.

And yet, I know only too well: if I give these thoughts the slightest extra space, if I allow my self-flagellation to gather strength and grow, if I lose focus and concentration, I will plunge headlong into the abyss. At such a moment I will see the entire village plotting against me, and at such a moment *they* really could, naturally enough, be everywhere.

But that is called paranoia, and for good reason.

I open my eyes. The man is sitting in front of me, his eyes still shut.

Is he one of them? I ask myself.

During the few moments I've had my eyes shut, the room has assumed more colour with the burgeoning day. The brick wall is slightly whiter, the copper of the Saviour's flank somewhat browner.

The man continues his prayer. He looks as though he could go on like that until the end of days, quite literally. Would a kidnapper pray with such intensity? Would he believe in impending Armageddon with the same fervour?

It doesn't seem very plausible. But how can I be sure? Eventually I realise there's an obvious way.

'There's a cancellation for tomorrow morning,' I say.

The man's eyes flash open. 'I'll be there,' he says, his voice sincere. Sincere and clearly invigorated.

The man looks outside. There's a renewed sense of alertness to him.

'I think that did the trick,' he says.

I allow him to explore this new, confident version of himself. He is not the kidnapper, I can see that now. I wait a moment longer.

'About your elk club,' I say.

'Shall we pray for them?'

I lean a fraction further forwards, my gaze fixed on the man's blue eyes.

'Elk hunters need rifles, isn't that right?'

2

I don't have a plan. Yet. But I know what I'm going to do. I'm going to bring Krista home. Nothing else matters. There was a time when I was indifferent to the meteorite, but not anymore. Now it's a necessity, and I need it. And the more I mull the matter over, the larger the role of the meteorite becomes.

Because:

Scenario 1: the kidnappers turn up at the museum with Krista and exchange her for the meteorite. From their perspective this option doesn't make much sense. After all, what am I going to do once Krista is free and the meteorite is hurtling away in a car? I'll call the police. The kidnappers won't get the head start they need. I don't think this is the plan. They won't bring Krista with them.

Scenario 2: the kidnappers turn up at the museum without Krista and wait until they have the meteorite. But why would I give it to them if I don't know where Krista is or whether they are still holding her?

Scenario 3: the kidnappers turn up at the museum and, one way or another, provide proof that they are still holding Krista and that she will be released at a designated time and place once I have stepped aside and allowed them to take the meteorite. Krista has doubtless identified them, so it doesn't matter where they release her: the kidnappers can have a head start as long as they like, but before long they will be apprehended.

I stand up from my chair, walk to the window.

The snow sparkles.

I've been thinking my way through an array of possible *modi operandi*, and they all seem to have one thing in common: for the kidnapper or kidnappers, Krista is a problem that won't be solved by simply getting hold of the meteorite. The realisation of this fact is chilling. And at the same time it means that, for as long as the meteorite is in my possession, there is at least a theoretical possibility that Krista is…

That she is…

Alive.

I can't take the thought any further.

I haven't left my office since I arrived early this morning. As before, I stick to my routines, but not because of the demands of this person or persons. It's another way of moving things forwards. I was promised the use of a hunting rifle; I'll fetch it this evening before going to the museum. Naturally, there's no way of knowing whether the kidnapper or kidnappers will be armed, but there's a more than significant likelihood. Round here practically every household has at least one rifle or shotgun, and more often than not both.

As I wonder what else I could do from my office, I hear Pirkko's steps in the corridor. They are coming closer, and eventually they come to a stop at my door. I turn from the window and sit down behind my desk. Pirkko knocks and steps inside before I have the chance to encourage her to do so. She is carrying a pile of paperwork, as usual. Papers that she could simply leave in my in-tray or, if I'm away, on my desk. She walks towards the desk and stops two metres in front of me.

'Morning,' she smiles. 'How are your muscles this morning?'

At first I don't understand what she's talking about.

'A bit tender,' I say. 'I haven't worked out for a while.'

'Your leg squats were very controlled. I've been meaning to say.'

'Thank you. Pirkko, I really…'

'The key is at the end of the movement,' she explains, then turns to the window and drops into a leg squat. I look on from the side, watch her profile. She stops at precisely the point where her knees reach a ninety-degree angle. She turns her head and looks at me. 'This was the biggest revelation for me, specifically as regards the thighs and buttocks.'

'It is…'

'Strength,' she says and starts bobbing up and down, a centimetre or two in each direction. 'Agility. It's never too late to start. Anything, that is. That's what I think.'

Pirkko is squatting in the middle of my office and looking me right in the eyes. I have to talk to her. But first things first; I have to get her out of that position.

'Looking good,' I say. Maybe it wasn't the best opening line.

'I knew you'd notice,' she smiles. Finally she springs back into an upright position. 'Nothing gets past you. Which is so important in your job. You take the time to listen to people, to accept them for who they are, especially people who—'

'That's nice.' I interrupt her. 'The thing is—'

Now I cut myself short. It's clear I have to make a choice. Either I can sort out the misunderstanding between us, or we can go through the day's business. In my experience, trying to sort out a misunderstanding will almost certainly be the more time-consuming of the two options. Both parties will have to have their say, then we have to form some kind of consensus and agree on how to proceed. It's not going to happen today.

We get stuck into the day's agenda. Eventually we get to the matter of choosing the cover material for the new hymnals. Pirkko walks round the desk and positions herself next to me. We are crouched over the table, going through the material together. I get the feeling the decision was made long ago.

Black leather it is, then.

Pirkko is about to leave my office when she stops and turns. 'The first client of the day,' she begins, then seems suddenly at a loss for words.

'What about him?'

Pirkko is about to say something but stops herself and smiles. She looks past me, the smile still on her face, hanging in the air, and I get the impression it wasn't even meant for me. The moment is quickly over. Pirkko turns and closes the door behind her. I walk into the middle of the room, look first at our Saviour on the Cross, then the clock.

Oh, happy hour.

I can't just sit here waiting for evening to come. I have to find some kind of advantage, anything, to gain at least some kind of leverage, something with which to fight back if necessary. I haven't the faintest idea what that something might be or where I might find it. And it's for this reason I am on the move and heading where I am heading. It's better to try something, anything at all, than sit around waiting, helpless.

I believe Krista would do the same. She would understand I can't just wait and count on the decency of the people who have taken her hostage. For a variety of reasons, I find it hard to trust their generosity of spirit.

The Golden Moon Night Club.

The dim lighting, the dark panelling and the music that carries your thoughts to the early hours. It feels like stepping into a cellar. I guess that's the desired effect, that time should disappear and only beer has any meaning. A handful of customers are sitting in the booths; there seems to be a clamour at the dartboard. I find a stool and prop up the bar in what is now my regular spot.

The space behind the counter is empty. It doesn't seem to bother anybody. I assume the bar staff have popped out the back for a moment.

I listen to the darts players arguing with one another. It quickly escalates from a discussion about one dart to many darts, from the darts to a pint of lager, then to whose round is next, and eventually to the injustice of the 1944 eastern border settlement and how someone should be made to pay for it. I stop listening to them and concentrate on more important matters. I wait a moment longer, and then I see her.

Karoliina arrives through the seating area carrying a metallic box. She walks briskly, almost hurrying, then notices me.

She smiles, looks content, says good morning, walks right behind me, almost touching me. Once she has walked round the bar she dashes in behind it, places the heavy-looking box on the counter and opens the door of the hotdog grill. As she opens the box and starts loading hotdogs into the rotating grill, she looks up at me.

'Breakfast?' she asks. 'Fresh sausage, just delivered.'

'No, thanks. I've already eaten.'

'I know; it's well past breakfast time. This lot only notice they're hungry by accident.'

I glance behind me. The three men have returned to their game of darts. Once Karoliina has placed the sausages in the grill and the cogs start rotating, she closes the glass doors and walks up to me.

'I would ask if you want a drink, but you left a full pint on the counter when you left yesterday.'

'I don't think I was in the mood for beer.'

'What about today? Are you in the mood for beer or something else?'

Her eyes give nothing away. Her hair falls in dark waves on both sides of her head.

'To be honest, I don't know. What's on offer?'

She pauses before responding.

'I've just made coffee. I can pour you a cup.'

Coffee sounds good, I tell her. She moves along to the middle of the counter and takes a full pot from the filter machine, pours the steaming coffee into two cups and asks whether I take milk or sugar. I don't. She adds a drop of milk to her own and returns with the cups. Nothing in her movements or her tone of voice makes me suspect she might be involved in the kidnapping or in preparing the robbery. She quickly glances around.

'Have you been thinking about things?' she asks. 'The things we talked about yesterday?'

I take this question as a good sign. Would the kidnapper still want me as an accessory to a robbery? Of course, it's possible, but it's highly unlikely.

'A lot,' I reply. 'But I'm still in the dark about a lot of things.'

'Such as?'

'Such as why you want the meteorite.'

Karoliina looks at me with what seems like a mixture of surprise and suspicion. 'Shall we speak frankly?'

'Why not?' I say. 'There isn't much time.'

'Can I trust you?'

'I'm a pastor. Anything you tell me is confidential.'

She thinks about this for a moment.

'Are you seriously asking me why I want that meteorite? What's that got to do with anything?'

'I'm deadly serious,' I say and pull my coffee cup closer. 'It affects how we proceed from here.'

'It solves my problems,' she says. Her voice is neutral and calm.

'It solves your problems? A million euros?'

She takes a cigarette from the packet on the counter, twirls it between her fingers.

'Show me a person whose problems wouldn't be solved with a million euros. And what do you mean, "how we proceed"?'

'What happens once … we have the meteorite?'

'We sell it,' she says, as breezily as if she were talking about pulling the next pint. 'I know how it can be done. Don't worry about that. Besides…'

'What?'

'What makes you want to get involved in this?'

'I have to.'

'Right,' she says and sips her coffee.

She looks like she knows what she wants, she seems sure of everything. I still haven't asked my main question. I take a sip of coffee; it's still too hot to drink.

I place the cup back on the counter and speak in an everyday tone of voice, as if I were talking about the weather. 'What about Leonid?'

Karoliina almost manages to hide her surprise. Only a tiny shimmer crosses her face. The cigarette is still between her fingers, clearly yearning to rise up to her lips.

'You know him?'

'I can't say I *know* him, but I've met him.'

'You know his name.'

'He introduced himself,' I say. 'Eventually.'

By now Karoliina has regained her composure. 'Leonid isn't a problem,' she says.

The darts group is braying again. Karoliina glances in their direction.

'I need to get out of this place,' she says. 'Thirty-six years of this.'

'Why don't you just leave?'

'Empty-handed? Head to Helsinki and beg on the streets? Join a housing waiting list, queue up at a food bank, something like that? We can't all be pastors with a job and a house lined up for us when we decide it's time for a change of scenery. No offence. I've left a few times, yes, and something always goes wrong. But not this time.'

'Haven't you got any family here?'

'My dad left when I was three. My mum's dead. No brothers or sisters. No man either – it's thin pickings round here. I've tried a couple of times, but I'm not going to make the same mistake again.'

'I understand.'

'I don't think you do,' she says. 'You're not from here. But it doesn't matter. All you've got to do is open the door.'

I shake my head. 'It has to look like a break-in.'

Karoliina smiles. There's something more than simply happiness in that smile.

'You're not bad for a vicar.'

I could tell her something else about myself and my calling – and some of the matters I choose not to reveal awaken very strong emotions within me, sentiments of which guilt is the smallest – but I'm not getting into that now.

I take my phone from my pocket. 'Can I have your number?'

Karoliina gives me the number and asks me to ring it. The phone next to the till buzzes. We are connected. We agree I will call her soon, once I have sorted a few things. I don't go into any more details, because at least for the moment I'm not sure what they might be. What's important is to understand the situation, to get a feeling for events, to look for and find something useful, anything at all.

I turn, and I'm about to slide off my stool when I catch a glimpse of the spinning sausages in their glass grill. I remember what I just heard.

'Local sausages, eh?' I say.

Karoliina turns her head and looks at the light-brown saveloys dripping with fat. Again I see the bruise on her temple.

'Want one?' she asks.

'I'd say yes,' I say, trying to keep my voice steady, though I can feel a certain agitation bubbling inside. 'But I'm still full. They look good, though. Where are they from?'

'Jokinen, who else?' she says. 'The grocer. He makes them himself in his own little factory. He even butchers the meat himself in his own abattoir.'

His own abattoir?

3

And so the pieces of the puzzle slot together. I maintain a brisk walking speed, even but relaxed. I'm not sure whether I'm being watched but I want to be on the safe side. The sky has turned a nostalgic blue, the sun has entered its short-lived afternoon arc. All the while, time is running out. Krista, I'm doing the best I can, I repeat to myself over and over. Then I run through the one thing I haven't seen, though it's been right in front of my eyes.

Jokinen.

His visit, his words. The things he told me about running his own business, how awkward he seemed sitting in our kitchen, how impossible it was for him to look me in the eye. All this was buried beneath a wave of jealousy swelling within me.

Things are tight as it is, we're just scraping by.

Jokinen's business is on a financial knife-edge. And that's just the beginning. The man has his own abattoir.

Jokinen, with all his delicacies, his home visits. The jovial grocer who chit-chats with customers and remembers their birthdays, who pops in to see people any day of the week, who knows people's homes, which doors lead where, the layout, when people are at work and when they're at home. In my case it was even easier: Jokinen knew I would be at the museum. I told him so myself.

Jokinen, I think. So it was him after all. I blame myself for dismissing Krista's suggestion I get to know him better. I would have known about the abattoir, and probably a lot more besides, much earlier on. But something stopped me making any closer acquaintance with him: instinct.

I arrive at the church hall and walk up to my office. I take the car keys from my desk, return to the car park and jump in the car. I start the engine, turn the car around and am about to put my foot on the accelerator when I see Pirkko standing at the front door of the building. She waves. I use the gas significantly more softly than I had been intending, steer the car nearer to the door and roll down the passenger window. Pirkko walks up to the car and leans inside. Her expression is one of confusion, perhaps even concern.

'Is everything alright?' she asks. Her breath is steaming so much that for a moment it obscures her brown eyes altogether.

'Why?'

'You left so … suddenly. I've just promised someone the three-thirty session.'

I glance at the dashboard, though there's no need. I know what the time is, and I know it's running out.

'I should have said. I'm really sorry but I have to pay a … home visit. It's an emergency, I'm afraid, completely unexpected.'

'Has something happened to…?' she asks, and places her hand on the edge of the door.

The movement is perfectly normal, but it catches my attention. Perhaps it has something to do with the way her fingers grip the top of the door, but there's a hint of insistence in her expression now. But that's not the most arresting thing.

'To who?' I ask. 'You mean my wife?'

Pirkko looks as though I'm speaking a foreign language but quickly regains her composure.

'Your wife? No, I mean … Well, *has* something happened to your wife?'

'I hope not.'

'Will you be back at work today?'

I am conscious of the passing seconds, how they turn into minutes, hours … Soon it will be evening. I have to get moving.

'I'll keep my phone on,' I say, though I'm unsure I'll be able to keep that promise. 'Who booked the three-thirty slot?'

I already have my foot on the accelerator when I hear Pirkko's voice.

'Timo Tarvainen. You know, the rally driver. Former rally driver, I should say. He hasn't competed since his accident. What a tragedy that was. The death of the map-reader and everything else.'

Jokinen lives outside the village. I take the road leading to Joensuu, then turn north. The spruce trees stand dark on both sides of the road; the day is slowly disappearing. A few hours of light are followed by almost twenty hours of darkness. Right now, it's hard not to think this says something fundamental about almost everything.

Snow billows up behind the log trucks in front of me. I overtake them utterly blind, trusting the flashing lights the drivers give me. I check the rear-view mirror every bit as much as I look ahead. Nobody is following me. I don't know how many people would be able to. I squeeze every last drop out of our Škoda, turn on to a narrower lane the width of one car. The lane has been recently ploughed. I keep going for another five minutes.

I have visited Jokinen's farmstead once before – like many idealistic people from the south before him who have moved out here, he bought an old farm complete with barns and outbuildings – but I've never driven right up to the house. I recall that Krista and Jokinen's wife Minna wanted to walk the rest of the way so they could pick blueberries. I stop the car at the same place as I did last summer.

I step out of the car and listen. The forest is silent, not even the wind is whistling through the darkening boughs of the trees. For a moment I think of the rifle that I still don't have. Then I set off on foot.

The farm's buildings come into view all of a sudden. I step out of the protective cover of the trees, and there they stand like an island in the middle of a sea of snow and, inconveniently, right in the middle of a large clearing. There's only one path leading up to the buildings, everything else is just flat, open terrain covered in snow.

There are at least four red-painted buildings: the two-storey house, a long, narrow barn, some sort of warehouse and the building I first heard about earlier today: the abattoir. That's the one. The stone foundations are tall, the windows wide and low; there's a grandness about the building, a chill, an air of finality.

I remain for a moment in the cover of the trees and watch the buildings. I wait for the blue moment between light and dark, and at this time of year I don't have to wait long. It's two-thirty in the afternoon when dusk begins to fall. I wait a while longer, then make a move.

When I'm halfway across the opening I see a light switch on in the ground floor of the house. I'm still relatively far away and can't make out anyone in the rectangle of light. If someone has seen me approaching and wanted to take precautions, switching on the lights would be the last thing they would do. I run closer, approach the front yard. I am almost there and run a bit faster – until I see the front door opening. I dive to the other side of the snow verge on the left and land on my stomach. Immediately I haul myself up, just enough to see over the verge. Jokinen.

He is only twenty metres away and he's carrying something in both hands. They look like water canisters. He walks across the yard and seems to be heading towards the smaller of two doors at the front of the abattoir. At the other end of the building is a larger door; it is tall, split into two parts, and bears some kind of warning sign. He lowers one of the canisters to the ground, opens the door, picks the canister up again and disappears inside.

The door remains open. I bound into a run. Just before the building, I stop.

I hear a voice from inside.

The clang of metal. Muffled cries of pain, like howling that can't quite get started, can't release, then turns into a whimper, gasping for air. Like a dog's bark, but without the power or determination, without the growl. Like something running out of strength, something whose final moments are approaching. I step inside.

The space is large and bare, the ceiling high, the floor and walls concrete. There are what appear to be fluorescent strips in the ceiling, but they are not switched on. The only light comes from a red warning light glowing above a door at the far end of the room. Again I hear the metallic clang, the faint whimpers. The sounds are coming from behind that door. The powerful red lamp hurts my eyes after the soft, blue dusk outside. It seems to take a lifetime for my eyes to adjust to the red room. I step across the concrete floor, head towards the door, and look around, try to find something heavy. But the room has been stripped of almost everything, it's like a cell or…

'Are you going to call the police?'

I spin around.

Jokinen is standing against the wall. He looks like he's been waiting for me. He is wearing a pair of plastic protective goggles. In his right hand he has a gleaming steel object that I can't identify. The object is long, it has a handle in the middle and tapers to a sharp point at both ends. Jokinen moves the object, swings it slowly back and forth.

'If everything's fine, then…'

'Everything was fine until now.'

'Everything's still fine, isn't it?' I ask.

'You're one of the authorities,' he says, the steel object in his hand now swinging in a longer curve. But that's not the most worrying thing. It's Jokinen's voice that grabs my attention. This is not the same jovial Jokinen who chats breezily in the store, who puts everyone in a good mood. This Jokinen is the opposite of the old one. His last statement wasn't a conversation starter; it was a judgement.

'Easy now. Let's have a look at what's on the other side of that door, okay?'

Jokinen is silent for a long while. His head moves slightly; the red light is reflected in his plastic goggles as though it were beaming from his eyes.

'I should have realised yesterday morning,' he says.

'Realised what?'

'That you knew something … Asking questions like that.'

The room is cool, the smell of disinfectant pungent. Our breath creates a faint steam, a brief flash of red. Jokinen's voice is cold and sterile – undeniably suited to the room. He takes a step forwards. I can't get back to the front door without passing him. I don't know whether the door is open and I don't know what lies behind that door.

'We can talk about this,' I say.

'I already asked if you're going to call the police. You didn't answer. What do you want to talk about?'

'But you can't just behave like this.'

Jokinen shakes his head. The goggles flicker as though they are on fire. He gives the steel object in his hand a shake.

'Pastor,' he says. 'You're always right, always know what to do. Always such a good, upstanding person.'

'I'm not a good person,' I say. 'I've made many mistakes. And I often don't know what to do either, don't know what would be best or good for people. In this situation—'

'You're making me angry,' Jokinen interrupts. 'I'll tell you straight. You're making me angry. You and your know-it-all wife. Both of you. Always think you're above everybody else, better than the rest of us. Always handing out advice.'

I remain silent. I don't remember giving advice for years. I have been so acutely aware of how little I know that giving other people advice is the last thing I'd do. I note that Jokinen is gradually moving closer in tiny, almost imperceptible steps. He looks threatening, powerful. He looks … for a moment I try to find a better word, but I can't think of one. He looks bloodthirsty.

'How did you find out about this?' he asks.

'I worked it out.' It's the honest answer. 'I put two and two together.'

'And who have you told?'

'Nobody.'

Jokinen seems to think about this. 'I don't know if you're telling the truth.'

His white protective coat looks redder the closer we get. I have to keep the conversation going. If possible, I have to steer it in such a direction that I can better engage with him, man to man, human to human.

'Does Minna know what you're up to?'

'She doesn't like it,' he says and lowers his eyes. 'Doesn't like it one bit. But she'll understand once we're out of the woods. To be honest I'm not sure why she's so worked up about it.'

'Maybe she thinks it isn't right.'

'She'll change her mind once the worst is over and we're in the clear again.'

'I don't know...'

'We only have one store, but there's plenty more where this came from,' he says indicating to the doors at the back.

'This?' I ask and get ready to spring into action. Jokinen clearly isn't going to listen to reason. He is utterly different from how I'd imagined him to be. He sounds like a lunatic. And if he sounds like a lunatic...

'Don't you start,' he says impatiently and takes another step in my direction. There are now only a few metres between us. His goggles are like red mirrors. 'Anyway, how do you recognise one from another? There are thousands of them out there, just find yourself another one.'

This is too much. I turn, take two long, quick strides towards the door, open it and step into a taller, chillier room. But in the cool blue lighting I'm not entirely sure of what I see. At that moment I hear a heavy thud, then Jokinen's steps behind me.

He lunges at my back and we both fall forwards. He tightens his arms around me. We hit the floor. I don't have time to put my hands out to break my fall, and my forehead bangs against the floor. I am on my stomach, Jokinen on top of me. I try to spin round. Jokinen says something – I can't make it out. I manage to pull one arm partially free and haul myself forwards inch by inch. Once my arm is completely free, I grab Jokinen in a headlock and twist. His arms release from around me. I rise to my knees and squeeze Jokinen's head in my armpit. I use force. By now he is on all fours; he is furious, battering his fists against my sides, my kidneys. I twist stronger still and eventually he stops. And there we are: me on my knees with Jokinen's head beneath my right arm, Jokinen on his hands and knees beside me.

I raise my eyes, then look up. We are so close that I can feel the warmth, smell the musk. My eyes rise from the legs to the chest, from there to the neck and muzzle and eventually to the antlers, which from this angle look metres long, like broken branches. I have to say it out loud.

'An elk.'

Jokinen is sitting in a chair at the far end of the room. The stag is standing in the middle of the room, snorting. It looks in turn at me and at Jokinen, and doesn't seem particularly pleased about what it sees. There's a bloody scratch on my forehead from falling over. Jokinen's half-metre-long steel meat cleaver is propped against the wall. I have turned off the blue light and switched on the fluorescent strips on the ceiling.

Up close the elk is even larger than I thought. Its head rises a full metre above my own, its antlers are like the naked boughs of a tall, skeletal tree. When it shakes its head, the balance of the whole room seems to shudder. Its dark-brown flanks shine like halves of a huge oak barrel; its legs look like gnarled telephone poles, tall yet in some way shaky and unsteady. According to Jokinen, the animal weighs around five hundred kilos. It's easy to believe.

Jokinen's goggles are dangling from his hand. His hair, which is normally neatly combed and patted down with gel, is dishevelled, jutting out here and there. His white coat is askew, twisted across his right shoulder and round to his back. Beneath his coat the two top buttons of his shirt have been torn loose. He looks like a man who has just been in a wrestling match.

'But why?' I ask him.

'It's January.'

I don't know what he is talking about, so I wait for him to continue. He sighs, raises his eyes from the floor to the elk.

'The hunting season stops at the end of December. This thing walked into the yard the night before last, in the middle of January. At the same time, the village shop is right there, and it's touch and go whether we'll be able to pay off our debts. And the market for organic meats is growing all the time. And as long as I can get my hands on appropriate meat and have the time to make the stuff, my handmade sausages fly off the shelf. I looked at that elk standing there in the yard, I worked out the weight of the meat and thought this might just be the answer to all my problems. And it stood there at the bottom of the steps snorting. It was like a gift from on high.'

The elk lets out a bellow, something between a yawn and someone clearing his throat.

'I enticed him in here,' Jokinen continues. 'And managed to get him in the pen over there.'

I realise Jokinen still thinks I'm here because of the elk. It's the elk he's worried about, not my wife.

'I was just about to butcher it,' he continues. 'I glanced out the window and saw the pastor heading up here at full pelt. I think I got a bit rattled. Sorry about that.'

Jokinen shakes his hand and goggles at the point where we were wrestling a moment ago. I remember something he said just before the attack.

'You mentioned my know-it-all wife, and said I'm always handing out advice. I can't remember ever giving you advice.'

Jokinen's posture shifts, he looks awkward – more awkward than before. 'I just lost it … I … couldn't think. The elk, the sausage, everything…'

'We can talk about that later,' I say. 'I mean, what made you say something like that?'

Jokinen looks at me. For a long time. Eventually he leans forwards in his plastic chair, props his elbows on his knees.

'Minna and I have had a difficult winter. She wants to call it quits, head back south. It's been a hard time in general. Minna and Krista are best friends. Minna said Krista had given her lots of good advice about things. I suppose I was so upset that I thought Krista had caused all this … whatever it is that's going on. So I tried to come round yesterday to talk to Krista, thought I might find out what's going through Minna's mind these days, if I could work out where we're going. But then I…'

'Then I came back from the museum earlier than expected.'

Jokinen lowers his gaze to the floor.

'You drove me away.'

'I'm sorry about that, but…'

'Then you turn up here trying to save the elk.'

I turn and look at the elk. The beast and I look each other in the eye – maybe. Then I turn back to Jokinen.

'You just told me hunting season is over.'

'The animal doesn't know the difference between December and January,' he says.

'We don't normally ask the elk for his opinion.'

'Just think, that's another elk-related car crash that won't happen now.'

'Is Minna at home?'

'She's gone to her sister's place in Helsinki,' Jokinen says, shaking his head. 'She's back and forth there all the time these days. Maybe it's for the best.'

The elk makes a sound, a yawn-like splutter. I see the clock on the wall.

'I have to go,' I say. 'But I have a favour to ask you.'

'What's that?'

'Tell nobody I was here, nobody at all. Not even … Just, nobody.'

Jokinen stands up. 'I won't breathe a word.'

I believe him. Five hundred kilos of organic meat says he'll keep his word.

4

Between Heaven and Earth a slender strip of blue thread lingers, the last vestiges of the day. I drive back to the village, take out my phone and check I haven't received any text messages or calls without my noticing. I haven't. I slip the phone back into my pocket.

The trembling in my hands continues. It's faint – other people probably wouldn't notice it at all – but I sense it all the same. It's a mixture of exhaustion and agitation, low self-esteem, guilt and panic. I talk to Krista out loud, tell her I'm on my way, wherever she is. I tell her she can trust me. I mean what I say, I just don't know how I'm going to make it happen.

There is nobody driving in the opposite direction, the empty road seems to hum, the soft snow puffing up behind the car. Again I think of all the people who might have taken Krista hostage. At the same time I warn myself not to leap to hasty conclusions. Jokinen might have a secret, yes, but it isn't one I need to investigate or even one I need to know about. I have to be more careful, more precise. The meteorite will be heading to Helsinki in less than twenty-four hours. The van that will carry it will pull up outside the museum at ten o'clock tomorrow morning. Before that happens, I have to get Krista back. There are simply no other options.

I recall the evening we managed to lose each other in Jerusalem. We had spent all day wandering the city in the parched July heat. Evening fell just as we were resting our legs, filling our stomachs at a restaurant and talking about everything we'd seen. Or maybe I did most of the talking that evening. I wanted to see the Dead Sea Scrolls; I'd written my thesis about them. Perhaps the fact that I'd chosen an archaeological as opposed to a purely theological topic was a sign of what was to come.

We had spent the morning in museums, wandering around the old city. Eventually we headed towards the city's new downtown area and ended up walking far beyond that too.

We stepped out of the restaurant. The darkness was striking – there was something almost physical about it, enveloping you completely, wholly. Krista said she fancied a Coca-Cola. She went back inside the restaurant. I waited in the street but she didn't come back out again. I imagined we'd take a taxi back to the hotel, because we were both tired, worn out by the walking, the heat. And so I thought that, while waiting for her, I might still use the bathroom at the restaurant. I quickly took care of my business, went back out to the street and waited. But she didn't appear.

I went back inside, but she wasn't in the small dining room. I asked the waiter if he'd seen my wife, the woman with whom I'd been enjoying dinner only a moment ago. Your wife just came in to buy some pop, the waiter replied, then rushed outside again. I returned to the street but couldn't see Krista anywhere. I pulled my phone from my backpack, only to remember that Krista's phone and wallet were inside my bag. While out walking we'd decided it was most sensible for me to carry everything in my bag. It didn't seem so sensible now.

The long street was dark, deserted in both directions. Suddenly I wasn't sure which direction we'd arrived from. I tried to think what Krista had done, which direction she might have chosen. I made a decision and set off. I picked up my pace and arrived at a crossroads. I called out her name. I could hear laughter from the darkness beneath the trees across the street. The walls of the buildings were covered in slogans and graffiti. I continued on my way.

The streets became narrower. Just one more corner, I thought many times, before ultimately returning the way I had come. I quickly noticed this wasn't what I had done at all. I lost my way along the narrow pathways. Again I took out my phone, this time only to notice that the battery was dead. The map application, which I'd been using all day, had sucked the battery dry.

I did everything I could to find my way back to the restaurant, but it was futile. We'd been warned about this part of the city, told that after dark it was best to keep away from here. I tried to convince myself that Krista was probably on her way to the hotel – if she wasn't lost too. And I was walking along a dark, narrow residential street when I saw it.

Golgotha.

A small, run-down hotel with an ancient neon sign outside.

I walked up to the hotel, stepped inside. Krista was sitting on the only chair in the lobby.

Later, once I'd managed to suppress the sense of stress and growing panic somewhere deep inside, we took to saying it was at Golgotha that we found each other again. Though I doubt either of us found the anecdote especially amusing, the memory remotely pleasant. I believe we both experienced an immediate, genuine panic about each other's wellbeing, and the specific place where we were reunited was more than just a trifling detail.

The centre of Hurmevaara looks different. But it hasn't changed; I just look at it from a somewhat different perspective from a few days ago. Everywhere I go I look for signs of Krista and try to see dangers before they can pose me a threat. I arrive at the church hall.

I turn the car round before switching off the motor so the bonnet is facing towards the village. I've parked in the space nearest the door. Although how can you define a parking space in winter? Who's going to sweep the snow away, reveal the painted lines on the asphalt and check whether the car is properly parked? I give a sigh. It seems I'll latch on to any passing thoughts to avoid thinking about my wife and the fact that I'm the one who put her in this predicament in the first place.

I get out of the car, walk up the steps and open the door. Many things remind me of everything I have forgotten since I became so paranoid: the familiar environment, the silent building, my own echoing footsteps, the plaster sculpture of Christ in the lobby, and beside it the former rally driver, his face almost as white as the Lord's. I remember what Pirkko said just before I left.

Tarvainen.

The three-thirty appointment.

The situation is surprising, unexpected, though I've always known there was a possibility it could happen. I say a stiff hello and he responds. Dark floodwaters surge and a storm rages between my ears. The lobby is perfectly silent.

'Pirkko said you had a slot at three-thirty,' says Tarvainen. He sounds different from when we met at the kiosk; now he doesn't sound remotely like the drunken idiot in whose car I flew through the air and raced along the snow-covered streets of Hurmevaara. His voice is neither harsh nor rough; he sounds like a man who has come to meet his shepherd.

Which, to put it mildly, feels ever so slightly conflicting.

5

A few minutes later Tarvainen is sitting in my office, his sponsor jacket round his shoulders, sunglasses over his eyes. I think the glasses are a bit of an exaggeration; the lighting in the room is dim in a way I might once have called soft, but now I think it disturbing, threatening even. Perhaps the threat I sense has more to do with my own thoughts and as yet unspoken questions – such as: how dare you sit there after getting my wife pregnant and kidnapping her? And where the hell are you keeping her now?

'I don't really know how this works,' he says.

That rather depends what we're doing, I think. I put myself in work mode; that seems the surest option.

'You talk; I listen,' I say.

But Tarvainen doesn't talk, for a very long time. I'm almost certain I caught the smell of alcohol in the lobby. Yes, it's here in the office too, filling the air in the room like liberally applied aftershave. An aftershave made from garlic and toilet cleaner. My mind immediately casts back to Krista's account of the terrific flight, the resulting euphoria and the momentary loss of control. Without his car, Tarvainen could hardly have waltzed into our family, and certainly couldn't have had quite the same effect. And I sense something else, too. Tarvainen isn't behaving like a man who's been playing around with another man's wife. I recall what Krista eventually said after I had pressed her on the matter: *He was extremely drunk. He called me Leena and probably didn't even realise what happened in those thirty seconds.*

Tarvainen doesn't know what he's done.

Regarding that, at least.

'I don't even believe in God,' he says suddenly. 'And you've got a scratch on your forehead.'

I'm not sure which statement to comment on first.

'I fell over,' I say. 'And these pastoral sessions are for the general public; there are no admissions criteria.'

Even kidnappers are allowed to pour their heart out – before I sort out my differences with them. But would the kidnapper behave like this, I ask myself? Would he be so hesitant? Would he sit there so meekly, stammering over his words?

'How about I just say what I came to say?'

'Perhaps that's best,' I nod. 'Everything you tell me stays within this room. I have a duty of confidentiality.'

Tarvainen shifts position in his chair, once, twice, and on the third attempt returns to the position in which he started.

'I used to be a rally driver,' he begins, but pauses instantly. 'This will take forever if I start there.'

'Start with what is worrying you the most,' I suggest. 'It might sound strange, but that's often the easiest place to start.'

'Sulevi.' Tarvainen lets out the word so quickly that it sounds as much like a yelp as it does a man's name.

It seems the mention of this name takes us both by surprise. I wait for him to continue, but he remains silent.

'Sulevi?' I ask.

Tarvainen sighs. 'He was from the village, just like me – from a house out in the sticks.'

He turns his head towards the window and looks outside at what must be the day's final glimmers of light. I get the distinct impression that behind those sunglasses the lights went out long ago. He turns his head. Maybe he looks at me.

'I used to be a rally driver,' he tries again. 'I'll have to start there. I always have been a rally driver, still am. Even though they've shut me out of competitions. For now.' He stresses these last words. 'I will drive again. Once I sort things out. Once … New car, new team. New … map-reader. Sulevi was my map-reader. From day one.'

I don't tell him that I already know this. And I don't mention that Sulevi is lying interred beneath earth and snow, in the graveyard at most 120 metres from where we are now sitting, forever liberated from the maps and drunken, unreliable driving companions of this world. I notice too that my stance towards Tarvainen is far from neutral. On the wall, slightly to the right of Tarvainen's sunglasses and sponsor jacket, the Saviour looks as though he wants to turn away from us. But this may be nothing but my own interpretation, the result of a slow-burning rage and a desire for revenge.

'We were driving a mountain rally course in France, a short trip. Sulevi was taking notes. He made one mistake. What he thought was a gentle right-hand turn was in fact a sharp right-hand turn, we went into the bend a bit too fast, I almost oversteered into the bend; if I had, we would have plummeted half a kilometre and come crashing right into the Sunday market in the village below. I shouted at Sulevi. He shouted at me. It turned into a … an argument. You have a duty of confidentiality, right?'

'Yes, I still do,' I nod.

Tarvainen straightens his jacket, pulling the sides together across his stomach, which sits like a gym ball above his belt. The room is filled with the bouquet of windscreen fluid. Of the companies whose logos adorn his jacket, half have gone bust or been devoured by large conglomerates.

'We were yelling at each other,' he continues eventually. 'And we were a second and a half from the lead. All I could do was put my foot on the gas. We got down from the mountain. I thought I could … It ended in a bit of fisticuffs.'

Tarvainen is silent.

'You stopped the car and started to—?'

Tarvainen shakes his head, interrupts me before I get to the end of the question. 'I drive,' he says. 'I'll drive for as long as the clock's running.'

'Right.'

'I was steering with my left hand and punching him with my right.' Tarvainen demonstrates this with his hands.

I say nothing. Tarvainen lowers his hands. For a while we sit in silence.

'It was a mistake. I didn't mean it, but I knocked him unconscious. Then, because I didn't have a map-reader – or because my map-reader was unconscious – I was driving as fast as the car would go and eventually I overshot a damn bend. The car flew into a river. Sulevi didn't wake up. They breathalysed me, took me for blood tests, sent me home.'

He lowers his hands, places them in his lap. From the angle of his sunglasses, I guess he must be looking at the small table or at the floor in front of us.

'Sulevi gave me direction,' he says. 'He showed me the way. I need to say it. That's what … I came to tell you.'

The Saviour on the wall seems to turn towards us again. Of course, I am simply imagining the movement, but still…

'And what was it all for?' Tarvainen asks.

Before I can answer, before I can say anything at all, Tarvainen is speaking again, his voice more agitated now, angry even.

'What was the use of it? I went and did it again. I might not have knocked anyone unconscious first, but the other night I was driving so quickly that the guy in the passenger seat had a heart attack. There are other mitigating circumstances too, but still. This is hell on Earth. All I want to do is drive.'

Tarvainen grips the armrests of his chair. He looks as though he's trying to wrench himself free. As long as Krista is missing, I can't tell anyone anything that might endanger her further or jeopardise my attempts to get her back. I can't tell Tarvainen that the man in his passenger seat was already dead by the time Tarvainen started showing him some tricks. And even if I could tell him that, I don't know how I could tell him I was in the car too, in the footwell in the back, my hand operating Grigori's scarf.

My former mentor – an old pastor, now deceased, and a man whose guidance I have missed these last few days – always encouraged me to remove myself from the picture so as to see what's really there. And so I try to see through the bitterness, the thirst for revenge, and understand what this is really about. Is Tarvainen the kidnapper? Is he aware that he has got a woman in the village pregnant – a woman who just happens to be the pastor's wife? Does he realise he has just revealed his secret – knocking the map-reader unconscious and thereby causing his death – to that same woman's husband?

The answers appear to me clearly. Tarvainen doesn't sound like he has the slightest idea about any of the things I need to know about right now.

'Rally or death,' he says suddenly.

'Excuse me?'

'Those are the options. My options. That's it: rally or death. If I can't drive, I'd rather die.'

I say nothing.

'And I don't believe in God either,' he adds.

'That's clear.'

'Doesn't it bother you?'

'Why should it bother me?'

'That people don't believe.'

'They do believe, in different things. You believe in rally.'

He releases his grip on the armrests. The position of his head and sunglasses shows that his eyes are fixed on me. For a moment. Then he shakes his head.

'I have to get a car, a competition car, and a winning team behind me. It'll need an initial investment of a million euros. I guess there's no point asking God for a new Turbo Toyota.'

By now the room needs the overhead lights; the glow from the floor lamp only half reaches us. I look at his sunglasses, behind which it must be very dark. Lighting that darkness is, perhaps, a glint from a metallic piece of heaven.

'I assume you've been weighing up different options,' I say.

'Of course,' he nods. 'It's just I haven't ... Well, now everything's become clear. Now that I've said it out loud. Rally or death. Maybe I should thank you.'

Tarvainen is silent for a moment, then gives another shrug. 'Thank you,' he says.

'You're welcome.'

It doesn't last long, but in the course of that moment something happens. I'm not sure whether I want to forgive Tarvainen, let alone whether I would be capable of doing so, but I feel something approaching that as I look at the former rally hero. Maybe that's why I say what I say next.

'Still, this doesn't exactly solve the problem of the map-reader.'

'What do you mean?'

'I don't know much about the division of labour in a rally car,' I say. 'But generally speaking, you could say it's not entirely irrelevant who is reading the map, who is giving instructions and directions. Whose instructions we listen to, what people ultimately trust.'

Tarvainen pulls a gleaming hip flask from his sponsor jacket, unscrews the lid and drinks. He sighs, wipes his mouth, screws the lid back in place and drops the flask back into his pocket.

'You remember that meteorite, the one that hit my car?' he says. 'It fell right on the map-reader's seat.'

6

The door closes behind me, I hear the soft click of the lock. Normally the sound is imperceptible, but now it seems to echo, to ripple like a wave from the gates of the church hall to the empty car park, and from there to the dark wall of spruce trees on the other side. I stand there and look around. Still nothing but –21°C and the intensifying darkness; no cars, nobody lurking in the shadow of the trees.

I walk down the steps and arrive at my car almost instantly. Perhaps I was a little paranoid, leaving my car ready for a quick get-away, but I understand the rationale. I know I couldn't possibly have noticed everything; I know I'm not at my best. Fatigue and panic inevitably show; even I can see it. In addition to worry and panic, my thoughts of Krista have now assumed new dimensions, not all of which are particularly welcome. They are dark, labyrinthine thoughts, scenarios of what might happen if … I can barely even put it into words. What if she … doesn't come home? And what does that mean? If a person is trapped beneath the ice in a frozen lake, or in a snowdrift with a bullet in their head, or tied up in a mineshaft, they quite understandably won't be coming home. They won't return, because they are dead. So the question is: what if Krista dies?

I start the engine, drive home.

Our neighbour is once again reading at her kitchen table. Framed in the window and beneath the lamp, she looks like a painting hung in a darkened landscape. I glance at the windows in our house. They are all dark.

I step into the porch, thinking in what order I should take care of the things I need to do before my night shift. I check my phone again only to note that I have received neither instructions nor renewed threats. It worries me. Alongside everything else.

I throw my outdoor coat from round my shoulders, open the door between the porch and the hallway, step inside and stop dead in my tracks. This cannot be happening. But it is, because there's no mistaking it. I take a deep breath through my nose. I don't need to hear the sounds, but I hear them all the same, whether I want to or not.

The sounds are coming from the unlit living room. They seamlessly combine with the scent; they are one. The greeting isn't dramatic; everything else is, and that's enough. I step into the living room.

Even in the darkness, I recognise Karoliina.

It seems as though she has had time to make more than a passing acquaintance with our house, because she flicks on the reading lamp above the bookshelf with apparent familiarity. She is sitting on the sofa, her right leg across her left. Her lipstick is like Christmas apples – red with a hint of black – and her hair is tied in a ponytail. The white of her hands seems accentuated by the black of her jumper.

'You haven't called me,' she says.

'It's been a busy day. The evening especially.'

'But you've been thinking about me.'

'Yes,' I admit.

'I've been thinking about you too. I came here to see you. The door was open, so I thought I'd wait.'

I am convinced the door locked behind me when I left this morning. But perhaps that's not the most pressing issue right now. I try to listen, to ascertain whether Karoliina is alone in the house. I try to keep my movements as relaxed as possible and position myself so that there's a wall behind my back.

'Where is she?' I ask.

Karoliina looks at me. The reading lamp lights her from an angle, so one of her eyes gleams, while the other remains indecipherable.

I listen to the silence. I know the sounds of our wooden house, I know how it breathes, how it reacts to human movements. We are here alone.

'Who?' she asks.

'My wife.'

'How should I know?' she says. 'I didn't come here to see her; I came to see you. I didn't even expect her to be here. I've got the impression things aren't going so well for the two of you.'

Karoliina's words strike me with full force once I realise I really did hear right.

'The impression?' I ask and take a step towards her. 'And where have you got the impression that things … "aren't going so well"?'

The coffee table is between us. On it sits a copy of Dante's *Divine Comedy*, exactly where I left it earlier.

'You hang around in bars,' she says. 'First thing in the morning. Alone. You drink whisky. You want the meteorite. And your behaviour is … preposterous.'

'Preposterous?'

Karoliina pauses for a moment.

'Oh, don't be such a priest. I've seen the same thing a million times. You're trying to make an impression on me.' Karoliina smiles. Maybe.

I say nothing.

'It's nothing to worry about,' she continues. 'And you have made an impression. You're quite cool for a priest. But we haven't got much time, so we have to agree on a few things.'

'Not before I know Krista is okay.'

She sighs. 'This is all very worrying,' she says and glances at the bookshelf.

'What is?'

'First you're like a cowboy, riding into town, appearing at the door of the saloon, trying to hit on the women and plan a robbery. Then, just when you need to put the plan into action, you start worrying about your wife.'

I have to admit there's a lot of sense in Karoliina's words – in one way. She doesn't talk the way a kidnapper would talk. She sounds genuinely frustrated. And she doesn't behave like someone with any real leverage. What's more, if she is not the one holding Krista, under no circumstances can she be allowed to get her hands on the meteorite. In short, if Karoliina does have a plan of how to get hold of it, I need to be a part of that plan.

'My wife has been a bit under the weather recently,' I say. Of course, this is true, and I have no difficulty saying it out loud. The next sentence comes just as easily. 'But she's tough.'

Karoliina shakes her head. 'When I leave,' she says, 'I'll make sure I leave for real, for good.'

I allow a few seconds to pass.

'So you have a plan?' I ask.

Karoliina stands up from the sofa. She walks round the coffee table, appears in front of me. Her proximity always has a physical impact on me: my heart beats quicker, my chest and stomach start to tingle. And it's happening again now. I simultaneously want to back away and move forwards. Desire has nothing to do with what is sensible or, for want of a better word, right. It's simply … desire.

'Yes, I have a plan, of course I do,' she says, and now I can smell the full force of her perfume. 'But … can I trust you?'

'I need that meteorite,' I say. It's the God's honest truth.

Karoliina appears to be thinking about something. Then she moves her right hand, and I feel her touch. And not just at the spot on my shoulder where her hand comes to rest, but through my whole body.

'If I'm honest, I'm a bit frightened,' she says.

'Frightened of what?'

'I can tell you this sort of thing, right? I mean, you're a priest, right?'

The light is shining from behind her. Her lips are dark, slightly apart. I can see their shape, their moisture.

'I have a duty of confidentiality, yes.'

Karoliina moves her hand along my shoulder. 'I'm afraid of him.'

'Of who?'

She opens her mouth, then pauses.

'Leonid,' she answers eventually.

'Right. Leonid.'

'Right. He forces me to ... He's a dangerous man.'

'In what way?' I ask.

'He is...' Karoliina begins and again looks me in the eyes. 'He's a criminal.'

'He wants the meteorite, is that right?'

I can hear her breathing. She moves closer all the while.

'Yes.'

'Is he working alone?'

'He is now that Grigori's dead. Someone shot him.'

I won't correct Karoliina by telling her that technically speaking Grigori shot himself, that he pulled the gun from inside his coat, pointed it at an unarmed civilian and pulled the trigger.

'Does Leonid know who shot him?' I ask.

'He says he does, at least. He's been talking about it nonstop, about how he's going to take revenge on the guy who did it, skin him alive, crucify him.'

A cold fist grips my insides. I try not to let it show.

'When you said Leonid was working alone...'

'Not quite alone. He's working with me.'

'You're afraid of him *and* you're going to steal the meteorite with him?'

'Yes and no.'

'What does that mean?'

Karoliina is right against me.

'It means I first want to be sure I can tell you my plan,' she says.

She presses herself against my body. She has closed her eyes. Her lips are so near my own that I'm certain I can already feel them touching. Our lips do not meet, but there's an electricity between them, and I can feel her breath against my face. She moves one of her hands, it comes to rest on my hip and it awakens something I haven't thought of for several days now. I close my eyes, lean back my head.

'Shouldn't it be the other way round?' I ask and open my eyes. 'Shouldn't I ask whether or not I can trust you? Shouldn't I hear about your plan first and then decide what to do?'

Karoliina looks up; our eyes meet. She moves her hand from my hip, crosses to my abdomen, then moves further down until she is gently touching the front of my trousers. Her bare arm turns slightly. Along the side of her forearm runs a long, freshly healed scratch.

'We will both have to work, but with regards to the future, it's for the best: we'll both be equally guilty.'

She speaks of guilt as though it were something to seek out and share with others. I can't possibly agree to this, but I keep my thoughts to myself.

'You are on guard at the museum,' she says, her voice now barely louder than a whisper. We are so close to each other that her voice sounds like waves on a beach. 'All of a sudden two people break in. One of them threatens you with a gun. You fight back, you manage to grab the gun and you shoot one of the intruders…'

'No…'

'The intruder dies,' she continues as though she hadn't heard me. I can feel her hand against my crotch. 'Despite your exemplary bravery, you still can't prevent the theft of the meteorite. One of the intruders escapes with it. It later transpires that the dead intruder is a Russian professional criminal. He has been seen around the village with a friend on several occasions. It is quickly established that he and his friend were working together. And now the accomplice is every bit as missing as the meteorite. One plus one. Two Russian crooks, one missing meteorite. Nobody will come looking for me – and they certainly won't suspect the brave guard on night shift who tried to protect the meteorite in the first place.'

'*Who* will shoot the intruder?' I ask.

'Leonid is a nasty piece of work. He'd do the same to us. If you won't do it, then…'

I have no intention of getting into an ethical discussion; there isn't time. And I haven't upheld the highest ethical standards myself in recent times. I still feel the same inexplicable, aching desire for this woman.

'Why wouldn't the surviving intruder kill the security guard too?' I ask.

'Because she needs the guard.'

'For what? She already has the meteorite, and blame has been deflected to the Russian crooks. Why does she need a pastor?'

'She needs him *because* he's a pastor,' says Karoliina. 'She needs an alibi, of course. Nobody will believe you could be lying. Everyone will believe you. And you'll give the police such a detailed description of the intruder that they'll be looking for the right man from the very next second.'

'The right man?'

'Grigori. Leonid told me Grigori's in storage, somewhere nobody would ever think to look for him. From our perspective – what could be better?'

I feel Karoliina's hand against my trousers as though it were against my skin, as though there was nothing separating us. I look her in the eyes.

Indeed, I think, what really could be better?

What could be better right now?

7

The driving instructions are anything but clear. The map application on my phone is no help at all. I try to combine the complicated instructions written on a piece of paper with the random coordinates provided by the app. I am somewhere to the north of Hurmevaara, an area even more sparsely populated than the rest of the village, speeding along dark, narrow lanes and trying to find myself, both in the instructions and on the map.

Finally I arrive at a long straight road that I recognise from the instructions. I slow my speed somewhat but still manage to drive past the small opening in the trees that I'm looking for. I brake, wait for the snow puffed up behind me to settle, then reverse and turn on to another narrow lane.

Matias Ihantola lives far away from everything. Which, I assume, is the point. He might well believe that such a remote location will give him an advantage should the world be struck by a pandemic, hordes of people, or a nuclear holocaust. I'm not sure I entirely agree with him, especially when we look at the final result: what must it be like to live life in a world that has turned into a battlefield, a world in which everything has stopped working?

I give my head a vigorous shake. My thoughts are not glowing with positivity, but, naturally, there is a reason for this.

The trees slowly recede. The house stands right in the middle of a clearing and is surrounded on all sides by forest, forest and more forest. Noticing an approaching car is easy. I can see Ihantola in my headlights. He is expecting me.

The house is very small; inside it is tidy and equipped in a way that can't help making a strong impression on me. Ihantola has prepared himself for the end of the world with great care and attention to detail. He clearly intends to survive long after the rest of the population has suffered plagues and floods of Old-Testament proportions. But in all these apocalyptic visions, there is one crack. And that crack is Matias Ihantola himself.

Never before have I seen him smile like this. Never have I heard the same levity, the sense of hope I now detect in his voice. Something has happened.

But the clock is ticking. What I have come to collect is…

'Exactly,' he says and raises his forefinger. 'The rifle.'

He disappears into a room that I assume must be the bedroom and returns with the weapon in his hand. I recognise it: a bolt-action Sako hunting rifle. He hands me the rifle. I take it and check it is loaded. It is not, and the chamber is empty. I look at Matias Ihantola.

'Right,' he says. 'I suppose I should have mentioned this.'

'Mentioned what?' I ask, though I can guess where this is going.

'I've been in such a dark place recently – ever since Kaisa took the children and left, in fact,' he says. 'And I haven't been hunting either. But then…' He scratches his thick stubble. 'The last time we spoke,' he begins, 'I realised something. And I want to thank you. I don't mean the praying. That was my idea; you didn't seem very enthusiastic about it. Which I find rather puzzling, to be perfectly honest, but let's not get into that. I finally realised that the way you relate to things … it made an impression on me.'

'The way I relate?' I ask. The rifle is still in my hand. I sense that time is passing and that right now I need to talk about something altogether different.

'Yes,' he says. 'The way you often say that you don't know or that you can only speak for yourself. It inspires … hope.'

'Really?'

'Oh, yes,' he says. 'After our last conversation, I realised I must think very seriously about the plastic in our oceans, the extinction of marine ecosystems, the atrophying of the seas, their death, which will come very soon, and how it is in fact our death too – but I didn't. I did as you taught me. I told myself that I can only do what I can do, and that everything else is beyond my reach.'

'I'm not sure I really…'

'That's it. You are a very positive person. You gave me hope. It is exactly as you said. And now I can say it too. What do I know? It's very liberating.'

'I don't…'

'And when I was supposed to think about artificial intelligence – because we already know there will come a day when machines can develop machines that are more intelligent than themselves, machines that can decide to commandeer everything connected to the web, turn everything against humans, and if humans try to resist they will destroy us with weapons and in ways that, obviously, we can't even imagine yet – I decided to think about it the way you would think about it.'

The steel barrel of the rifle is pointing at the door, where I should be heading right now. But Ihantola's monologue keeps me rooted to the spot.

'And how would I approach it?' I ask.

'You would sit calmly in your chair and maybe you'd say that you don't know.'

I'm about to say I'm not at all sure I would do that, but I realise this wouldn't please Matias Ihantola. The silence of the house is arresting. We are so far from other settlements, so far from everything, that the silence is like an air-tight seal around us; it comes in from outside, its pressure greater than any of us can withstand.

Ihantola nods decisively and continues. 'You realise there could be a market for this kind of philosophy these days? It's the antidote to everything the usual snake-oil salesmen are touting: certainty, self-confidence, omniscience. And these days, with people thinking they know everything about everything, always taking a stance, shouting over one another because they are more right than the person in front of them, imagine how refreshing it would be if someone said simply, "I don't know."'

'I don't know…'

'That's exactly what I mean,' he says. He is clearly only getting started.

I have to stop him. I turn the rifle in my hands, show it to him.

'The cartridges,' I say. 'You have cartridges for this thing, right?'

He hesitates, and his expression is overcast with that same anguish I've seen in him before.

'Right,' he says. 'Like I said, I'd been having dark thoughts…'

He reaches out his right hand, and now I realise what he's been holding throughout his monologue. He holds his fist between us and opens his fingers, slowly. In the palm of his hand is a .308-calibre bottlenecked cartridge.

One cartridge.

I look at the cartridge, then at Matias Ihantola.

'I feel I should apologise,' he says, his voice a little hoarse. 'But I'll say thank you instead. This was for me. My insurance for the end of days. I don't need it anymore.'

He looks me in the eye as he drops the cartridge into my hand. His eyes are wet with tears.

'You have given me hope,' he says. 'Thank you.'

8

Mercy. I hear the words of my former pastor mentor. Mercy means that we can help others by virtue of our own faults and shortcomings. And if not by virtue of them, then at least despite them. We can be of use despite ourselves.

These words come to mind on an empty road as, once again, I speed back towards Hurmevaara. Matias Ihantola seems like a changed man. It looks as though the deeper into despair I have sunk, the more positively he has begun to view his own existence.

The single-cartridge rifle is a source of some disappointment. I don't have time to get my hands on more cartridges, let alone look for a new weapon. In the event that I actually need the rifle, I will quite literally have only one chance. The rifle is in the footwell behind the front seat – for now. The phone is in my lap in case I should receive a text message regarding Krista's whereabouts.

I arrive at the museum a minute before my shift starts. I decide to leave the rifle in the car for a moment longer; I have no desire to answer the questions it might elicit. I relieve those on evening shift; they loiter in the doorway longer than I would like. They chat about the meteorite's last night at the museum.

And this is the last night.

In the morning a van will pull up outside the museum door and take the meteorite to Helsinki, and from there it will travel to London. These are the meteorite's last few hours in Hurmevaara.

The security guard on the evening shift tells me many times over how exciting this has been, explaining that the meteorite has shaken the village out of a daydream. I could tell him a few things that would raise the excitement factor considerably. But I decide to say nothing and take small, hopefully imperceptible steps to steer him and the museum's part-time caretaker towards the front door and to guide them out into the yard. Finally they are outside in the freezing night, their breath steaming, and the door locks behind them with a click. They walk off to their cars. I can hear their chatter for a moment further; apparently there's no shortage of things to talk about.

Of course, the meteorite's final night in the village gets me thinking too, but in a wholly different way. What's more, I realise I don't suspect either of them of involvement. They don't even seem to see this side of the story; I can hear it from the way they talk, in what they talk about and how they behave in front of me and when in proximity to the meteorite. In recent days people like this have been in a minority in my circle, I muse. I seem to be surrounded by a whole list of people whose behaviour has changed beyond recognition.

I soon hear their cars. They start their engines almost simultaneously; the second speeds away more urgently than the first. Then the sounds of their cars fade into the evening. I wait for a moment and open the door.

It's going to be a bright, starlit night.

The stars glow and twinkle, almost trying to reach down to the Earth. I walk to my car, look around. This is a risky business. The letter said I would receive a text message once they see I have arrived at the museum. But I'm not sure I believe this. Nobody has been following me for the last few hours, of that I'm absolutely certain. Nobody could have followed me all the way out to Ihantola's house without my noticing. Rather, I assume that the kidnapper knows what time my shift is due to start and will turn up and assess the situation. It's only a question of how soon this will happen. I can't see anybody. I fill my lungs with fresh air, wait for a few seconds. I open the car door, take the rifle from behind the front seat and return to the museum, the weapon in my hand.

They say that the darkest hour is just before dawn. Maybe. But there are also moments when the whole idea of dawn seems only theoretical, something it's pointless to wait for because the real battle will take place in darkness.

I make some last-minute preparations at the museum. I eventually decide to conceal the rifle halfway between the meteorite room and the exit; I position it as part of a display of military uniforms. I am about to hide the gleaming, rust-free barrel of the rifle beneath the sleeve of an old army coat when my phone beeps as a text message arrives:

Where are you? The lobby is empty.

I make sure that the rifle is firmly propped in place, easily accessible yet hidden from prying eyes. The telephone is in my hand; I quickly search for the number and receive an answer immediately: *the number you entered cannot be found*. This means with almost one hundred percent certainty that this is a prepaid account. I don't know whether I can draw any other conclusions from this except that it seems I'm not dealing with total amateurs.

Keeping the phone in my hand, I take a deep breath and walk into the lobby. I approach with caution. I don't want to walk straight into an ambush. Because the lights are switched on, I can't see outside as well as I'd like to. But I do see that, except for my own car, the car park in front of the museum is deserted. I turn and look towards the forest. The large windows reflect the lobby and my own image, but still I can see the pure, untouched snow cover stretching all the way to the edge of the trees. I take a few steps forwards until I am standing in the middle of the lobby. At the same time I realise how lucky I am. I managed to smuggle the rifle into the museum just in time. I stand there for another thirty seconds or so, then my phone beeps again:

Exchange at 0230.

Don't try anything, don't be smart.

Just act normally.

The next instructions will arrive at 0215.

You are being watched.

Acknowledge that you understand.

I respond immediately:

I understand. Is Krista OK?

I look in both directions. I can see no movement, no human figures either on the side facing the village and the car park, or the side looking towards the forest. I move calmly. Somebody knows where I am, someone can possibly even see me. It's just gone nine o'clock. I do the things I would normally do: I brew some coffee in the staffroom, walk the length of the museum, making sure all the doors and windows are locked. I return to the staffroom, keeping the phone within arm's reach. The phone beeps just as I return to the lobby with a mug of steaming coffee.

Joel, it's Krista.

I am fine. I'm allowed one message.

To prove it's really me: Dubrovnik.

I know immediately what she means. We've been planning a trip to Croatia this summer. So Krista is … somewhere. I can't – and daren't – imagine that she is safe. The message came from the same unlisted number. A few seconds later I receive the first message again:

Exchange at 0230.

Don't try anything, don't be smart.

Just act normally.

The next instructions will arrive at 0229.

You are being watched.

Acknowledge that you understand.

I sit down in the caretaker's chair, again acknowledge receipt of the message and that I have understood it. I place the coffee cup on the table and take my books out of the desk drawer: the Bible and James Ellroy's latest novel. I place them on the table in front of me, though I know I can't bring myself to open either. The coffee gradually cools at the corner of the table. I am neither hungry nor thirsty, I am not tired.

I am waiting for my wife.

And I wait until 2.19 a.m., when one of the windows smashes to smithereens.

9

The sound of the window smashing comes from the western end of the museum, the side nearest the forest. I stand up, a thousand thoughts whirling through my mind. The first are volleys of questions laden with curses. Then, once I'm already running, I go through the various scenarios and everything that might conceivably go wrong.

It certainly can't be Karoliina. To my mind we had an agreement, an understanding. On the spur of the moment I came up with a plan of my own, though one I have no intention of carrying out. I spoke for a long time as we stood there next to one another, close to one another. I said I would send her a text message from the museum once the coast was clear, but before that neither of us should be tempted to go off script. She brought her face even closer to mine, until eventually I felt her lips against my skin. She whispered into my ear that never before had she waited in anticipation for something like this, saying that I was exactly the kind of partner she'd been looking for. Then she moved away from me, pulled on a jumper and coat and left. For a good few minutes I remained sitting in the armchair in our half-darkened living room in silence, calmly steadying my breath.

This is a complicated situation. I have a rifle, yes, but it only has one cartridge. If I use it, I'll be up against the kidnapper with nothing but a prop. That cannot happen. I need something in my hand, something heavy. I remember that in the first room there is a life-sized war-time mess, and on the table in the mess is an old iron kettle. I pick it up and run off again.

The intruders didn't choose the western wing of the museum at random. Admittedly, the window they had to break is rather big – it's what you might call a panorama window – but the route to the meteorite is shorter and more direct. I approach the meteorite room, trying to move silently, and make my way behind a large anti-aircraft cannon. Now I am only one door away from the meteorite room. I hear footsteps.

I'll have to improvise, that's for sure. But how much?

The meteorite is housed in a new glass cabinet, much stronger than the previous one. The casing is taking a battering. I creep from behind the cannon towards a wall of bazookas, then make my way behind them until I reach the wall of maps opposite the meteorite room. I edge towards the doorway, crouch on one knee and peer into the meteorite room.

There's no mistaking the enormous man. He is attacking the glass cabinet with a hammer. There's power behind his blows. The thick glass is cracked and will soon be in pieces. I can't see anyone else in the room. I wait and listen. All I can hear is Leonid smashing the cabinet and the squeak of his shoes against the floor. Whichever way you look at it, his behaviour is utterly mindless. And if he's operating alone, it's even more mindless. And that's what it looks like. Except for him, the room is empty.

The glass smashes and clatters to the floor. Leonid picks up a hiking backpack, which looks like a school satchel, and prises the meteorite from its stand. I know the meteorite weighs less than four kilos. He stuffs it into his bag, closes the bag with a drawstring and clips and shrugs it over his shoulder.

I can't fathom what is going on. Leonid takes a few steps towards the window. I give him a head start, clench the iron kettle in my right hand. Once I am sure he is walking so quickly that he won't hear my steps, I position my legs so that I can leap out behind him and—

I recognise it immediately. It is exactly the right size and weight, and all it needs is the support of a familiar voice. The barrel of a gun is pressed forcefully into my neck.

'Change of plan,' comes the voice. 'Stay where you are.'

I am leaning slightly forwards, my left knee still touching the floor. Leonid stops and spins round, and from his expression I realise he was expecting this sudden turn of events. I have rushed headlong into an ambush, though that is specifically what I have been trying to avoid. I have experience of ambushes. And still I made a mistake like this. Before long I realise why. I can't smell any perfume. I haven't given the matter the least thought; I've internalised it. The perfume was supposed to warn me.

'Get up. Slowly. Don't do anything unless I tell you to. And keep that pot in your hand.'

'It's a kettle.'

'Then hold your kettle. Stand up.'

I shift my weight to my right leg and slowly push myself upright. The barrel moves away from my neck.

'Walk into that room, the one where the meteorite was.'

I try to turn, to look behind.

'Don't turn around. Walk. Calmly.'

Leonid watches as I go. It's hard to read his expression. The vitrine is in smithereens on the floor. I stop before stepping on the shards.

'Forwards,' says Karoliina. 'Right up to the cabinet.'

'There is no cabinet,' I say.

'Of course there isn't. You smashed it,' she says. 'Smash your kettle against that pedestal.'

I glance over my shoulder. I recognise the pistol she is holding. It's the same gun that was once in Grigori's hand – and it was pointing at me then too. Karoliina is wearing a woolly hat. The hair visible beneath the hat is wet; that would explain the lack of perfume.

'Smash it,' she says.

I look over at Leonid. He might be smiling. I'm not sure I would smile if I were him; I don't know if I could trust anything I'd agreed with Karoliina. But a person in love will see whatever they want to see, even if it ends up killing them. I weigh the kettle in my hand and try to gauge my distance from Karoliina. About six or seven metres. There's no way I'll be able to reach her before she has a chance to pull the trigger. And I'm not sure I'd hit her if I tried to throw the kettle.

I decide to buy some time. I can basically guess what she's up to: she wants it to look as though I decided to steal the meteorite, but that my accomplice shot me and disappeared with the meteorite alone. I turn and strike the pedestal with the kettle a few times.

'What do you call that?' Karoliina shouts. 'For the love of Jesus, you look like you're doing the dishes. Hit it, man.'

I hit the pedestal another few times, so hard that my hand hurts. I hit it because every blow gives me the extra seconds I need to think. The noise of metal against metal hurts my ears; it's dizzying. The room is echoing, booming. I stop. My ears are ringing. I guess this must be the case for all three of us.

None of us could possibly have heard the arrival of a fourth person.

10

Karoliina and Leonid cannot see the masked man. He is standing behind them. They look at me. The broken window is behind the man; that's how he has come in. All four of us are in some kind of infernal chain, each part of which is linked to all the other parts. The masked man is aiming a rifle either at me, Karoliina, Leonid or all three of us. Probably all of us.

'Don't move,' he says in a booming voice. 'Or I'll shoot.'

Karoliina turns her head slightly, keeping her pistol aimed firmly in my direction. Her expression is a mixture of rage and disbelief.

'Drop the gun,' says the man.

Karoliina's head is turned towards him. She must be able to see the rifle. The pistol is pointed at me. Long seconds elapse. Eventually her fingers relax and the pistol drops to the floor.

'Kick the gun to the side,' he says.

Karoliina stands on the spot. Again a few seconds pass. The barrel of the rifle rises slightly, a shot explodes and plasterwork falls from the wall behind us. Again the rifle seems to point at all of us at once.

'Kick it.'

Karoliina kicks the pistol, and it glides a few metres across the floor.

'The bag,' the man says, this time to Leonid.

Leonid is standing on the spot, just like Karoliina was a moment ago. I get the impression the rifleman is starting to lose his temper.

'What the hell's wrong with you?' he hisses from behind his rifle. 'Simple instructions, dammit. The bag. Now.'

At this the man seems to realise something himself.

'*The bag*,' he says, this time in English. 'You. Bag. Give.'

Now I know the identity of the rifleman behind the balaclava:

Tarvainen the rally driver. His booming voice had me fooled for a moment. But I recognise his English from the TV sports round-up; I can see him standing by the track, shouting commands, a baseball cap pulled tight over his head, the foreign words tumbling from his mouth like clumsy metallic car parts. Leonid removes the bag from his back and holds it in his hand.

'Throw,' Tarvainen continues in English. 'Bag. Me. Now.'

Leonid throws the bag as though it were a sock or a towel. It clanks on the concrete floor in front of Tarvainen. The rally driver points the rifle at us and cautiously bends down towards the bag. He takes his left hand from the shaft of the rifle and grasps the straps of the rucksack, all the while succeeding in keeping the rifle aimed and ready with one hand.

'Pastor,' he says. 'Walk over to the pistol, lift it by the barrel and drop it into that cannon.'

At the far end of the room is a large field cannon. Its barrel is pointing towards the edge of the roof at the other side of the hall. I walk towards the pistol and pray that Tarvainen doesn't notice one thing: the kettle still in my hand. Once I reach the pistol, I hear Tarvainen's voice again.

'Slowly,' he says. 'Pick up the pistol and point it at yourself.'

I crouch down, grip the pistol by the barrel so that it is pointing somewhere around my stomach. Then I stand up straight and look at Tarvainen.

'Walk calmly towards the cannon,' he says.

I walk towards the cannon with the kettle in my other hand. The green steel barrel of the cannon is thick, the hole at its end like a black chasm. The barrel rises up at a steep, forty-five-degree angle.

'Lift the pistol carefully and drop it into the cannon,' says Tarvainen.

I move my arm slowly, raise it almost as far as I can reach. The mouth of the cannon is quite high from the ground. The pistol reaches the opening; I place it further inside and let go. The slide gives a metallic echo, then quickly dies down. I keep the kettle huddled against my body. I'm not exactly hiding it, but I don't want to show it off either.

Tarvainen begins backing off towards the window. He is still pointing the rifle at us. Shards of glass crunch beneath his winter boots. Then in a flash he is outside and only the barrel of the rifle remains inside the museum.

'If I see someone following me, I'll shoot,' he says, and now I can hear the drink in his voice. Until now he's managed to conceal it.

'I'll shoot if you come after me,' he shouts once more.

Then he disappears.

I don't have a plan of any sort.

What I do have is an iron kettle and a sprinting start.

Leonid has turned and is facing Karoliina. I can't see what Karoliina is doing as I run towards Leonid. He turns and sees me all in the same movement. He is quick, his hand disappears inside his coat and pulls out a knife. But I have speed on my side, that and what I've got in my hand. I swing the kettle.

It thumps Leonid square on the chin with a dull clang. He falls to his knees, the knife flies from his hand, clatters as it slides, glinting, across the museum floor. I continue running towards the window and glance over my shoulder. Karoliina has reached the field cannon and has reached her hand inside. I peer out of the window, hear an engine starting and dive outside.

Tarvainen is sitting on the back of a snowmobile and slams his foot on the gas. He has the rucksack on his back, the rifle slung across his chest. He doesn't look behind him as the snowmobile hurtles further from the museum. I make my way to the other side of the museum, run to my car pulling the keys from my pocket. I manage to start the engine, reverse, turn the car and set off after him.

I steer the car to the main road, and before long I can see the back light of the snowmobile flickering up ahead. The vehicle is travelling between the trees, parallel to the road. Thank goodness the stars are brighter than on any other night this winter – and thank goodness there's a full moon. If there was even the slightest snowfall or if clouds covered the sky, I wouldn't see anything.

I need that meteorite. I glance at the clock, aghast, and pull my phone from my pocket. I simultaneously try to see what is happening in the forest – where the snowmobile is heading, and struggle to put together a text message. It isn't easy. Tarvainen is driving at a terrific speed. I really have to put my foot down just to keep up with him. He knows how to drive. I've only managed to type two words when the phone beeps as a text message arrives:

Bring the meteorite out.
We are in the car park.

I shout out loud. 'No, no, no, no, no!'

I can't turn around and I don't have the meteorite. I delete what I've already written and glance to the sides. The back light has disappeared. I brake, the phone falls from my hand. I reverse, the engine howls, the wall of spruces suddenly opens up and I can see the snowmobile far across the other side of the fields. It is heading towards…

Lake Hurmevaara.

Tarvainen's house is on the shores of Lake Hurmevaara.

Who steals a million euros, then takes his loot and drives straight back home?

Answer: a drunken rally driver. Maybe.

After crossing the field, the rear light again disappears into the forest. I grope in the footwell for my phone and finally find it beneath the passenger seat. I send a text message, then try to make a call. I set off and hold the phone firmly against my ear. It rings. Nobody answers.

At the intersection I turn right. I drive along the road for ten minutes and arrive at the Hurmevaara junction quicker than ever before. I take the road leading to Lake Hurmevaara, twisting and turning as it winds its way towards the lake. There isn't a single straight section in the road, and I really have to focus on driving.

Regardless of the hazardous conditions, I look at my phone and try to call again. It's futile.

When I arrive at the point where the road veers off towards the western edge of the lake, I search online for Tarvainen's contact details. These are easily found. Neither his address nor his telephone number are ex-directory. This suggests the rally driver didn't give the idea of becoming a meteorite thief much prior thought.

The final kilometre up to Tarvainen's house is the fastest that night. I am familiar with the house from hearsay. It was built with the fortunes of a rally career, money that, judging by what I've seen, has long since run out. The house is large, wholly unsuited to its surroundings, and is positioned almost on the water's edge. Perhaps the edge of the ice would be a more appropriate term at this time of year. In the glare of the moon and stars, the angularity of the house, its brightness and its large glass windows make it look like a miniature airport without a runway. I drive past the house but cannot see the snowmobile. The house is unlit.

After a few hundred metres I make a U-turn and drive back towards the house. From this angle I get a better view of the strip of land between the house and the shore. The snowmobile is parked on a steep incline, its bonnet almost right up against the house. The lights are on in the window in front of the vehicle. Tarvainen is in one corner of the house, so I surmise that I can drive along the main path and approach the house from the opposite direction.

The path seems to lead down towards the house and the shoreline. I switch off the car's headlights. As soon as I turn on to the path, I shift into neutral and switch off the motor. I open the window. The car glides silently forwards on the narrow, snow-covered pathway. I almost make it all the way to the house without hearing a sound.

And when the sound finally comes, I see the glass of the windscreen crack around a bullet hole.

11

The first shot makes a hole in the windscreen, the second penetrates the bumper and the third punctures the left front tyre. I unclip my seatbelt, open the door and dive out into the snow. I manage to reach the safety of the trees and don't hear any more shots. Now I hear cursing. I stand up carefully and, from behind a thick spruce, look towards the house.

Tarvainen is standing on the upper-floor balcony, battering his rifle against the floor. I've seen the same kind of panic before when a firearm malfunctions. A faint light glows behind him, making his movements look like a violent theatre of shadows. I remain in the shelter of the trees and wade through the snow, which reaches halfway up my thighs. Eventually I arrive at the front yard and walk round the side of the house. Tarvainen is still on the balcony. He seems to be peering towards the car and the yard. Perhaps he can't see that the door on the driver's side is wide open.

I make my way along the side of the house, turn the corner and reach the back of the house, where the snowmobile is parked almost right against the wall. Its motor is still clicking with heat in the frozen night, the key is still in the ignition. I remove the key. If Tarvainen wants to shoot my car to pieces, he can give me a lift back to the village. Assuming I need a lift at all, that is – assuming Tarvainen doesn't shoot me dead.

There is a door to one side of the snowmobile. It is unlocked.

The lights are on in the downstairs room. The room has large windows facing the lake and a big open hearth, which doesn't appear to have been used recently, and such a cornucopia of rally paraphernalia that it almost feels as though I've stepped into a motorsports museum. There must be dozens of trophies. And medals. And photographs showing cars turning corners almost on their sides or flying through the air, photographs in which Tarvainen is holding a trophy aloft or spraying champagne in the air, or standing arm-in-arm with rows of smiling people. Tarvainen himself never smiles.

Something about the room makes me stop. It's not that I stand still wondering about it, but the truth is that only a moment ago this same man saved my life. Karoliina and Leonid wouldn't have left me alive to tell anyone about the break-in or the people carrying it out.

I walk up the steps as quickly and silently as possible. Despite my best efforts my winter shoes make the wooden floorboards creak ever so slightly. I get halfway up and peer into the room above from floor level.

The living room is large and open-plan, and the space is still bright, though it is lit only by a single floor lamp in the corner. Otherwise the room is empty. I walk up the remaining stairs and try to locate Tarvainen by sound. I just about work out the location of the balcony from which Tarvainen opened fire and take a few cautious steps in that direction. I assume that if the rifle was working, Tarvainen would have taken another pot-shot – either at the car or into the woods. Then I hear a clatter from a completely different direction.

Tarvainen is in the kitchen. I approach the doorway and peer inside. The kitchen is a large rectangular space; Tarvainen is at the far end of the room, by the windows. The rucksack is firmly strapped to his back. And there's something in his hand. When the lights from the kitchen counter illuminate him from the right angle, I recognise what it is. A large Chinese kitchen knife, the shape of a cleaver. I take a deep breath, exhale and step inside.

'We have to talk,' I say.

Tarvainen spins round. He doesn't look surprised; he looks furious, utterly livid.

'About what?' he asks, by now sounding considerably more inebriated than at the museum. Perhaps he downed a few celebratory drinks on the way home. He has also unbuttoned his black overcoat, beneath which I can see the sponsor jacket of yesteryear.

'About lots of things. I want...'

'The meteorite.'

I don't answer. He's right, of course.

'I want to thank you,' I say and take a few wary steps in his direction. 'You saved my life. Back at the museum.'

Tarvainen staggers. It's obvious that he is profoundly drunk. I don't know how he managed to steal anything or steer the snowmobile so skilfully. But on the other hand I understand: every member of my small family has first-hand experience of his skills behind the wheel.

'You're welcome,' he says. 'Now get out of my house.'

'One more thing,' I say. 'Well, two things. First, I need that ... rucksack.'

'I knew it, dammit.'

'What did you know?'

'I knew you were the same as all the rest of them.'

'Of course I am. But—'

'You want the meteorite. Everybody wants it. But it's mine. It belongs to me now.'

'I need it,' I say honestly. 'I need it to save my wife, Krista.'

Tarvainen's expression doesn't flicker.

'And another thing,' I continue. It's extraordinarily hard to put this into words, and even more so to make myself say it. 'I want to forgive you.'

He clearly hasn't the faintest idea what I'm talking about.

'I want to forgive you,' I repeat. 'We all make mistakes. Now put the knife away.'

Tarvainen does the opposite. He raises the knife, brandishes it in the air. The enormous blade seems to gather all the light in the room; it gleams like a lamp pointed right at me.

'Out of my house!' he shouts.

I shake my head. 'I can't leave without that meteorite.'

Tarvainen cries out, bellows something indistinct, and lowers the hand with the knife. He is standing only three or four metres away, and I catch his familiar scent: raw liquor, a mixture of old and fresh. The blade of the kitchen knife flickers again, and I prepare myself to wrestle him. But Tarvainen takes me completely by surprise and throws the knife underarm. It flies towards me, and I just have time to drop the snowmobile's keys to the floor and start to raise my hands.

The knife hits me in the front, sinks through my coat and shirt right in the middle of my chest. And there it remains, I don't know how deep. Pain erupts through my body, it feels as though my chest has been torn open, breathing is impossible. And of course, I'm more than aware of why this is: there's a giant Chinese kitchen knife stuck in my chest. But understanding this doesn't make me feel any better, doesn't alleviate the dizzying pain.

Tarvainen is running, somewhere, it sounds as though he is hurrying down the staircase.

I grip the handle of the knife, it feels worse than anything I've experienced before. I close my eyes and wrench it out. The knife makes a sucking sound as it exits my chest, the sound of a starving person slurping thick soup from the side of a bowl. I drop the knife to the floor. It is covered in blood and I can feel the warm flow on my chest. I manage to breathe for the first time since the attack. It is difficult, my chest hurts as though someone were tearing it open. I turn and head after Tarvainen.

What should I think of this man? In the space of one night he has both saved my life and tried to kill me. Twice.

I reach the ground floor and make my way outside. Once in the yard I can see footsteps in the snow, and when I raise my eyes I see Tarvainen in the glow of the moon and stars. He is running across the frozen lake. I glance at the snowmobile; naturally he tried this first, but, as I then realise, the keys are still on the floor upstairs.

I try to catch up with him, but there's no way I can run as fast as I'd like. Shouting is even more difficult. I can see the flags, and now I know where Tarvainen is running.

The fishermen's flags, marking holes in the ice.

The famous Lake Hurmevaara sprats.

At first I wonder whether Tarvainen sees the flags at all, but he must surely see them. Now I realise what is happening. Tarvainen corrects his course. He is running directly towards one of the flags. He approaches the flag, and I try to shout out.

Tarvainen is so close to the flag that he could almost touch it. But he doesn't have the chance. The ice buckles beneath him and he disappears into the hole. I see his upper body, like a barrel bobbing in the middle of the lake; the rucksack makes his chest bulbous and heavy, and it sinks more slowly. But it sinks all the same, and eventually Tarvainen disappears from view.

I stop, gasp for breath. I cannot run, I can only walk slowly.

A hand appears above the ice, then disappears again, leaving only the moonlit night, the stars and the smooth, gleaming surface of the endless lake.

I recall Tarvainen's words.

Rally or death.

12

I am bleeding and the snowmobile is shuddering beneath me. The headlights illuminate the surface of the snow. I can't drive at full speed, because I can only steer with one hand. The other is clasped to my chest. In Tarvainen's downstairs living room I found equipment to make a crude bandage. I taped a pile of disposable sauna towels to my chest with duct tape, I wrapped the tape round my body a few times and jumped on the snowmobile.

I hold my hand against my chest to protect the makeshift bandaging, to try and hold it together. But it's impossible. The bonnet of the snowmobile rises and falls with the landscape, it wobbles from side to side as I swerve along the narrow forest tracks. I have to stop the mobile, the pain sucks the breath out of me. I pull my phone from my coat pocket and call the kidnapper's number. Nobody picks up, and no new text messages have arrived. I press the accelerator again.

I don't want to think about my situation, but even without actively bringing it to mind, it appears to me in all its brutality: I do not have the meteorite, I do not know where Krista is or whether she is okay. There's an open wound in my chest, and I am now unarmed.

I approach the museum along the main road through the village. My logic is that I'm less likely to attract attention coming along the main road than if I were to approach the museum from the forest – assuming, that is, there is still someone at the museum waiting for me. Be that as it may, that is the place I must visit first. It's my only hope.

I try to keep my thoughts on the task at hand, but I guess I must still be in shock. My mind is racing, my emotions bubbling to the surface. I'm driving a dead man's snowmobile along a snow-covered road in a remote eastern-Finnish village, I am bleeding profusely, and my wife has been kidnapped. You never plan for things like this. I slow down a bit, eventually bring the vehicle to a stop and switch off the engine.

The museum car park is empty. I see the car park first, then the museum itself. In a way, everything looks just as it should: the lobby is fully lit, the office window is dark, and light from the meteorite room seems to spill out into the woods on the other side. I climb off the snowmobile. Moving is difficult. My whole upper body aches as though someone were squeezing my sternum in their fists. I walk towards the building and stop only when I can see into the museum through the broken window of the meteorite room. I wait and listen. It seems as though the noise of my arrival hasn't attracted the locals. I wait a moment longer, leave the shelter of the trees and walk towards the window.

The display room appears empty. Once I am certain of it, I think of walking round the museum and entering through the front door, but I realise this is unnecessary given the circumstances. Karoliina and Leonid wanted to get their hands on the meteorite, but the meteorite has gone. I climb in through the window, trying to avoid the shards of broken glass. It's impossible. The floor is covered with glass from the broken window and the smashed glass display cabinet. I see my iron field kettle. The room looks as though a group of vandals has performed a military strike. The next room is as it should be; nothing has changed. I walk up to the row of uniforms, move the grey sleeve of one of the coats, take my rifle and listen again. Finally I am convinced I am in the War Museum alone.

My condition is getting worse by the minute. I know it and can feel it, the pain in my chest becoming more acute all the while. I know I need to get to a hospital, fast. But I'm also painfully aware that the nearest hospital is an hour's drive away and that Krista is still missing. In the staffroom I find a packet of low-dose painkillers. I swallow half the packet with cold water and rinse my hands. Everything I have touched is stained with blood. I too am covered from head to toe in blood and must surely look like I did after my encounter with the roadside bomb in Afghanistan. I wipe the blood from the screen on my phone to see if there are any new messages. There aren't.

I feel woozy, I need to sit down. Sitting hurts too, as though a fresh knife is being thrust into my chest. I undo my coat and look down.

It doesn't look good. It looks like…

Papers in the breast pocket. I look at them without touching. They are covered in blood, but I can still make them out. I wipe my hands on my trouser leg, pull the thin pile of papers from my coat pocket and place them on the coffee table. They have remained just clean enough. I look at them with a sense of deep confusion as a fragile hope begins to awake within me.

The left-hand paper is the threatening letter taped to the door of the church hall. Along the lower edge of the paper runs a black line left by the printer, so faint it is barely noticeable. The middle paper is the letter left on our kitchen table. That too shows a faint line at the bottom. The paper on the right also shows a faint line at the bottom of the page, but the content of that piece of paper is of a very different nature.

My personal workout programme, compiled for me by Räystäinen.

It is almost four in the morning. Driving the snowmobile causes me excruciating agony, but there is no other vehicle at my disposal. And I don't care. I don't think it really matters what I think or feel. Perhaps it's only right that I feel like this. I don't know. That aside, I now know exactly what I have to do. Krista, only a moment more, I say to myself. I'm on my way.

The lights are on at Hurme Gym. At this time of night I doubt it's because there's anyone doing a series of squats or working on their abs. I climb from the snowmobile, grab the rifle and trudge through the deep snow down the hill through the dense forest. I approach

Hurme Gym from the side: the gym is situated in a building at the eastern end of the industrial park. I approach from the west. I make my way along the wall, the rifle at the ready.

In the middle of the building there is an opening in the wall, presumably some kind of loading bay. When I arrive at the opening, I peer inside and am startled. A Volkswagen Jetta is neatly parked right beside the loading area. The same Jetta, in fact, that I saw at the church-hall car park just before discovering the first letter. But this car doesn't belong to Räystäinen; he has an SUV. And that vehicle is nowhere in sight. There are several different tyre tracks in the snow. Is there someone else inside too, someone other than Räystäinen?

I pull the phone from my pocket and search for the registration number. I notice my hands are trembling. It's not just because of the cold, I know that. The car belongs to Räystäinen's wife, who, according to the registration details, lives at an address in Kajaani, hundreds of kilometres to the north. It takes a moment before I realise I haven't seen Tarja round the village for a while – or anywhere else, for that matter. Then I recall Räystäinen mentioning that Tarja would be happy to take his SUV but nothing else. So that's what he meant: Räystäinen has been using his wife's car. I push the phone back into my pocket and see that the door of the loading bay is standing ajar.

I hear a series of dull thumps, regular and with metronomic precision. When I open the door slightly more, I hear a whirring sound. The sounds come together, and I get it.

Räystäinen is running.

On the treadmill at the front of the gym. The door is at the rear of the room. Räystäinen has his back to me. His pace is somewhere between a jog and a run. I raise the rifle to my shoulder and step inside. I walk towards the machines, the rifle aimed and ready, occasionally turning to look behind me. From the corner of my eye I can see myself in the various mirrors around the gym. A bloodied man with a rifle in his hands and a missing wife.

I approach Räystäinen from the side now, and begin to walk

towards him. He is glistening with sweat, his steps thumping regularly, but there's something heavy on his chest, something weighing him down. And this isn't the only thing pulling him forwards somewhat. His hands are attached to the railings at the sides of the treadmill, taped round the wrists so that releasing them by himself would be impossible. I approach him one careful step at a time. Then stop.

His chest has been taped too – almost like mine. The tape is holding up something strapped round his abdomen. From beneath the tape run a series of strings, each of which is attached to the railings.

I walk round one of the exercise bikes and approach Räystäinen, my rifle at the ready. A moment later he sees me to his left. Something in his eyes lights up.

'Help me,' he gasps and continues running.

I point the rifle at him and allow my eyes to scan the gym.

'Is there anyone else here?' I ask once Räystäinen is directly in front of me.

He shakes his head. The movement is minimal. He looks like a man who is trying to conserve energy. Droplets of sweat fly from him, his face is covered in red-and-white blotches.

'Help me,' he repeats.

He doesn't speak so much as utter sounds through frantic breathing. That's what it sounds like, at least.

'Where is Krista?' I ask.

Räystäinen continues running. I can see he is building himself up to speak.

'They … took…'

'Who?'

'Karol…'

'Karoliina and the big man? They took Krista?'

Räystäinen nods.

'You took her first,' I say. 'Isn't that right? Why?'

'Help,' he shouts.

I point the rifle at him. 'Did you take her?'

He nods.

'Why? Why did you take Krista?'

'Money … Bankruptcy … The gym…'

My finger is on the trigger. My mind is consumed with rage, a rage born of jealousy. It is a dark power, cold and numb.

'You took my wife because your gym is about to go under, is that it?'

Räystäinen gives another nod, small and almost imperceptible. He continues running. I look down at his chest and examine more closely what has been strapped to him. The strings tied to the railings are all attached to a metallic pull ring that I recognise instantly. Beneath the ring is an oval object that I can readily identify despite the tapes covering it. I know a grenade when I see one. I can also say with some certainty that this is not the grenade that was stolen from the War Museum.

The set-up is actually very simple. If Räystäinen speeds up, the string behind him will tighten with fateful consequences: the pin will release, the lever will rise, and the grenade will explode. If he slows down, however, the string in front of him will tighten – with the same result. Räystäinen himself is bound to the treadmill by the wrists, so he can neither escape nor untie himself. All he can do is keep running.

I lower the rifle. 'Is Krista okay?'

'Yes … just now…'

'She was okay a moment ago?'

A nod.

'They took … her … and my house keys … Can you help…?'

It's a question, I realise that. I think about this for a moment. With the rifle still in my hand I walk to the reception, open the fridge, take out a bottle of sports drink and return to Räystäinen. I open the bottle and raise it to his lips. He gulps it down like a thirsty dog or a horse. The bright-blue liquid splashes all around us, but most of it ends up in his mouth until the bottle is empty.

I look at Räystäinen, the kidnapper, the writer of threatening letters.

'What time does your first customer arrive?'

'What?'

'What time does your first customer arrive?'

'Six.'

I look at the clock on the wall. It's just gone four. I walk towards the front door.

13

The hum of the treadmill, the beat of the steps, regular and deliberate, the heavy breathing, the rattling and spluttering. It takes a moment before I realise that this is my own heartbeat, my own breath. I am no longer anywhere near Räystäinen; I am on the other side of the village. The wound in my chest feels as though it has spread throughout my body, radiating pain with every heartbeat. By now my breathing is nothing but panting; I'm literally sucking in the air.

I sit on the snowmobile for a moment longer, then shrug the bag over my shoulder, pick up the rifle and start walking. It's not far to go. The stretch of forest between the two roads is only two or three hundred metres across. In my present condition, however, that's some challenge. Not to mention the items I'm carrying: the rifle and the sports bag with the four-kilo dumbbell. The house comes into view, and I stop. I go through my plan once more; it is simple and based entirely on the premise that I can take the pair by surprise. The lights are on, so there are people at home – whatever that means on a night like tonight. The last fifty or so metres up to the house are nothing but a stretch of thin birch trees, dried and riven with hoarfrost and providing only minimal cover. I hope nobody is looking out of the window or moving around outside the house.

It's a 1970s red-brick bungalow, and I approach via the backyard. I reach the boundary of the moon and the artificial light, and cross over. The electric light seeping through the curtains makes the snow look jaundiced; I raise my feet through this golden-yellow snow and make my way onwards. As I finally lean against the brick gable wall, I am shivering with cold and exhaustion.

For a moment I try to breathe as quietly as possible, with the result that I end up having to gasp for breath more frantically than before. All I can do is pant and hope there is nobody there to hear it. I move towards the back door.

The terrace at the back still bears the trappings of summer. Now the patio table, the deckchairs and barbeque are covered in a layer of snow a metre thick. I reach the table and notice three things. A narrow path leads through the snow from the table to the back door. On the other side of the table is a tin can from which faint smoke rises. And the air is filled with the smell of tobacco.

This is the smoking area.

And with the smoking area in such regular use, the same must apply to the back door. And in that case I doubt the door is locked...

I crouch down, lie as low as I can behind the table. The door opens and closes, light spills out into the yard as though thrown from a bucket. Footsteps crunch against the snow. I hear the sound of a cigarette lighter. Then I hear nothing. Of course not. How much noise does someone make smoking a cigarette? My problem is a simple one. Right now I dare not breathe. Before long I will have to.

The smoker shifts position, the snow again crunching beneath footsteps. I realise I will have to take a breath in two seconds, three at most. The decision has been made for me.

I stand up without knowing what to expect. In the same movement I lift the rifle, prop it against my shoulder and aim...

Right between Leonid's eyes, it would appear.

He is standing at the other side of the table, almost diametrically opposite me. For a moment he stares into the black hole at the end of the barrel, then raises his eyes, as if to widen his perspective, looks me in the eye. We remain surprisingly calm, given the situation must be a surprise for both of us.

'Quiet,' I say in English.

Leonid says nothing. Smoke rises from his cigarette. The lamps behind the curtains must be very bright, because there's plenty of light on the terrace.

'Let's go inside,' I say and wave the barrel an inch, two.

Leonid does not move.

I sharpen my aim. 'Or shall I go in alone?' I ask.

Leonid looks at me for a moment longer. Perhaps he sees the blood on my clothes and face, but eventually he turns. The snow crunches again. I walk round the patio table and follow him, the rifle aimed and ready. Leonid grips the door handle.

'Stop,' I say.

Leonid keeps his hand on the handle. Again I am forced to improvise. And I have to hurry. My condition is worsening all the while. I know it's only a question of time until my strength runs out, and that's when I'll make a mistake, one that I might not be able to correct.

'Let's go inside slowly and calmly,' I say. 'Stay right in front of me. I want you to remain between me and Karoliina at all times. Every second. You understand?'

Leonid doesn't answer. I nudge the end of the barrel into his back. I think of Krista, and I guess I must have shoved him with considerable force.

'Yes,' Leonid replies. 'In front.'

'Good. Open the door.'

Leonid opens the door slowly. It's bright. Leonid steps inside, and I follow behind him.

We are right in the middle of the living room. I see both Karoliina and Krista. Seeing Krista causes a whirlwind inside me, something I try hard to control. She sees me. She is sitting on a long sofa, her face turned towards me, Leonid and the door. One of her eyes is red and swollen; it looks as though she's been in a boxing ring without any protection. The bruise takes the most direct route right into my heart, wrenching my chest open, just like the knife before it. I force myself to focus.

Karoliina is sitting with her back to me and Leonid, and she is holding a pistol. Again I prod Leonid in the back. He gets my drift and stops. I stand slightly to the side of him, just enough so I can aim the rifle at Karoliina too.

She turns. 'Shut the damn door…'

She sees us, and her expression shifts from annoyance to confusion, from confusion to burgeoning interest.

'Reverend,' she says, this time in Finnish.

'I have the bag,' I tell her, turn my body somewhat and show her the bag behind Leonid's back.

Karoliina looks first at the bag, then at me.

'And I have your wife,' she says. 'You should thank me for that. I followed Räystäinen. I saved her.'

'Krista,' I say. 'Stand up and walk behind me.'

'Krista,' says Karoliina, and raises the pistol towards Krista with startling speed. 'Stay right where you are.'

Krista remains sitting on the sofa. She says nothing. I recognise her expression. She is tired and annoyed. She might be frightened, but more than that she is furious. I perfectly understand her. On my chest I sense that any minute the sauna towels and duct tape will no longer serve their purpose. More of my own warm blood seems to be pumping out across my chest and stomach with every heartbeat; it feels as though I am bathing in it. The trembling is getting worse all the while, and my hands are quivering so much that I'll need six cartridges, not one.

'I want the meteorite,' says Karoliina.

'You can have it in exchange for my wife. You give me Krista, I'll give you Leonid and the meteorite.'

'Leonid?' she asks. She sounds genuinely bewildered.

Leonid naturally hears his name and realises we are talking about him. I assume he and Karoliina exchange glances; that's what it looks like. After that, everything happens very rapidly. Karoliina moves more quickly than at any point before. She swings the hand with the pistol.

'Darling…' Leonid manages to utter before the back of his head separates from the front.

In the wintery quiet of the house, the shot is like an explosion. Leonid falls backwards, and it's like watching a building collapse;

I am about to end up beneath him. I can't fire – I have to lower the rifle and save myself from the weight of this towering man. My movements are slow and cumbersome, of that I am painfully aware. Karoliina fires again. Leonid takes another two bullets, of which he will be wholly unaware. At the same time he saves my life.

I made an error of judgement, that much is clear, and now I'll try to correct it.

I leap up, dive to the side and land on my stomach on the other side of the wall. It's not the optimal position by a long shot. The pain surging through my chest now feels like a roaring fire as I come thumping to the floor. The force of the landing is only heightened by the weight of the bag over my shoulder. I can't breathe. The rifle is still in my hand.

I realise I am on the floor in the dining room. I spin round and end up on my back between the wall and the dining table. I force myself up, first to my knees then to my feet. I instantly have to steady myself against the wall, then raise the rifle. I realise I only have a few moments before I lose consciousness. I press my back against the wall, trying to muster as much support as I can; Karoliina is round the corner, but she's stopped shooting. Just as I wonder why, I hear her voice.

'The meteorite,' she says loudly.

'You'll get the bag,' I say, trying to gather my strength. 'Once I get Krista.'

I move closer to the corner, peer round it. I am as quick as I can possibly be, given the circumstances. I see Krista and Karoliina at the other side of the living room. Karoliina has positioned herself behind Krista. Leonid is on the floor, the pool of blood around his head is almost black. Perhaps it only looks black to my eyes, like everything else will be in a moment. I glance around. The kitchen is at the far side of the dining room. From there there's a door leading to the hallway. I lower the rifle, take the bag from my shoulder.

'Here's the bag,' I say, drop the bag to the floor and kick it into the living room. It requires every ounce of strength in my legs just to make the four-kilo bag move. The bag slides towards Leonid's torso. 'If you put down the gun and let Krista go, I'll allow you to pick it up.'

Karoliina is quiet for a long while.

'I've got a better suggestion,' she says. 'Krista and I will fetch the bag together. Then Krista and I will leave together and I'll let her go once I'm far enough away.'

Of course, there's no way I can allow that. And it's probably not part of Karoliina's plan either. After all, she just shot Leonid.

Again I glance into the kitchen, at the doorway at the far end. If I can just make it that far … If one cartridge is enough…

I manage to pull off my winter shoes and place them so that the tip of the right shoe is visible from the living room.

'All right,' I say. 'I'm standing here waiting.'

'Joel, no!'

Krista's voice. She has seen close up what happens to people who hang around Karoliina.

'Krista,' I say as forcefully as I can. 'We'll be home soon.'

'We're going to pick up the bag now,' says Karoliina. 'Then you can go home.'

When I hear them moving, I make my own move. As my sock touches the floor, I realise I don't have many steps left in me. My movements are unsure. I can't feel my feet. My upper body feels essentially paralysed, the pain now throbbing, searing. I step along the side of the wall, arrive in the kitchen. I can hear the sound of winter shoes coming from the living room. The floor doesn't like it; the laminate creaks audibly. Which is a good thing from my perspective. My own steps are quiet, but they are limping. Just before reaching the doorway, I stumble. I gather my strength, reach the doorway. Then I focus on making my next movement as streamlined as possible.

From the kitchen door I turn into the hallway, which leads directly into the living room. The hallway rug is thick, soft and silent. I stand on the rug as firmly as I can, aim the rifle and wait a few fractions of a second. Then I see Krista's profile. A few more fractions of a second, then…

Karoliina's gun hand comes into view; she is almost right against Krista. First the hand, then the arm, and finally the shoulder. I try to force the trembling from my body. I only need a millisecond more. I concentrate, concentrate … and finally the rifle is steady. The shoulder appears at the other end of the hallway. The rifle gives a blast.

Karoliina staggers from the force of the shot. There's power in a hunting rifle, power that I guess is meant to neutralise a large animal. But Karoliina does not keel over. She spins round ninety degrees, the pistol still raised, and shoots. She shoots and hits her target. The bullet hits me in the upper body. I lurch backwards towards the front door, the now-useless rifle falls from my hand. The pistol is still aimed at me. I tried my best, I think, but I lost and now I'm going to die. But that isn't the worst of it, I think. The worst is that I was unable to help Krista.

At the end of the hallway is a light growing brighter and brighter. In the living room the sun is rising, I think to myself. I stare at it from the other end of the dark hallway, and it looks like spring and summer all at once, as though something large is opening up behind the figures at the end of the corridor, as though nothing but brightness and warmth are rolling in from afar.

Before the warmth and brightness fully envelop me, I see something else too. Karoliina is turning towards Krista but doesn't manage to complete the movement. Krista's hand moves, her fist is quick, she strikes Karoliina's chin with a surprisingly clean right-hander. There's a strong element of payback to the punch. Karoliina topples to the floor as though she has suddenly decided to go to sleep.

Krista runs towards me. She touches me; her touch is that same growing light and brightness to which I can now give a name. It is love. I want to tell her this, but I cannot speak. And there's no need. Here we are.

Just a moment longer.

Then the light engulfs us both and I finally feel warm again.

TEN MONTHS LATER

October is resplendent. The autumnal sunlight is at its most melancholic, its most beautiful. It sets the windows alight, magnificently warms the dark wooden pews, making the space seem taller – and taller still, as though the white panelled ceiling were slowly rising, up and up, until it was very close to the sky, almost touching.

The old wooden Hurmevaara church is full again. It's taken some getting used to. Not least because the pews began to fill up again after I came back from sick leave. I began to realise that the swollen congregation was here because of me.

I climb up to the pulpit. The steps creak – the wooden boards are uneven, worn and smooth. I gaze out into the church. I recognise many of these people by name, but every Sunday there are new faces too. I don't know what to think about the fact that they all know what happened to me. But precisely because they know, I speak.

I always speak of how hard it is to do good, how so often when we have good intentions we end up making mistakes, how life is really a complicated affair and never offers easy answers to what we might call the larger questions. I speak from experience.

And that's what I talk about today too. About how we can never know how life will turn out, and why that's a good thing. I have to admit that many of my experiences sound more like thrillers, and that perhaps that is one of the reasons my sermons are so popular, but still … the stories I tell are only a part of what actually happened. When giving my sermon, I always stress that people are free to give their own meaning to what they hear, just as everyone can believe that their own life is guided either by chance or divine intervention. Or neither. That's what I do too. God and the universe will cope, I think.

But how should I know?

I say that too.

And I end today's sermon with a thought with which I am particularly occupied at present.

Do not worry, do not be sad.

It surprises me too that I've started worrying about the future. I have survived stepping on a mine, being stabbed, shot, and lived through countless other unexpected events, and still ... But this time I am not worried about myself or my own future.

Once the service has ended, I shake hands with the congregation, listen to their joys and concerns, the ins and outs of their lives, then help Pirkko and Matias Ihantola to lock up the church. I remind myself that this little episode was all an egocentric misunderstanding on my part. I imagined Pirkko was interested in me while all the time she was trying to get close to Ihantola. I thank them for helping with this Sunday's service, which once again was excellent.

And then I walk home.

Krista and Samuel are at the kitchen table. Samuel is eating. At least, he's trying to, and Krista does her best to make sure they get there in the end. I give her a kiss on the cheek, on the lips, and Samuel on the top of his head, otherwise my face would be covered in regurgitated sweet-potato purée. I sit down at the table with a cup of coffee.

'You can take a nap, if you want,' I say to Krista.

'And what will you two get up to?'

'I don't know,' I say, though I have my suspicions.

Krista looks at me the way she sometimes does. Sometimes she calls me the jigsaw man when we're lying naked next to each other in bed. It's an apt description, a very appropriate name for me. My body is etched in scars from head to toe. Whenever I visit a public sauna, people ask what it's like to wrestle with a bear.

'How did the service go?' she asks.

'Full house again today.'

'And what did you tell them?'

'How hard it is to do the right thing, and that's precisely why we should strive to do just that.'

'I love you, Joel,' she says.

I look at her.

'I love you too.'

Krista stands up, takes me and Samuel in her arms, kisses us both. Then she walks upstairs. Samuel is waving his arms around, flailing in his high chair. Samuel is a miracle – our miracle – and blissfully unaware of it. I continue feeding him, trying to drink my coffee. The coffee grows colder; Samuel eventually finishes eating. I wipe him and his surroundings clean. I'm not sure whether there's more food on the table, my son or the wooden floorboards.

I lift him from his chair, take him in my arms and pick up a blanket from the living room. We walk out into the yard.

It's high noon, calm and sunlit, perhaps the last warm day of the year. Tomorrow's forecast promises wind and rain, and a thunderstorm in the evening. There's a hint of the coming storm in the air – everything is still, like being at the foot of a giant wave. From down here, everything feels fine, but above you a white-crested disaster is brewing.

I don't know why I think things like this today. Perhaps it's because of the news I heard this morning. Karoliina's appeal to the high court might be successful. She could be out of prison in a year, if she really can prove she acted in self-defence. It's entirely possible. She has convinced everybody that she was acting under duress from Leonid, that she was unaware of what he was planning, and she still maintains she doesn't know what happened to the meteorite or what the robbery was all about. She has even managed to convince people that it was only once she was in hospital that she heard the meteorite might be that valuable. And all the while she has claimed that her life was being threatened, that she was in danger and that everything she did was merely to save her own life. In this light, Leonid's death becomes involuntary manslaughter and my shooting her is common assault. I can live with that.

Far more difficult might be the matter that Karoliina whispered to me when we met during the trial. She passed me in the corridor, accompanied by a police officer. Her head turned a fraction, just enough for me to smell her perfume. I doubt anyone else noticed the comment, let alone heard it. Karoliina said she would be back to pick up the meteorite.

Which is at the bottom of Lake Hurmevaara.

I put Samuel down, and he lies wriggling on his blanket, waving his hands, rolling over, trying to crawl. The sun warms the blanket, like a large oven glove just taken from the side of a pot.

Karoliina knows that I know the whereabouts of the meteorite. Nobody else does. When Tarvainen's remains were found on the opposite shore in the spring, the rucksack was no longer on his back. Although he had lost so much, people were far more interested in the location of the rucksack than in the rally legend whose best days were firmly behind him.

Why didn't I tell anyone which fishing hole Tarvainen had fallen into, indicating the rough location of the meteorite? I think it must have more than a little to do with everything that lump of rock caused: greed and death. But it won't be at the bottom of the lake forever. One day it will fly again, perhaps once the sun has finally been snuffed out and gravity no longer exerts its force on the Earth, when the planet collides with other planets and smashes into infinitesimal boulders of different sizes or is sucked into a black hole and turns into a point the size of a pinhead, a spot that will simply sleep for billions of years until something else unexpected happens.

Because things always happen.

Like now.

Samuel is doing it again. He never does this when Krista is around. He is on his stomach on his blanket. He raises his head, and suddenly he seems completely focussed. He looks forwards, his eyes unflinching, and—

He flies.

He makes surprisingly recognisable sounds: the ignition, the howl of wheels. Then the acceleration, the changing of gears. The motor – my son – pushing himself to the limit. The car reaches its top velocity. Samuel cruises along at full pelt, right ahead.

He looks as happy as a human being just under six months old can look.

Driving his race car.

To the limit.

ACKNOWLEDGEMENTS

Before I say thank you to certain important persons and people, I would like to – as I believe they say in English-speaking countries – take stock. *Little Siberia* is both my third and my eighth book. It is eighth if you count all the way from the beginning (and most people who know their maths do), and yet it is also my third if you count from *The Man Who Died*, which was published in 2017 in English-speaking countries. The original Finnish version came out in 2016 under the title *Mies joka kuoli*.

So why count from TMWD, as I call it when I write to my agent and wish to be seen as someone with their finger on the business pulse? I suppose this has to do with the change I made after my fifth book, *The Mine*. By that time, I'd written five very dark, very noirish crime novels. I felt I needed a change, that I needed to bring forth an element I had used in a much more subdued manner before. That element was humour.

The Man Who Died turned out to be a success. I think I can say that. It was even nominated for The Best European Crime Novel of the Year in France and for the Petrona Award and The Last Laugh Award in the UK. Most importantly, quite a few readers seemed to like it. I followed that book with *Palm Beach Finland*, which made *The Times* say 'Tuomainen is the funniest writer in Europe' so I wouldn't have to say it myself.

Anyway. I'm hoping *Little Siberia* can be seen as part of the same continuum, even though I know it is also quite different. I wanted to try some new things. I thought it would be interesting to write a crime novel with a priest as the main character, and make that story both dark and darkly funny. I wanted to explore some philosophical questions, some life stuff too. I feel now that it was an important book for me to write. I'm happy I wrote it and I'm proud of it too.

I hope you enjoy(ed) it.

And, so, even though I write my books alone (by this I mean that I literally sit in a room all by myself and make up the whole thing in my lonely head), I do receive invaluable help and assistance along the way. I have been blessed with some truly excellent company. In geographical order, they are:

Helsinki

Jaakko Launimaa edited the original Finnish version. He saved both me and the main character Joel Huhta from gravest perdition. Thank you, Jaakko.

David Hackston translated this book from Finnish to English. Trust me when I say this: Finnish is the hardest language to translate. And yet David makes it seem like it's the most natural thing. To say that David is talented is an understatement. He is downright fantastic.

Stockholm

I can't thank my agent, Federico Ambrosini from Salomonsson Agency, enough. Same goes for everyone at Salomonsson. You're the best.

London

Karen Sullivan is simply amazing, and I'm happy and incredibly privileged to call her my publisher. She is the hardest-working person in publishing and yet she finds time to be funny and supportive and kind when a writer needs it. Thank you for everything, Karen.

West Camel keeps things on track with steadfast and precise editing. I'm grateful for the support you've given me – and all Orenda's authors. Thank you so much, West, it's a delight to work with you.

Mark Swan has created all my Orenda covers. He is an artist and a wizard. See any of my books for proof. Thank you, Mark.

UK & US

Bloggers – thank you. Thank you for reading, for spreading the word, keeping the flame alight. It means so much. Without you, I don't know where we'd be. Well, I do know, and it isn't pleasant. Thank you for keeping the (reading) light on.

People I've met and keep meeting along the way – thank you for making the 9.00 a.m. panel, for coming up and saying hi, for the kind words and for *reading the books*. I can't tell you how happy it makes me. I might write the books alone, but, truth be told, I write them for *you*.